HOME
TRUTH

HOME TRUTH

JANIS STOUT

SOHO

Published by
Soho Press, Inc.
853 Broadway
New York, NY 10003

Library of Congress Cataloging-in-Publication Data

Stout, Janis P.
Home truth / Janis Stout.
  p.   cm.
ISBN 0-939149-66-4
      I. Title.
PS3569.T659H6   1992   91-46594
813'.54—dc20   CIP

Manufactured in the United States
10 9 8 7 6 5 4 3 2 1

Book design and composition by
The Sarabande Press

Save yourself; others you cannot save.

—Adrienne Rich,
"Snapshots of a Daughter-in-Law"

for my sons

HOME
TRUTH

1

When they called from the Home and said they were making arrangements to send Sister home for Christmas and needed to know which bus she should take, I didn't know what to say. It hadn't really hit me till then that with Mama gone this was going to be my responsibility. The calendar hadn't really hit me yet either. It seemed like a long time yet till Christmas. I had a lot of other things to work out before I was going to be ready to schedule Sister's visit. Break the idea to Stan, for one. He wouldn't have even thought about it. I knew that. I put down my mixing bowl and just stood there. I didn't know what to say.

"Well?" the woman prodded me.

"It's not a good time," I said, stalling.

I looked out the back window at the kids, playing on the swing set. Just like Mitchy and me at that age, I thought. There was about the same difference in our ages. We would have been playing out in the back yard the first week of a warm Texas December too, like Gail and Davey were now, with Mama watching us through the window like this, holding the telephone receiver in her hand, or maybe holding a letter from the School, and trying, the same as I was now, to plan for Sister's Christmas vacation. And how to cope with it. And maybe thinking to herself, the same as I was, I can't handle this, life is complicated enough already.

I stuck my finger in the cake batter and licked it off, trying to think what to do. If she came Christmas Eve and stayed over till the twenty-sixth or twenty-seventh, that wouldn't be bad, she would have her Christmas at home and I could surely handle her for that long.

But really it wasn't a good time, not at all. Things were already touch and go with Stan and me. This might just do it, he might just walk out again.

"It really isn't a good time for me," I repeated. "I'm not sure I can do this."

The woman on the phone was not impressed. Everyone in the blind unit had to go home, she repeated. Everyone. The unit would be closed for Christmas. Anyway, their clients needed that time with their families.

"Yes, of course," I agreed, still stalling for time, trying to think.

Maybe she could go to Aunt Doris's? Not that that would be the same as going home. For that matter, coming to our house wouldn't be like going *home*. But she probably didn't even remember Aunt Doris. To tell the truth, I hardly remembered her myself. Outside, Gail pushed Davey off the swing. I tapped on the window and shook my head.

"So we need to make arrangements," the woman insisted. She had the bus schedule right there in front of her, and she was going to read it out for me, so I could choose a time.

"Look," I interrupted. "I'm not sure she can come here."

There was a pause.

"Then where would you suggest?"

"What if she had to stay there? Not that that's good, I mean I know she wants to come home for Christmas and all, but what if she had to? I'm not sure I can work this out. What do you do with people who don't have anywhere to go?"

"Everybody has someplace to go," she said. "They have to."

I wanted to say, but what if they don't? But then, like an inspiration, some hint in what she had said earlier came back to me. "You said the blind unit was closing. Does that mean just the blind unit? What about the rest?"

"Oh well, the retarded unit will stay open, of course, but—"

"Then if she had to she could go there for a couple of days, right? I'm not saying that has to be it. I want her to come here if I can manage it. But if she had to?"

"She's not in the retarded unit, she's in the blind unit."

"Yes, but she's retarded too." I had her there; she couldn't deny that.

She didn't try to. She just said it didn't make any difference.

Raising her voice a little, she repeated, "Lisbeth is not assigned to the retarded unit."

"But she *is* retarded," I said, raising mine more. "If that unit is staying open and she can't come here, why can't she go there? I mean, she does qualify. She is retarded."

There was an exasperated sigh, and she went over it again slowly, the way you do when you explain something to a child who's being dense. "Lisbeth is in the blind unit. Our clients have to be counted one or the other, and she's with the blinds, not with the retardeds. That's how she was admitted." She paused. I wondered if she was listening to what she had just said and asking herself, as I was, how much sense it made. "Besides, it isn't a couple of days, it's three weeks. So when do you want her to come?"

Three weeks! Christmas was one thing; I knew Sister wanted to be with family for Christmas, naturally she did, but three weeks? There was no way I could have her here for three weeks. I just couldn't. I had my hands full as it was. Besides, I remembered all those Christmases when we were kids, how she always spoiled everything. She couldn't handle the excitement. She always arrived home for the holidays wound up tight as a spring, and the spring always broke. Some little something would happen, and she would go off into screaming fits, and Mitchy and Beep and I would hide under the bed. I didn't want Gail and Davey having to go through that. But after all, that was a long time ago, when we were little. She was twenty-eight years old now. I was twenty-seven, and Sister was twenty-eight. Surely twenty-eight-year-olds didn't have screaming fits! Something kept twitching in my memory about one Easter vacation when I was in college and brought a boyfriend home, and she spilled her Coke, and then . . . But I pushed that recollection down.

"Look," I said. "Let me call you back. I'll call you sometime tomorrow."

She said she needed to know *now*.

I knew what that meant. She was reluctant to let me off without a commitment. Like a good salesman, she was trying to close the deal while she had me, for fear I'd wise up and never buy. Finally she gave in and said all right, I could call her back tomorrow. "But it'll have to be by nine o'clock, you hear? By nine o'clock, no later." Then before hanging up, just in case I was trying to pull a fast one, she threw out a warning: "We'll send her home in a police car if we have to."

When Sister was little, we used to hear stories about kids at the School having to be sent home in police cars, otherwise their families wouldn't take them. Imagine, we said, children whose own families wouldn't let them come home unless the police brought them! So had I come to that point myself now? It wasn't a good feeling.

Sister might be slow, she might not understand a lot of things, but she would understand not being wanted if I refused to take her for the holidays. That had always been a big point for us: No matter how much trouble we had with her times at home, we must never let her think we didn't want her. And I wasn't going to let her think that now, either. I owed her that much: not to let her think she wasn't wanted. And I did want her. Or at least I wanted to do right by her. I thought how, if they told her I wouldn't let her come, she would roll her blank eyes, and clench her hands in her lap, and say, "Oh, can't go, huh?" I couldn't let that happen.

I divided the cake batter evenly between two greased and floured pans, patted their bottoms, and set them in the oven, then put the bowl in the sink and ran water into it. It was two o'clock, over three hours yet till Stan would be home from work. Time enough that I could take a nap with the kids, maybe. Not that I did that as a rule—hardly ever, in fact. But it seemed like a good day for oblivion.

I drifted out to the back yard and sat on one of the swings, so low to the ground that my feet doubled under me in the hard-packed rut worn there not so much by my own two, who were too little to kick the ground and swing high, as by the children who had lived there before. If I had tried to imagine, before I got married, what it would be like to stay at home with small children—if I had actually thought about it in any detail—I would have imagined grass under the swings, not these worn ruts. But I didn't. I was a junior at the state university in Arlington, and Stan was finishing the automotive course at the technical school where Mitchy was going. Mitchy introduced us. Stan had soft, broody brown eyes and a heavy drawl, and he could play the guitar and sing old Western songs, songs from the 1930s and the Light Crust Doughboys. Being in my proletarian phase at the time, I thought it would be great to be married to a man like that. Earthiness, the vitality of the common people, all that.

I had seen the children run behind the garage when I came out the back door, and I could hear an interested-sounding murmur from behind the ligustrum bush. "Where are you?" I called. "What are you up to?"

Gail answered, in a strained voice, "Nofing."

But Davey ran out wide-eyed from behind the bush and reported breathlessly, "Ga poo-poo."

I bolted out of the swing and rounded the bush just as she topped off a neat little mess. She looked at me solemnly while she stood up, struggling with her overalls. She managed to get one strap over the shoulder, but the other remained looped under her arm, bunching her T-shirt out above it. "Had to go potty," she explained matter-of-factly, and stuck her finger up her nose. Davey hugged himself and squealed. Clearly, he felt delighted to have a sister who went potty behind the ligustrum bush.

"Don't you know better than to do that outside?" I demanded. "You're supposed to come in to the bathroom when you need to go."

"Had to go potty," she insisted. Then, putting her head down, she charged into Davey, who was still celebrating the event with a hopping dance, bowled him over, and hurled herself down beside him. Together, they sang ecstatically, "Poo-poo, poo-poo," and rolled over and over in the grass.

I looked at her mess there on the ground and wondered if I really *had* to dispose of it. It was pretty well shielded by the ligustrum where it was, and it looked basically no worse than the dog's messes, which I hadn't cleaned up either for several days. The week before, when I had let Gail go play down the street with several other three- and four-year-olds and she had messed smack in the middle of Ginny Edwards's not back but front yard, there had been no question. I wondered if an urge to go potty outside indicated emotional disturbance.

9

"Let's go take a nap," I suggested. They sat up and looked at me noncommittally. Davey gave a tentative shake of his head. "I'll take a nap with you," I offered. That seemed to strike them as a good idea. They got up and took my hands, one to a side.

Inside, the house smelled wonderful from the baking cake layers. I peeked through the glass panel in the oven door while Davey tugged at my jeans and saw that they were rising from the edges toward the centers and just beginning to brown. It would be another ten minutes yet. I hoped I wouldn't forget to come back and take them out if I went on now to lie down. I could have set the timer, but I hated the buzz when it went off.

Davey was still pulling at my leg. "Davey," I asked, "do you need to wee?"

"No!" he cried, with an emphatic shake of the head. "No! No!"

I looked then and saw that he was wet, standing with his legs wide apart over a puddle.

"Oh, Davey! Why didn't you go potty? Why didn't you tell me?"

He looked momentarily rueful but, seeing that Gail was watching, laughed and stamped his foot in the puddle, splashing the refrigerator door.

That was too much. I yelled "Bad boy!" then jerked his pants down and slapped his bare bottom, a little harder than I meant to. Which did nobody any good, of course, but just started him bellowing.

By the time I washed up the floor and the refrigerator

and got him changed, the cake layers were done and I could set them out to cool before we went back to the bedroom.

We lay across the bed on our stomachs. The kids rooted around and giggled for a while, but soon snuggled up against me and contented themselves with reaching over my back now and then to poke each other. I put my face against them, first one and then the other. They smelled warm and pungent, like sourdough bread. It seemed amazing to me—it often seemed amazing—to think that they had really come out of my body and now here they were, full of their own life and smelling yeasty good. After a while they fell asleep, breathing through their mouths with a faint snoring sound, and I lay there with them for a while, looking at the ceiling, starting to worry again. This time, there was no danger of my going to sleep and failing to start dinner on time.

I thought about how it would be to have Sister with us for three weeks. Starting with the morning, I tried to think through the day, step by step, from the time she got up and came to the breakfast table to the time she had a bath and brushed her teeth and went to bed. I tried to think of everything she would do and everything she would need to have done for her—from helping her find her place at the table and cutting her pancakes into bites and averting collisions on the way to the sink to wash her hands after the pancakes, to testing her bathwater and hanging up her towel and turning her hand over every time so the toothbrush wouldn't be upside down when she squeezed toothpaste onto it, then helping her pull back the covers without pulling them clear off the bed. Then I tried to put all of that up against everything I did for Gail and Davey every day. It wasn't clear that she would need much less than they did, or any less. And all added together it was too much; I couldn't do it. It would be like having another two-year-old to look after, except it would be a two-year-old in a hundred-and-forty-pound woman's body, a body thick and ungainly, not quite feminine but still a woman's.

How the children would take to her was beyond imagining. They might regard her as a new playmate or a new toy, they might treat her as the natural butt of hitting and pinching games, they might turn jealous of my attention, they might be afraid of her—there was no telling.

When I had reached this point, I slipped out from between them and went to the kitchen to mix up a meatloaf.

Meatloaf was a good thing to have because Stan liked it, and a good dinner was essential if I was going to talk to him about Sister coming. Which clearly I had to do if I was going to make that phone call in the morning. I made cornbread to go with it, and as an afterthought stirred up a package of chocolate pudding.

It was while I was stirring the pudding on the stove that I thought, What am I doing? Why am I doing this? It was exactly the kind of thing I used to despise so in my mother, that old kowtowing, shortest-way-to-a-man's-heart-is-through-his-stomach routine. Oh, how I used to hate that! I would come in from school and see her there in the kitchen, working over the stove, perspiring, watching the clock, with that certain set to her mouth, always that same tight, set mouth, and I would know what was up.

There was something she had to tell Daddy, or something she wanted to ask him to do, and she was getting ready to soften him up. I would tell her, Why don't you just say it, whatever it is. You don't have to ask his permission, just tell him, you're an adult the same as he is. She would shake her head and go on with what she was doing. I didn't understand, she said. And of course I didn't—then.

Now I understood. Here I was, doing exactly the same thing she had done, trying to soften up my husband before I told him the bad news. And the bad news wasn't my fault in the first place, so why did I feel like apologizing? It seemed perfectly natural; that was the hell of it—it was so natural. But I hated it anyway, and I hated myself for doing it.

Stan came in at a quarter to six. He said, "Hey, hon," and went on through to the bathroom to wash up. When he came back, he got out a beer and came up and touched it against the back of my arm before he opened it, to make me jump. Then he nuzzled my neck a little and gave me a quick feel. I was mashing potatoes. "How's my babe," he said. I said fine, just fine. He went to sit down by the table, took a chug of his beer, and started looking at the *TV Guide.* I kept on with getting dinner ready. After a few minutes he asked what was the matter.

"Tell you later," I said. The children were coming in, and I didn't want to start on it then.

He took one look at them and knew they'd been asleep. Which was no wonder, since they'd only been up about five minutes and were still bleary-eyed and tousled. This was one of Stan's sore spots. He hated for me to let them sleep late in the afternoon. He wanted me to have them good and tired so they'd go to bed early. As soon as he saw them he cut his eyes over at me and said, "Have you been letting them sleep right up till dinner again?"

"We lay down together. They just had a little nap. They'll go to bed all right."

His mouth was set and his jaw thrust forward a little, the way it always got when he was in a temper. "I've told you and told you, Meg, I want them ready for bed early. I need to unwind in the evening, and I can't do it with kids crawling all over me."

Whenever I used to get really put out at Stan, I would go over to the window or the door and look out, with my face right up near the glass, to block out as much of the room as I could, and I would imagine him yelling and waving his arms, all red in the face and his eyes bugging out—which was the way he got sometimes, luckily not too often. And I would imagine myself saying the most audacious things to him, things I would never say out loud, and when I did he would get littler and littler till he was only about an inch tall, but still red in the face and waving his arms and yelling. And sometimes I would imagine myself just stepping on him.

This time, what I imagined myself saying was, Why are you so afraid you'll have to spend a little time with your own children? Do you have any idea what it's like to go through one day with these two? No, you don't, so don't tell me about letting them take a nap. But what I actually said was, "I know, hon, I know you need some time to unwind. It just happens sometimes."

But he wouldn't let it go. "It wouldn't 'just happen,'" he pointed out, "if you didn't let it happen."

14

"Something came up."

"What? What came up?" The way he said it, I could tell he didn't believe anything had come up at all. He was deliberately backing me into a corner.

"I'll tell you about it later, OK?"

"What's the big deal that you can't tell me now? Is it you don't want to talk in front of the children? Is that it?"

"You don't have to raise your voice."

"We can spell out the scary words. M-O-N-E-Y, R-E-N-T. Is that it?"

He ran his fingers through his hair in a frazzled way that made me feel momentarily sorry for him, though that didn't stop me from being mad. I knew he felt like things were crowding him sometimes, especially money, though he still insisted, stubbornly and I thought unreasonably, that I shouldn't get a job, he could handle it.

"It's not money," I told him. "Just something that came up. I need to talk to you about it later on."

I was wishing I hadn't mentioned it, but it was too late now. I needed to stall, to think how to go about it, but I knew he couldn't stand to think I was holding out on him. Stan always liked to know what was going on; he couldn't abide uncertainty.

Fortunately, Gail and Davey had waked up enough by then that they wanted to be played with. They wrapped their arms around his legs, one on each, and whooped. As fast as he had gotten mad, he got playful and sweet, and started swinging them around his body, under his arms, across his back, the way they liked. It was as if he had forgotten the whole thing.

That was one thing about Stan that was always hard for me to accept—he changed so fast; his moods were so unpredictable. In the time it took me to decide how I was feeling about something, he would have gone through two or three of those quick reverses. So I never knew what to expect. He liked to play with the kids and think of himself as a good father. Then that fit would pass and he couldn't be bothered. But of course children have to be bothered with, every day, every hour practically. That's what wears you down, they're so unrelenting. Whereas Stan could be cool as ice one minute and in a frenzy the next. He looked solid as earth—short, short-legged, thick, heavy-browed. To look at him, you would never think he was flighty. But we never knew where we stood with him. I guess the children didn't know that they didn't know, but I did.

He stayed in high spirits all through dinner. He lined up peas on his knife blade and let them roll down into his mouth like little balls, and grinned while the children begged him to do it again. Davey banged his spoon on his high-chair tray and rolled his peas off onto the floor. Gail, perched on the bench on her knees to reach the table, threw her head back and shrieked laughter, dangling her blond mop halfway down her back. Beyond her, in the window, I saw us mirrored against the darkness outside. The American Family, I thought—this is worth it all.

After dinner Stan lay on the sofa with the newspaper and let them drive little cars all over him while I did the dishes. He seemed to have forgotten our argument. But when I came to get the kids for their baths, he pulled me down to the sofa and wanted to know what this big news was that I had to tell him.

I kissed him and ran my finger down the back of his neck. "Let me do this first," I begged. "Then I'll tell you about it."

I put them into the tub together and let them splash a little while I gathered up their clothes to put in the hamper. The knees of both pairs of overalls were grass-stained, and the bibs held reminders of lunch and dinner. A brown smudge down the inside back of Gail's was evidence of her back yard toilet stop: She had pulled up her overalls and left her underpants wadded in the legs. The records of our day. They would be washed away in the Kenmore tomorrow.

When I came out, Stan was watching football. I sat down beside him and curled up my legs on the sofa, prepared to wait till the quarter was over. But he hadn't forgotten. He looked over at me in a way that said, without words, Well? Get on with it. So I told him. "They called today from the Home, where Lisbeth is. They're starting to line things up for Christmas."

"So?"

"So they need to know when she can come. She'll need to be with us for Christmas."

"No way," he said flatly. "What do they think this is?" His eyes fastened back onto the action on the screen, but when the play was over he turned them on me again. "Now. Did they just phone you up and tell you that?"

I told him about the superintendent's secretary calling and saying Lisbeth had to leave for the holidays, that the Home would be closed.

His response wasn't much different from my own. "That's crazy. They're bound to have people that don't have anyplace to go. They won't just put them out the door. You know they won't."

"That's what I thought too," I told him. "She said the retarded unit will have some people staying over, but the blind unit will be closed. She said Sister can't stay there because she's not in that unit."

"If your sister's not retarded, Einstein wasn't a genius. I mean, it's obvious, right?" He looked back at the TV, trying to get back into the action. The quarterback was scrambling.

"Of course she is, I know that. But they say that doesn't matter. She wasn't admitted retarded, and so she can't stay at that unit, she has to come home."

"Well, this isn't home. Let her go somewhere else."

"Where?"

"Hell, I don't know! What do you expect me to do, figure everything out in two minutes? Jesus!"

I wasn't sure if that last was for me or for the quarterback, who had just been sacked. There was less than a minute till halftime. I waited.

When the teams started to the locker room, Stan went to get a beer. He came back with it and put his arm around me and pulled me over against him. "Look, babe," he said. His voice had become that gentle croon he always used for smoothing over difficulties. It was a voice I had learned not to trust, though I always wanted to.

"Look, I know you want to be nice to your sister and do the right thing and all that. But what I'm saying is, face facts.

We've got our hands full with the kids. I'm thinking about you, now. What would you do with her here for a week, on top of everything else? You're running yourself ragged as it is, sweetheart." He stroked the top of my head with the point of his chin, making little crooning sounds in his throat, but keeping his eyes on Bryant Gumbel, who was talking standings.

"But she doesn't have anywhere else to go." I could have added that anyway it was three weeks, not one, but I decided to let that go for now.

"Do you think she knows the difference? All right, all right, maybe she does. What about Mitch and Beep?"

I didn't even bother answering that. Mitchy with his late hours, his musician friends in and out; Beep with her roommate, her job, her evening classes.

He gave my shoulder a terminal sort of squeeze, signaling that he was ready to wind this up and get set for the second half. It was all right with me; my neck was cramping from the position he was holding me in. But I needed to get it settled. "I have to call them back tomorrow," I said.

"Well, call them then. It's settled. She can't come here." His voice had a hard edge to it.

"Stan, I can't just turn her away. She's my sister."

"She's Mitch and Beep's sister too, right? Let them solve a problem for once. We have our own problems to solve. Or had you forgotten?"

He stood up and stomped out to the kitchen with his beer can. As the teams came back onto the field, he returned with a laying-down-the-law look on his face.

"I'm not having her here, Meg. That's too much to

expect. Besides, think about the kids. They shouldn't be around her. It's enough to give them nightmares. I know you don't like that, but it's the truth. There are places for people like that. They don't belong with regular people. So just put it out of your head."

I thought of Sister's clouded, milky white eyes, her mouth off to the side and twice too big for her face, her sparse hair standing in chicken-feather tufts, her shambling body. I didn't like having her around either. I hadn't liked it when I was a child. She hadn't actually given me nightmares, but she did seem scary at times, she really did. Mom never knew it, I maintained a steely exterior, but my acceptance of Sister and my childhood kindnesses to her were pitched over deep chasms of aversion. It was the same now; it wasn't exactly that I wanted her here, it was more that I would feel bad about not having her. Guilt, you might say. All right. I felt sorry for her. She had so little—she couldn't see, she couldn't live like other people. And I couldn't do anything about any of that. Having her with us for Christmas was at least something.

But I knew Stan well enough to let it go for now.

Later, when he came to bed after the game, he woke me up to make amends. Or no, not even that, because he wouldn't have believed he needed to make amends. It was more like this: He was making sure I'd be thinking of him as the great lover, the doting husband. That was Stan's style. He expected only his good moments to count. Maybe at heart we all do.

At first I thought oh no, not that. I mumbled that I was sleepy, and started to turn over. But then, drowsy as I was, I realized this was an opportunity and I'd better wake up and use it. So instead of either putting him off or sighing and letting him do his thing, I gave him a good time. I did all the extras, said words I hated and went down on him without even being urged to. He rolled his head on the pillow and moaned.

Then afterward I lay with my head on his shoulder and made little mmm's of pleasure and whispered how much I wanted to keep him happy and how much I loved being with him and with the children, and how I felt pulled in two directions at once. These weren't really lies. They weren't lies at all, just truths told for a purpose.

He lay there breathing all slow and spent, and said yes, yes, oh he knew it was hard, and I was the sweetest little girl in the world, and of course I felt like I had to take care of Lisbeth, there wasn't anybody else to take care of her, he knew that.

So then, when I knew I had him on the ropes, I hit him with a hard one: "I keep thinking how awful it would be if one of ours let the other be lonely and unloved or something after we're gone." As if I could even imagine such a thing!

He was already drifting off to sleep, but that brought him back just enough. "Right," he breathed. "Oh God, that's right. They've got to stick together. We'll manage somehow."

So I had won that round. Or you might say I had lost it—in the old, old way. I moved away to my side of the bed and lay there looking into the darkness of our bedroom and wondering which.

2

EVEN THOUGH I had already decided there was no use trying to drag Mitchy and Beep in on this, I wanted to talk to Mitchy before calling back the woman at the Home. Not Beep; there was no use talking to her. She couldn't do anything about it if she wanted to. But I was hoping Mitchy might help out a bit, take her over to his place for a few days or something.

Mitchy's hard to get. He comes in at three in the morning after playing piano at a late-night club and goes to sleep with his telephone under a pillow. I went to the club where he was playing once. He's good, he really is. He plays that ripply bar-style piano and keeps a little patter going with the customers. The empty glass he kept beside the keyboard for tips didn't stay that way; there was something to put in his pocket every time he took a break. When he came back he always put a couple of quarters or a dollar back in, priming the pump. But I don't know, I don't think it's what he had in mind when he quit auto mechanics school to be a musician.

Sometimes when I try to call Mitchy I get his answering machine with its friendly spiel over a musical background: "Hi, this is Mitchell Taylor. I can't come to the phone right now, but if you'll leave your number . . ." I never do. It would be such a disappointment to him to hear my voice on the recording when he's probably hoping every day for a call from a New York booking agent.

This time I was lucky; he answered himself on the third ring, his hello emerging from a prolonged yawn, so I knew he had been asleep. I could imagine his eyes gummy and his hair, the same faded red as my own, standing in tangles and rooster tails. "Oh, Sis," he yawned. "What's going on?"

"Not much," I answered. "Just the usual. Here."

Gail had just crawled damply into my lap. Like me, she is a slow waker. I held the phone to her ear, and she listened a minute before pushing it away. "Nobody talked," she reported. I listened. Sure enough, nobody talked. Mitchy must have been waiting too, at the other end, or else he had leaned his head against the wall and gone back to sleep with the receiver in his hand.

"Here, Mitch, it's Gail," I said, and held it to her ear again.

That woke them both up enough to exchange the basics. When I took the phone back, I asked when he was coming to see us. "Oh, don't know, don't know," he said. "Been pretty busy."

"Gail says make it soon." In truth, she hadn't said a

thing, she was too busy ramming her hand into the Alpha-Bits box on the table. But I felt sure she would have said that if she had understood what grown-ups considered it proper to say at such times.

"Listen, Mitchy, something's come up. Lisbeth—"

"Oh, Lord!"

"Lisbeth's coming here for Christmas. They called yesterday."

"So?"

"So that's a problem."

"Well, yeah. When was Lisbeth not a problem?" He yawned again and, I imagined, scratched his freckled and red-haired chest. I waited.

"Tell them she can't come," he suggested. "Tell them they'll have to do something else, you have your own children to look after."

"But we're her family. She'll feel so bad if we don't let her come. Anyway, they say she can't stay there for the holidays, and I don't know anywhere else she can go."

"Yeah, well, neither do I."

"Stan thought maybe you and Beep could take her for part of the time. You know, share the wealth."

"Yeah? So Stan said that, did he? The Honor Graduate said I could take care of my big sister so he wouldn't have to look at her, is that right? Well, what does he know about it?"

Mitchy always calls Stan "the Honor Graduate" when he gets ticked off at him. It's because Stan finished mechanics school and got a good job at a Buick dealership and he didn't, he dropped out.

"Don't get mad," I said. "I just thought—"

"You just thought you'd run it by me, right? Well, you ran it by and it kept running."

"Hey, come on, Mitchy—"

"The answer is no." He hung up.

I sat there and told myself it was no use crying, I should have known he would react that way. How else could he? After all, there wasn't much of a way he could look after Sister. He had to go to work, and when he was home from work he had to sleep. So how could he manage her? It was just that I didn't know how I could either.

By this time Davey had arrived and was trying to climb over the tray into his high chair. He had just made it when the phone rang. I knew who it was, of course. I didn't even bother with hello, just picked it up and said, "Yeah?"

"Look," Mitchy said, "she's going to be here a week, two weeks, right?"

"Three," I said, but I don't think he heard it.

"She could come here for a night or two on my days off. Maybe she could go to Beep's for a night or two. Maybe the roommate'll be going somewhere for Christmas. That'd spread it around a little, wouldn't it?"

"Beep can't handle her and you know it." I thought how Beep always was with Lisbeth. Two minutes and she had had it. It was impossible.

"What, then?"

I sighed. "You've stolen my line."

"No, I mean it. What are you going to do?"

What was *I* going to do, I got that. He had offered to help, of course—Mitchy's basically sweet—but that left the real responsibility right where it had been, with me.

"I don't know," I said. "Put sheets on the roll-away bed and hope for the best, I guess."

There was a long pause during which I could distinctly hear him scratching himself. Mitchy has to scratch to think. If he ever had to make a major decision, he'd flay himself. Finally he said, "I wonder if Mama thought about this when she took off," and hung up again. Mitchy doesn't believe in good-byes.

I wondered too if Mama had thought about this. I wondered about it while I cleaned up the breakfast things and got the children dressed, and while I put clothes in to wash. What I decided was, this was exactly the kind of thing she would have thought about. Not that she didn't care about our having to take on something we weren't prepared to handle and really couldn't handle, because it was too big a problem for anyone to handle and besides, we had all our other, ordinary complications. Not that she didn't care what it would mean for me, specifically, being the oldest. The oldest, that is, other than Lisbeth. But she must have looked ahead too, and seen countless more years of feeling trapped and enslaved when Sister was at home and guilty about her own sense of relief when she wasn't. And she must have seen how it wasn't doing any good anyway, since Lisbeth was still the same as ever, or worse, even after she had poured herself out for her that way. And she must have realized she wasn't up to it, she had simply reached her limit.

It had been nearly a year now since Daddy had reappeared, as abruptly as he had vanished, and taken Mama away with him, and none of us had heard a word from either of them since that day. It was absolutely astounding.

Odd—after struggling for years to establish my independence and show I didn't need her, now, having done that pretty successfully, I was wishing Mama was here to help. And not just now that this matter of Sister's Christmas visit had come up, but at various times, with various things, with the children, with Stan. I needed a mother now in a way that I hadn't when I was eighteen, twenty, twenty-one.

The story of Mama's leaving is a strange one; I don't claim to understand it. It starts, really, when Daddy left. I was thirteen, which made Mitchy eleven and Beep just eight. We never knew why he went, any more than we knew where. One day he just wasn't there. Mama got a letter in a plain envelope with no return address, postmarked right here in Dallas, saying he wasn't hurt or in trouble, he just wasn't coming back. She cried and raved and cried some more. But we didn't cry at all. Maybe we were too stupefied, and just plain scared. And disgraced too; we felt that acutely. None of our friends at school had been abandoned by their fathers. Not absolutely and out of the blue like that.

After she got over the initial shock, Mama seemed to get along all right. But then, what did we know about how she got along? We were just kids. For all we knew, she might have been crying all day while we were at school and all night while we were asleep. But she had always been the one who managed for us really, not Daddy, and she seemed to do all right.

She became an Avon representative and a Tupperware representative and a magazine representative—I don't mean in succession, but all at once. Anything that promised a little money while letting her stay home after school hours or on days we stayed home sick, she signed on to do. I can still see her sample bags and her sensible shoes and her brisk skirts and shirt-style jackets—it was the age of polyester knit—and our car trunk piled with boxes and bags of catalog-order merchandise for delivery. It's a wonder she didn't take cold cream to the ones who'd ordered cake boxes and send food container orders off to the *Good Housekeeping* circulation department. But she seemed to juggle everything without a slip. And we got by. Of course, there was always the problem of Sister, always some kind of crisis or another, always the worry of what might happen, what if the School turned her out, what if . . . we didn't even know how to finish the question. We only knew we wouldn't be able to handle it.

We grew up, more or less. I started college; Mitchy joined the musicians' union and started auto-mechanics school, both about the same time. Beep finished high school and got pregnant and then got un-pregnant; I got married and had a baby. And then one day Daddy showed up again— from Alaska, he said. All those years when we didn't hear from him except to get a fifty-dollar or hundred-dollar bill in a Christmas card once a year, he had been in Alaska. And in three days, just three short days, he was gone again, and Mama with him. She went off with a stranger—because that's what it amounts to, after twelve years. And not just went off with, but eloped, practically climbed down a ladder from her bedroom window, or would have if it had been a two-story house, leaving a note behind: "I have gone off with your father, don't know where, Meg can take over my Avon." That was it. And not a word since.

And I didn't want the Avon anyway.

Talking with Mitchy had got me to thinking about Mama and what she and Daddy might be doing, where they might be. Sometimes I wondered if they were even still alive. They could have driven off the road in the desert somewhere; we would have no way of knowing. Mostly I liked to think of them having a good time together, a better time than they had had before. But there was a little resentment mixed in with that too. They had ridden off into the sunset and left me to take care of their problems as casually as Mama had assigned me her Avon customers. I didn't want their problems. I felt like yelling, the way I used to when we were kids, "Mama! Come take care of Sister!"

After I got the children dressed and off playing in their room, with a promise that we would take the red wagon and walk to the store in a little while, I decided I might as well get it over with, and called the woman at the Home. Just a shade huffier than she had been the day before, she saw fit to tell me I didn't seem to have a very good outlook about this. I could hardly believe it—I was actually being scolded by long-distance telephone. Their clients, she said, had as much need for love and a family as anyone else. What could I say? Of course they did. I told her it was just that there had been problems lately.

We settled on a date and a time, and she volunteered that they would make sure Sister had enough medication when she came home to last her through the holidays. Well, I would hope so! The last thing I needed was for her to have a seizure while she was here. I thanked the woman excessively and praised her work, told her what wonderful things we thought the Home was doing. Then after I hung up I wondered why I had faked it like that, why I hadn't just told her what I thought of her and her assumption that she could just drop this on me whenever she felt like it. The answer was obvious. I hadn't done that because I couldn't risk offending her. Because they might get mad and not let Sister come back after Christmas. Then I wouldn't know what to do for sure. Because there wasn't anywhere else for her to go. Because it would all fall on me, now that Mama was gone.

After talking to the superintendent's secretary, I needed an outing as much as the children did. I put Davey in the wagon, and Gail alternated between riding and pulling, and we went to the store for the day's supplies: peanut butter, bread, bananas, two cans of green beans. We were in no hurry. It was a bright, breezy day, perfect sweater weather, and I was happy for them to burn up their energy climbing in and out of the wagon so they would be ready for a nap after lunch. Stan was right. I needed to turn over a new leaf on the matter of their daily schedule.

On the way home they were happy to stay in the wagon, because then there was the bag of groceries they could dispute possession of. They sat with their legs apart and their arms wrapped around the bag, first one of them and then the other. I devised a plan of switching it back and forth every third house. "Der!" Davey would exclaim, with great satisfaction, every time the bag came back to him. Gail would look concerned—I guess she thought he might unaccountably throw it overboard—and when she got it back she would cling to it with an air of great conscientiousness.

It must have been all that switching of the groceries

and the long discussions of fairness that went with it that kept me from noticing Mitchy's car in front of our house. We were starting up the driveway when I heard him shout, "Hey, aren't you even going to say hello?"

"Mitchy!" I cried. "What are you doing here?"

Gail promptly climbed out of the wagon, considered whether to abandon the groceries to their fate, and after some wavering decided in favor of Mitchy. "At's all," she stated, and made a run for him. Davey was too busy being pleased with sole ownership of the bag to notice. He wrapped his arms and legs around it and crowed again, "Der!" I realized belatedly that the loaf of bread was going to be hourglass-shaped.

"Hey, Sis," he said, as he came up. I had never particularly liked being called Sis, but I was too glad to see him to object. "What's going on?"

"You know about all there is," I answered. Suddenly I felt touchy, offended, and struggled to keep from showing it. Funny, I always do try to keep from showing it. Maybe that was my trouble with Stan. I tried so hard not to show things that he never knew they were there. Or else he got mixed signals.

By then Davey had realized what was going on, and he climbed out too, and went for Uncle Mitch. Mitchy carried the two of them up the driveway to the back door while I pulled the wagon with the groceries. Even the dog was excited, and ran back and forth along the fence, barking.

"Just like twenty years ago," he said. "If it wasn't for these two." He nodded toward the wagon. "You remember how we used to go to the store for Mama and take the

31

wagon? You always pulled. I didn't want to. Our wagon looked just like this one."

"It was this one," I told him.

"You mean it? This is our old wagon?" He put the children down and knelt down to look. I noticed the hairs on the back of his neck, showing he needed a haircut. That was something new; he used to wear it so long that his neck didn't show at all.

"It sure looks beat-up enough, all right. I can believe it's our old one. I'm just surprised it hasn't rusted out before now." He grinned and shook his head over it. "That's neat, your having our old wagon."

"It couldn't have been twenty years ago, though," I pointed out. "That would have made you five and me seven. You don't think Mama would have let us walk to the store by ourselves when we were just five and seven, do you?"

"Well, we weren't much more than that. Maybe six and eight. But we used to go to the store and take the wagon. I can remember that."

We went in and made peanut butter and jelly sandwiches, and he cut a banana into his, the same way he used to. Gail said his sandwich was silly, then asked me to make hers that way. I poured big glasses of milk all around. Afterward we raided the cookie jar, and the cookies were oatmeal chocolate chip, just like we used to have at home. By then the kids were sleepy, and I took them off for their naps.

When I came back, Mitchy was still sitting at the table, just sitting. He looked up and said, "I might as well not have grown up. It hasn't done me a damn bit of good."

It caught me by surprise. "I wish I hadn't sometimes," I

admitted, and immediately felt tears well up. I dropped into a chair and put my face in my hands and cried for five minutes. I don't know why I did that; it was crazy. But things had just gotten too much for me.

Mitchy was always a good person to cry with, and he hadn't lost his touch. He just sat right there and let me go on, accepted it without fussing over me or making me feel silly. He could hold up to being cried to. After a few minutes, he put his hand on my head and said, "Poor Sis!" I shook my head; I wasn't through yet. But his doing that made me feel better right off. I wanted to have my cry out, but it wasn't so bad anymore, it was almost a luxury.

At just the right time he stuck a couple of Kleenexes in front of me, and I was able to stop crying and blow my nose.

"Well!" I wavered. "I don't know what that was all about." I was feeling pretty embarrassed by then.

"Things pretty bad, are they?"

"No, not bad. Just not good." I felt my lips start to tremble again and could barely finish.

"How are you and Stan doing?"

"Oh, I don't know. Fair. Not bad, not good. I get scared sometimes."

"Yeah," he said. "So do I. About everything."

We talked some, mostly about Sister and how hard it had always been to know what to do for her. He remembered those holiday visits too, the same as I did. He said that when Sister would have a specially bad day, he used to go to bed and keep his eyes open as long as he could, just looking at the light under the door or at the little bit of light at the window, whatever there was to look at, because if he let them close, the next time he opened them he might look out and see nothing at all—a blank, or a darkness like the dark ceiling of his room after even the hall light was out. Then he would be like her. He said it mockingly, making fun of himself for being afraid like that, but it wasn't a funny thing to remember.

And we talked about Beep too. He wanted to know if I had seen her new boyfriend. I hadn't. Mitchy was worried about her. "Concerned," I guess, is the word. He didn't like the whole thing. The new boyfriend was ten years older than Beep if he was a day, maybe closer to twenty. He said he wasn't married, but if that was true why wouldn't he give her a home phone number? And she had shown Mitchy a gold chain he had given her, with some kind of diamond drop on it. It looked expensive. Mitchy was uneasy. What could I say? I was uneasy too.

He stood up and stretched, showing the flat belly that I wished was a family trait, and said he had to go do a couple of lessons.

I went to the front door with him and told him next time not to make it so long. He stood there and looked out at nothing in particular, as though he didn't want to leave. He was so young. Just two years younger than I am, but he looked like a kid. He always did look a lot younger, to me. Or maybe I just always felt a lot older.

After a minute he sort of shook himself and said, Well, he'd better be going, sure enough. He looked at me then, with his flecked-hazel eyes all empty, just looked and looked, as if he wanted me to know what he was meaning without having to say it. But I didn't, I couldn't. And I guess he gave up on me, because then he heaved a deep breath and asked did I remember how Sister used to play "Find-us" and we would turn it into a real blindman's buff. Uncomfortably, I did. "That's how I feel sometimes," he said. "Just like she must have felt then. Like I keep going after things, but they keep moving away."

He started down the walk toward his car, then turned back to say he'd be in touch about taking over with Sister for part of the time she was home. I shouldn't have to do it all, he said. He hesitated again, then asked, speculatively, "Where do you think they are? Mama and Daddy, I mean."

I shook my head. I didn't have an answer for that. And I didn't see him again for three months.

3

୦ଏ୦ଏ୦ଏ

"Find-us" and "Take-off" had been Sister's favorite games. Actually, I guess they were just about her only games. There was very little we were ever able to figure out for her to do.

Mostly it was Daddy who played with her. That was his one household chore. He didn't take out trash or gather up wet towels like we did, and Mama did all the real house-keeping and cooking—did it doggedly, resentfully, with a fierce pride in her own ability to go on being unfairly treated. Daddy never took us to the doctor or disciplined us or went to conferences with teachers either. He and Mama had a clear division of labor: He earned money and mowed the yard, she did everything else. But whether through some complicated process of negotiation that we were never aware of or just through the accidental formation of a habit, he did take on the duty of keeping Sister occupied while

36

Mama got dinner ready and while she cleared the table and washed the dishes.

He must have simply stumbled onto "Find-us" in the course of trying to think what to do with her. She was always groping things out anyway, finding things. Or especially finding people; finding us, even if we crouched very small and hoped very hard not to be found, even if we were very quiet. Most of all if we were very quiet. So all he had to do was make a game of it by giving it a name and a regular, repetitive format. Because Sister was devoted to repetition; she lived by it. I guess repetition was a way of making her world stay put, so she could get hold of it.

I can remember one summer night—or maybe a composite of many nights, but I remember it as one—when the three of us, Beep and Mitchy and I, were out in the back yard running around and falling on the grass while Daddy sat on the back step with Sister and smoked. I must have been six or seven at the time, because I remember Beep being there, but very little, just toddling. And it must have been during Sister's summer vacation, because she would have been gone to the School by then. She went when I was six. There were lightning bugs out, I remember that. I can close my eyes and summon up that night, just as clear as if it were last week, and see the lightning bugs blinking on and off, first one place and then another, above the bushes, over by the driveway. The grass must have been full of chiggers. It always was, in the summer. We never noticed them when we were playing, only later when Mama stretched us across her lap and dabbed our bites with rubbing alcohol or the dreaded Mercurochrome, with its glass wand.

One thing that puzzles me about that night, as I remember it, is why I see Mama in the kitchen window. Because if it was summer, it would have stayed light a long time, and I don't know why she wouldn't have finished in the kitchen before time to turn on the lights. Maybe she had had a bad time with Sister that day, or with the baby, Beep, who would surely have been just a toddler then, and hadn't been able to start supper when she should. Or maybe Daddy had persuaded her to go get Sno-Cones or soft ice cream before she started the dishes. Sometimes he came up with ideas like that. Who knows? Anyway, I know that it was dark enough outside for there to be lightning bugs and for me to see her in the square light of the window.

Sister had been fretting, I remember, and Daddy had been trying to ignore her while he smoked his cigarette. I can remember the red glow of it, among the tiny yellow glows going on and off, on and off. He had that look that kept me away from him sometimes; that may have been another reason why Mitchy and I kept running around and falling down. But then he threw his head back, exhaled, and ground out his cigarette on the concrete strip that ran from the back steps around to the garage.

"Okay," he said. "Take off."

With a kind of crow, Sister got to her feet and shuffled a little way out into the yard, then turned and shuffled back, bending forward from the knees and reaching out, down, sweeping the air in front of her to find Daddy again. He sat still, quiet as could be. Only if she had veered off or was about to bump into something would he make a sound, and then just the least sound, the merest throat-clearing or finger-tapping. The trick was for her to make a true about-face, after she had "taken off," so as to go straight back to where she had started without drifting to one side or the other. When her feet encountered the concrete strip, she knew she was getting close. It was probably good training for her, or would have been if she had been able to benefit from training. And I guess it was a real challenge, judging from the way her face split into a grin when she went straight to him again.

Sometimes it seemed as though she could play that game by the hour. Out away from Daddy (always him, never anyone else, for that game), back, out, back. Really, it was wonderful the way she could stay on course, or if she strayed off, the way she could locate him again on just the slightest cue. And of course we always praised her extravagantly for her successes, even Mitchy and me, at no more than five or six years old. And the more we fussed over her, the more excited she got and the farther she went from home base, which was Daddy. She made little proud crowing sounds, and her slow shuffle became a jerky, hesitating trot—a slow hurry, you might say.

That night that I'm remembering, with the lightning bugs and the soft, woolly stars and Mama in the window, Daddy must have been feeling really low. He did sometimes, I think. I remember him having, pretty often, a certain look that I now think was a look of feeling trapped, a look that said 'What's the use?' I think that's how he was feeling that night, because I remember how his face didn't change at all when he told Sister, "Great, terrific," and his voice didn't soften one iota. But he kept at it, he kept playing her game, and Mitchy and I kept running and tumbling and knocking Beep gently over on the grass, and Mama kept looking out at us over the dishes. And when she saw that we were looking at her, she smiled. But if she didn't know we were looking her face had no smile at all.

Then Sister began to get tired of the game. Oh, she kept it up, all right; she always kept something up once she was started on it, until somebody started her on something else. That was a whole problem in itself. But she began to fret in little wordless, whining syllables while she went out and straight back, out and straight back. Mama was still at the sink, in the lighted window, washing dishes. Or maybe she had taken the stove burners apart to scrub, maybe that was why the whole thing was taking so long. Because instead of quitting and taking Sister in for her bath, Daddy stood up, lit another cigarette and walked partway out into the yard with her. Mitchy and I, sitting on the grass, panting, knew what was coming. The other game, Find-us. Really it was a variation of the same one. It was like Take-off but different.

To start this game, Sister stood still and Daddy moved. He walked away from her a few steps, walking normally, so that she could hear him, then said OK and veered off another way, but this time moving softly, as near silently as he could. The challenge was for Sister to find him anyway, after he had moved. She would listen, listen, for the least signal, the slightest shuffle of a foot or the merest click of his tongue, for his very breathing. Then she would close in on him, arms outstretched, ready to grab. He would tickle her or swing her as she caught hold of him, and she would whoop with laughter.

Sometimes Daddy turned his part of this game over to one of us, Mitchy or me, or to both of us—hence its name, Find-us. We liked taking over for him, but there was an element of hazard to it too, because when she came groping for us and found us, she grabbed hard, shaking us or pinching or tickling or all at once. She seemed very big to me then; her hands were everywhere, impossible to elude. And she was totally without restraint, while I, even if I had been strong enough to fend her off, knew that I had to be careful with her. My only resort was to laugh and laugh and laugh— the shrill laugh, as I remember it, of panic.

It was as a kind of equalizer, I guess, or maybe just because we were kids and jealous of all the attention she always got and full of kids' meanness, or maybe because we had seen Daddy giving himself up to gloom that we took the game a step further that night. Instead of one silent move, we started making several, eluding her with quick jumps and other tricky maneuvers. That made the game great fun for us, but frustrating, even more frustrating than usual, for Sister. She knew what we were doing. Daddy knew it too, of course, but he turned us loose anyway. Even while he kept playing we had been making little raids on the game, dashing in and tapping her, making it hard for her to concentrate on finding him. And finally he just backed out of it and left her to us.

We took turns at first. I remember that when it was Mitchy's turn I looked back and saw Mama's face again in the window, frowning, anxious. But we were too far gone into the game; I couldn't take it easy now.

We darted and ran, giggling, unable to keep still a minute, no longer even trying to be quiet. Sister whirled and lunged at us, chortling. I remember how she came at me when it was my turn to be It—bent over, stretching out her arms and shaking them in a wild witch-doctor dance, clenching and opening and clenching her hands. It was a game, only a game. I laughed till I screamed.

And still that wasn't enough. The faster she lurched after us, the faster we spun away. We began to dash in on each other's turns, we broke all the rules. Even Beep, who should surely have been in bed by then, dashed and nipped at her like a puppy. We were all like puppies, baiting a lumbering, friendly old bear. Daddy stood off to one side, quietly laughing around his cigarette.

Then it happened. Sister reached too far or tried to go too fast. Her feet were never quite under control anyway. She fell on her face, and not just on her face, but on top of Beep. Beep screamed and kicked. Sister, after a minute of stunned shock, roared.

Mama's face disappeared from the kitchen window and reappeared flying out the back door. A huge dark lump was already coming up on Beep's forehead, and Lisbeth's lower lip was bleeding. Mama dabbed at it with the hem of her dress and tried to comfort both of them at once, shushing and patting and saying sweet, soothing things that had no effect whatever.

The rest of us stood around doing nothing. There was nothing we could think of to do. We knew it was our fault.

We had let the game get out of control. Mama, I remember, looked at Daddy in the middle of the uproar and said to him, "Well, Frank, you did it again."

Again? I thought. Again?

After they got Sister in and Mama was getting her to bed, Daddy came back out and sat on the step with Mitchy and Beep and me. Beep took over his lap, where I wanted to be, and went to sleep with her face against his undershirt. But he blew smoke rings for us, and we got to sit close against him, one on each side. I held off sleep by making faces at Mitchy. But I felt miserable and overcome by a great dread. All too soon Mama came out and said it was bedtime, but for probably the first time in my life I wouldn't go, and when they tried to make me, I cried and held onto the doorknob. It was dark in that bedroom. The more they tried to make me go in there, the louder I cried. I positively screamed, clenched my fists and screamed, and wouldn't let any of them touch me. I remember Mitchy cowering against the opposite wall. And no wonder; I had never done such a thing in my life, only Sister had. Finally Daddy reached past my flailing fists—I tried to fight him off—and picked me up and carried me bodily to bed. Then he sat on the side of the bed beside me, and he promised to stay there until I was asleep and not let anyone turn off the light.

It was Sister's hands. That was what had done it. It was being grabbed and held and clutched and pawed and not being able to fend those hands off. How could I have told them that it was just that, nothing but that? They wouldn't have understood. I didn't understand myself; I only felt it. It was later that I remembered how I had felt and realized what had set me off.

It was her hands. All my life, as long as I could remember, she had been grabbing me and groping over me. If I got a cookie—or an apple or a glass of Kool-Aid or any other good thing, but say a cookie—Sister was all over me, groping with those seeing fingers of hers over my face, my mouth as I chewed, out my arm to where I was holding the rest of it, finding my hand no matter how elusively I waved it around. If I tried switching whatever it was that I wanted to keep from one hand to the other, she used both of hers— insistent, exploring fingers—to find and unclench each of mine. She was like one of those rubber bathtub mats with rows and rows of little suction cups—she fastened herself onto me until she found whatever I had and pried it out of my hand and stuffed it into her own mouth. And always, every time it happened, I had that same feeling of panic. When I read about dragons and goblins in those monstrous storybooks that people seem to think are good for children, I always imagined them with great damp clutching hands that no one could get away from.

There's a story Mama used to tell about me, as far back as I can remember, about my refusing a cookie, saying I wouldn't take one unless my sister got one too. I was a little thing, she said, not more than three or four, but already such a little mother toward Lisbeth (she always used that very phrase—such a little mother) even though she was a year older than me. I'm not sure it ever happened. I don't recognize myself in that self-denying little saint Mama liked to picture. But if it did happen, I know why. It was because I would have been better off making sure she had her own cookie in the first place, so she wouldn't fasten onto me to get mine.

One day when I was about twelve years old, and Sister had been away at the School, off and on at least, for years, we all drove to Austin to see her. I don't know if it was a school holiday or Mama just let us miss a day but, anyway, we went.

Daddy was at his best that day, I remember. He always tended to be at his best in the car. He would sing and tell jokes and think of games to play. The rest of the time he was silent, silently demanding attention, severe. We never knew what he was thinking about, or if he was thinking anything. But in the car, going somewhere, he was great fun; he made us believe, for the moment, that he was a jolly dad.

It was after three in the afternoon when we got there, nearly time for school to be over for the day. They let me out at the front while the rest went to park the car. I don't know why me. Maybe I had fretted and wiggled more than Mitchy and Beep, so they thought I needed it more. Or maybe I had wiggled least, so I was being rewarded. I don't know. Anyway, I was supposed to go in and wait in the main hall to find Sister when she came out of class. They would park and walk back. I think they had some bit of business to take care of in the principal's office.

I found the hall, and I thought I knew where to wait, to watch for her. I stood there, cowering from the reverberations of my own solitary footsteps in that empty tile hall. There wasn't another soul in sight; there wasn't a sound.

Suddenly there came a prolonged, ripping buzz, and

doors banged, and the hall filled with noise and bodies, pouring out of every door. They shuffled, shambled, groped their way along, some sweeping, sweeping canes in front of them, some few stepping out, high-kneed, in a terrible parody of self-confidence, a cross between stepping out and holding back. I backed against the wall as they bore down on me. The reason, though I didn't know it, was that I was standing by the end of a bank of lockers. They all needed to go to their lockers at the end of the day. But I didn't know why they all came that way, right at me. The first ones bumped against me, apologized, sidestepped, went on. They were used to it; they bumped into people all the time.

I was small for my age, skinny and short both. They all seemed big; they seemed huge. They loomed over me. I pressed myself against the wall, trying to stay out of the way. But there was no eluding them. These were not pretty, pathetic waifs, you understand, blind but otherwise perfect. That's not the way it happens, usually. Some of them were elongated, skinny, cadaverous, with black sunken hollows where eyes should have been and small, pointed heads. Others were grossly fat, with bloated, clumsy bodies, thick and lumbering, and broad, blank faces with wet, shapeless mouths. There were twisted, beaked bird faces, bare scalps with random tufts of hair, raw winey birthmarks, pus-oozing eye sockets, faces like lumps of modeling clay squeezed and poked by an incompetent modeler. To me, they were a mob of monsters, bearing in on me. I stuffed my fist into my mouth, for fear I would scream and they would all, all of them in the width of that now huge corridor, turn on me at once.

But there was no way to elude them all. One and then another and another came guiding themselves along the wall to where I stood. They bumped against me, they noticed me and knew I was not one of them, they crowded around, talking to each other about me in what seemed to be a language of their own, syllables I was too scared even to recognize as words. Their hands went over my face and my neck, into my hair, down my arms. Their fingers were like fast-growing tentacles of ivy. They had me.

I must have screamed. I had to have screamed, because Daddy said later that he and Mama came running. But by then I had broken into a sweat, and the light had narrowed, and the floor had come up to meet me. The next thing I knew I was waking up on the principal's cracked brown couch, and they were all—Mama, Daddy, the principal— clutching me, feeling of me, holding a wet cloth on me. I woke up screaming and remembering that night in the back yard and Sister's hands.

It was only then, for the first time, that I realized how awful she looked—like those monstrously pitiful others in the hall—and how she had always terrified me.

4

AT BREAKFAST a couple of days later, Stan asked if the people at the Home had given me any trouble when I told them Lisbeth couldn't come. You could have knocked me over. So much for bed persuasion!

When I didn't answer, he looked up from his plate and said, "Well? Didn't you call them?"

"Sure I called them," I said. "I told you I was going to, the next day."

"And? Did they give you any trouble?"

"I told them OK, she could come. We set it up."

"You what?" He set his coffee mug down hard. "Meg—Jesus!"

As usual, I felt tears gathering behind my eyes and nose, and I knew my voice would be trembling soon. I hated that! Why couldn't I learn to argue without crying? But I felt attacked, blamed; I was being put on the spot and I could never seem to take that without crumbling.

He looked really mad, as if I had done this just for spite. "What on earth did you tell them that for?" he demanded. "After we talked about it! You knew I didn't want—"

"After we talked about it is right!" I cried. "You said OK! You said she could come! You agreed!"

"Damn it!" He was practically yelling by this point. "I did *not* agree! I said she could *not* come here. You know I said that!"

"Later," I insisted. "When we talked about it later you changed your mind. We had an agreement." At least, I thought we had had an agreement. True, it was an agreement I had cheated to get. But that had been part of the game from time immemorial. It was understood and accepted that wives would cheat that way. That was our equalizer.

I could tell he knew what I meant and didn't want to talk about it. Leaving his half cup of coffee, he stood up, flung his chair back, and marched off to the bedroom to brush his teeth and stow his comb and wallet in his pocket. When he came back through, he stopped only to point his finger at me—close enough that I noticed the grime around the nail—and tell me, through clenched teeth, "If you do want this thing to work, you're sure going about it funny."

"This thing," of course, was our marriage.

With that he went straight out the door, started the car, and backed out of the driveway. But then, instead of tires squealing as he took off down the street, I heard the car come back up the driveway and heard him throw it into park—there was that distinct shift to a higher pitched whine. Then he was back and totally different from when he walked out, his eyes soft as suede and his mouth no longer set in a line but drooping, all misery. He picked up the chair he had knocked over, pushed it neatly under the table, and came around to put his hands on my shoulders.

"Sorry, sweetheart," he whispered. He ruffled my hair for good-bye and went out again. The car door slammed shut, the car went into gear, and this time when he backed out he drove away.

I poured myself another cup of coffee.

What I had just seen was typical Stan: sudden rage, sudden sweetness, the quick shift. It was something I had never learned to cope with, and I had a feeling I never would. What I had learned, though, was to adopt an ironic tone. Typical Stan, one of Stan's better performances, Stan's thing again, today's episode; these were the phrases I said to myself after one of those unsettling scenes, trying to assume a detachment I didn't feel. Underneath I was as unsettled and upset by it as ever, every time. And if I let these quick shifts of mood, which were as natural to him as peeing standing up, get me down every time, what was the outlook? How could I hold up to twenty or thirty years of it? I imagined myself going off someday, like Mama, only alone.

I guess it's just the usual thing for people to idealize each other before they're married, and then learn better. Anyway, it was sure true for me, with Stan. Even if I hadn't been so crazy then, so full of big ideas from a couple of sociology classes that dating was more like a workbook exercise than a personal encounter, I would just naturally have idealized him. Any girl would have. Sandy haired, hazel eyed, broad but not stocky, and always a trace of engine grease around his fingernails and a sheepish look on his face—the all-American boy, only not quite a kid anymore. Which made him twice as attractive to someone who was still a kid herself, only she didn't admit it. And he joked and whirled me around by the waist and told me he had never done those things before, those certain wonderful things we did in the back seat of the car, or at least not when they meant anything, not till now. In a way it was his first time too, since I was the first one they had meant anything with, so there was the potent charm of newness combined with his having enough practice to know what he was doing. How could I not idealize him?

So now we were having the usual rude awakening. It happens to everybody. But as I sat there among the crusting plates and forks, with the bright relentless sun showing up every dusty ledge and every grimy handprint, it seemed very rude indeed. Or actually, we had had our rude awakening when we separated for a while back in the spring, and it had been too much for us, we had gone back together. And now we were having it again.

The thing is, Stan was sweet, he really was, but only sporadically. That was the problem. His sweetness came in fits and starts, whereas I needed somebody I could count on to be steadily sweet, or at least civil.

I was still sitting there at the table, and the plates were still crusting, when Davey came in. He climbed right up into my lap and hid his face against the bacon-spattered lapel of my robe. I thought, uh-oh, that again. Davey had been having ear infections one after the other since he was six months old. We had just gotten through three weeks without earaches—the best he had ever done. But I knew it was too good to last.

As usual in the morning, the odor of ammonia nearly made my eyes water.

"Peuw," I said, "you smell like wee." Of course, I couldn't very well expect him to stay dry at night, when Gail didn't yet either, but I could at least make him aware of the problem. I gave him a little pinch in the tummy when I said it, though, so he would know I wasn't really scolding him. Then I stood up, with his arms and legs wrapped tightly around my neck and waist, and carried him back to his bed to get his night diaper off. While I was at it, I decided to check his temperature. It was 103—and that was at the start of the day. What would it be by late afternoon, when temperatures always go up? His skin felt hot and dry. After I fastened his diaper, he reached up for me to pick him up again and then rooted around on my shoulder, whining. I asked him, "Is that old ear hurting my baby again?" He thrashed against me in answer.

It occurred to me how disproportionate an amount of time and worry ears get, when you have young children. Ears are so small in comparison to heads and legs and backs. It's as if an auto mechanic spent all his time on turn signals. But thinking so didn't make the problem go away. There we were, poised at what looked like the start of another ear cycle. I knew the signs; no use trying to ignore them. I might as well give up and call the doctor.

Sometimes I wondered what had happened to old-fashioned child rearing, with old-fashioned self-reliance in coping with childhood diseases. What had our grandmothers, or their mothers, done when the baby cried and batted his ear? My own mother, I knew, had relied on our doctor as much as I did, maybe more. Daddy used to say we were doctor poor. Which was one of Stan's gripes too.

I gave Davey two baby aspirin and set him up with some dry Alpha-Bits and a glass of juice while I got on the phone, but he didn't want to eat. He only fretted and crushed the Alpha-Bits, one at a time, and scattered their sweet dust over the floor around his high chair. Gail, who had changed her own wet things before coming in, chose to scold him and explain how bad it was to make the floor dirty. She tried brushing the Alpha-Bit dust into little piles and then picking it up in pinches, which she deposited back onto his high-chair tray. It was not an efficient operation, and Davey didn't want his breakfast debris returned. He screeched and kicked at her every time she came close to deposit a little pinch of sugary dust. She ignored him. Now and then she stopped to dab a wet forefinger into what she had gathered and lick it off. Davey screeched louder, "No!"

While all this was going on, I was stuck on hold. When the receptionist finally did come back on the line, she tried to give me an appointment two days off. I told her that wouldn't do. The doctor was booked up, she said. I raised my voice: This was not a checkup, I had a sick baby and he needed to be seen today. She under*stood,* she insisted, but the doctor was booked up. Now, if I would see Dr. Krawitz instead . . . Of course I would. That was fine. Eleven-thirty? Eleven-thirty it was.

I was pleased as punch to get an appointment with Dr. Krawitz, who had come into practice with old Dr. Hill, my own baby doctor and Mitchy's and Beep's, just a few months ago. He had seen one or the other of the children twice now, and I had passed him in the hall a couple of times when taking them to Dr. Hill. Dr. Krawitz was much younger, maybe thirty-five, and to my Texas eyes, at least, distinctly foreign looking. Not only foreign looking, but in any usual sense decidedly not handsome: small, bony, big-nosed, heavy-lipped, hairy-wristed. But he had the most wonderful big brown eyes, so dark they were almost black, and he actually looked at me and talked to me—talked *to* me, not *at* me—in a low, bass-violin voice that would have made chicken pox sound appealing.

I began to think about what I would wear to take Davey in for his appointment.

First I needed to call Stan, to ask him to bring me the car. I had had an old junker while we were separated—that was one of the things he provided—but it hadn't been running for some weeks, and though he kept saying he was going to fix it up, he hadn't gotten around to it. I knew how he hated to be called at work, but that was just too bad, I had to.

Sure enough, he sounded crabby as all get-out when Jack called him to the phone. His hello was more or less a snarl. I guess he had known it would be me.

"Hey," I said, "I've got to take Davey to the doctor at eleven-thirty. Can you bring the car home?"

"What do you have to take him to the doctor for? He seemed fine last night."

"I know he did, but he woke up with fever. I guess it's his ears again."

"Don't you have any ear drops left from last time?"

I knew what he was getting at; we had been down that road before. But I wasn't about to take any shortcuts.

"He may need to have fluid removed," I insisted. "Besides, you know it won't clear up without antibiotics, and they won't prescribe antibiotics without seeing him."

"Shit! That's twenty-five bucks, you know that. Or more. I ought to start just signing my paychecks over to the doctor and not bother with the bank."

"Yeah, well, can you bring the car home?"

"What time's your appointment?"

I told him again.

"Eleven-thirty! Good Christ, Meg, use your head. I can't take my lunch hour that early, and I've got a carburetor apart here. Change it to this afternoon. Or tomorrow."

I probably could have, to afternoon anyway, but I didn't feel like it. He had no business acting like getting Davey to the doctor wasn't important enough for him to bother with. There was Davey, lying on the sofa with his blanket, sucking his thumb and looking all hollow-eyed. I heard somebody in the background, not Jack, say, "Hurry it up on the phone, there," and heard Stan answer, "Yeah, I'm about through." No wonder he hated for me to call him at work. But I couldn't let that make any difference now.

"I'll take the bus down," I told him, "and pick up the car. We'll meet you when you get off work." I knew he hated that too. He liked going out and getting in his own car and driving home himself.

He said "Shit" again and hung up.

We were just two blocks from a bus stop, and though I didn't ride the bus very often, if I ever really had to get somewhere I could. Of course, you can't get everywhere by bus, not in Dallas anyway; for instance, I couldn't get to Dr. Hill's and Dr. Krawitz's office. But one place I could get to was the Buick dealership where Stan worked. It was right on the route. And fortunately, I had my own car keys, so I didn't have to bother him when I got there.

When I told Gail we were going someplace on the bus, she was greatly pleased and went to get out her purse, a huge old worn-out one of mine with a big safety pin holding the strap on. I could hear her throwing toys out on the floor of her room, looking for it at the bottom of the toy box. I began to feel happier myself, and thought of my orange sweater that I wore only when I felt up to it. It seemed a shame for Davey's fever to be the occasion of an orange-sweater day, but that's how these things happen sometimes.

By eleven, when we went to catch the bus, he was feeling enough better to play grab-Gail around my shoulder—which made it a lot harder for me to carry him, of course. His thirty-five pounds already felt like a hundred. But it was a bright, cool, wonderful day, one of those days when everything has sharp outlines and even shuffling old ladies begin to feel like picking up their feet. I enjoyed being out and going somewhere, even if it was just to the doctor's office—especially since I had a crush on the doctor. We sat on the bus-stop bench and swung our feet, and Gail got up every minute or so to look down the street and report that the bus wasn't coming yet. I gave Davey another chewable aspirin while we waited. When the bus came, after five minutes or so, and we got on, I remembered to get a transfer to add to the collection in Gail's purse.

The doctor's reception room was jammed. I had to sit holding both of the children on my lap, knowing without doubt that this was doing nothing at all for my orange sweater or my brown corduroy slacks, or for my hairdo either, for that matter. But apparently Dr. Krawitz was used to seeing worse. He smiled at me, meeting my eyes in a confidential way, when we passed him in the hall on our way to an examining room. We hadn't had to wait long; in fact, we were called in ahead of several who were there before us. But they were probably waiting for Dr. Hill. Two of them scowled at me when the nurse called us in, and if they hadn't been attractive I might have told them my secret.

The first thing the nurse did, of course, was to weigh Davey and take his temperature. The way he cried, you would have thought he was scared to death. I couldn't help laughing—he never cries when I take it at home—but the nurse didn't seem to approve of my attitude. I guess she expected me to fuss over him and talk baby talk.

"He just looks so funny," I explained. "Bellowing away with the thermometer sticking out of his bottom." She stared at me, stony-faced. Ah, well, I didn't want her to think I was weird. I held his thrashing fists and patted one arm.

Wiping the Vaseline film off the thermometer, she held

it up, turned it a little, and said, "Why he doesn't even have a temp! I thought you said you had to get him in today."

I felt a little sheepish and mumbled something about aspirin, but the set of her mouth told me she wasn't buying it. I saw her write beside the date in his record, "Mother says temp 103 this A.M. (?), says pain left ear (?)." She went out, shooting the file into a rack on the door.

Gail had been taking it all in, but now went back to her picture book, one of those with things to feel worked into the pictures—pieces of sandpaper, fluff, whatever. We didn't have any like that at home. I sat down on one of the two straight metal chairs and held Davey, wrapping my arms around him to keep him warm. He had nothing on but his diaper, of course. Doctors' offices are always good about having you undress kids and then wait in a cold room.

After about fifteen minutes—longer than we had waited in the reception room—Dr. Krawitz came in, personable as ever. He mussed Gail's hair and asked how we were today. He looked at the chart. "Those ears getting you again, are they? Tell Mama to lift you up here so I can take a look."

That was how he always was; he never said a word that didn't fit the standard bedside manner. He pretended to talk to the children and referred to me as Mama. And yet I always felt, or chose to feel, that there was a little ironic tinge to it, as if he were saying, Yes, this is the game we have to play, but you and I know it's only a game. I had convinced myself that he thought of me as special in some way—that he thought of *me,* period, not just of Patient X's mother—and that he liked to see me, and on the strength of that conviction I acted as though we were actual acquaintances. Just in little ways, nothing out of order. I asked how he'd been, how he was liking Dallas—just a word here or there that wasn't strictly necessary. And then he looked at me with those big, brown, slightly foreign eyes, as if he were seeing someone worth talking to, a little, anyway. I stood beside him at the examining table, patting Davey's legs while the nurse held his arms down and Dr. Krawitz peered into his ears and down his throat, and the hem of the stiffly starched lab coat brushed my pants leg. It was almost a sexual experience.

Oh, yes, Davey did have an ear infection. I couldn't help glancing, in a see-there way, at the nurse. Some people, he said, and frowned slightly, might lance ears like these—I knew he was thinking of Dr. Hill, but we two didn't have to spell things out—but he didn't like lancing unnecessarily. He would prescribe antibiotics, though; maybe he had some sample packages there that he could give me, and he'd give Davey an injection to get him started. "All right, big fella," he quipped, "you won't like this, but it likes you." Then, while the nurse prepared the syringe, he looked at me directly and said, "Do call me if you have any problems."

Not just "call me," I noted, but "*do* call me"; the difference seemed significant. I thought about it while I dressed Davey and got us out through the reception room. And "any problems": Did that include boredom? frustration? failure to reach orgasm?

Just joking, of course. Nothing to it. But then, I scolded myself, even if I was just joking, this was getting ridiculous.

I started the car.

Ridiculous or not, all this wishful thinking had me

revved up and restless. It was a beautiful day, and I had the car, for once, a car that actually ran, and the last thing I wanted to do was to turn around and go home. I looked back at Davey. After all, he was supposed to be sick. But his two doses of aspirin had brought his fever down. The flush in his cheeks was gone, and he was jabbering with Gail and pointing at things out the window.

Where to go was another question. The zoo was too far, and Davey probably wasn't up to that big an outing. It was too nice a day for an indoor shopping mall. Then I remembered a nice little area of shops, sort of an outdoor pedestrian mall, where a street had been closed off and plants in oversized pots had been hauled in and grouped here and there with wooden benches around them. A nice little area. The shops were expensive, but I wasn't going to buy anything anyway, just walk around and look. We could look at windows for a little while and have an ice cream cone and still have plenty of time to get dinner started before time to pick up Stan. I checked the mirror and felt glad I had dressed a little better than usual.

Sure enough, it was just as nice as I remembered. There were yellow chrysanthemums blooming around the crepe myrtle trunks in all the planters, and plenty of shade and sun, both. The children got into the spirit of the occasion and ran up and down, giggling and watching each other. At first I tried to keep Davey quiet, but that seemed cruel when he was having so much fun, and it was easier to let him go. They stopped at some of the windows to press their hands and faces against the glass and look in at the displays of candy, coffee mugs, scented soaps, wooden toys. It seemed that everything looked wonderful to them—and to me too.

Along with our ice cream, we had an oversized cookie to share—nearly three dollars in all, but I felt like splurging. And while we were sitting down eating our treats, a smartly skinny girl in tight slacks, high heels, and a dozen or more hoop bracelets came by, with a sort-of-nice-looking man considerably older than she was. I was just appraising her and making my own guesses about *that* situation when I realized who, under the makeup, she was.

"Beep!" I called. "For gosh sakes!"

I jumped up and advanced toward her, breaking off part of the chocolate chip cookie, which landed on the pavement between us.

She turned around as if thinking she should have known she couldn't get away with it, something would happen to spoil everything.

"Well, if it isn't Meg," she said flatly, and brushed my cheek with hers. "The happy mother. And the two happy tots."

They eyed her over their ice cream cones, probably wondering who she was. They couldn't have known; she hadn't been around since Easter or before.

We stood looking at each other, both of us, I guess, groping for something suitable to say to a sister on her way to becoming a stranger. She introduced me to the man she was with, no doubt the boyfriend Mitchy had told me about, the one he hadn't approved of. From the looks of him, I didn't either. He was polite enough, but seemed less than enchanted to be meeting a housewife and her grubby kids. Oh, I could tell that was the kind of thing he was thinking. We certainly weren't any credit to Beep in his eyes.

"Why don't you go on and start looking at shirts, hon?" she suggested. "I'll be along in a minute."

He said he was glad to have met me, and seemed even gladder to take her suggestion. I caught the little look he gave her as he turned away, telling her not to be long.

"Well," she said, sitting down. "So how're things going?"

I asked if she wanted a piece of cookie. She didn't.

"It's so great to run into you like this," I said. "I'm so surprised."

"I took a day off."

"You look great."

"You too," she said. It was one of those things people say without meaning them. Because she couldn't mean it, I knew that. The way her friend—boyfriend, if you can call a man with gray hair boyfriend—had looked at me, I felt boring and tacky. She looked around at the stores, people passing, whatever.

Someone came along with two cocker spaniels on leashes, and the kids ran to pet them. I called after them to leave the dogs alone, but the owner had stopped and seemed to admire Gail and Davey in much the same way they admired her dogs, as if she wanted to pat their heads and pull their ears.

"Cute kids," Beep remarked. She stood up to go. "Have you heard from the folks?"

"If anyone did," I pointed out, "it would be you." I

asked myself if that was true; it had just popped out. "Did you know Sister's coming home for the holidays? If you can call it home."

She shook her head no.

"I thought Mitchy might have told you."

"I don't see Mitchy very often."

"Hey!" someone called. The voice was almost familiar, not quite. "Did you lose something?"

For a minute I couldn't place the skinny fellow in blue windbreaker and old jeans, coming up to us with Gail and Davey by the hands. I only knew that I ought to have a name for that cheerful face, and that with the sunlight striking it his light hair looked very nice.

"Rob Brewster," he prompted. "You know me."

Ah, yes! A graduate student for whom I had typed two long papers back in the spring, while Stan and I were separated and I was scrambling for money. I had tacked up a few notices at U.T. Arlington and S.M.U. and made a little money typing dissertations and theses, or mostly term papers, actually, at home. Rob had been my best customer. I had typed three seminar papers for him. He had come by several times to drop things off or pick them up, and once he had stayed to have a glass of Coke at the kitchen table and tell me about his plans to go on for a doctorate. I had been acutely aware that he was probably a couple of years or more younger than I was.

"Rob! Of course. It's so good to see you!" I looked away, feeling somewhat flustered. "Were these two wandering off?"

"Oh, I don't know, maybe not. I just saw them and

figured that meant you were somewhere around here, so I grabbed them up and came looking." He almost grinned, but closed his lips into a more sedate smile when he saw Beep, as if conscious of some need to draw back.

"Beep," I turned and linked my arm with hers, drawing her in, "this is Rob. Rob, my sister Glenda." I felt all awash in good luck. I had come out for an hour with the children, and the sky was blue, and I had run into not one but both of these beautiful people. I felt like the center of a great network of acquaintances: If I turned around and looked, people would be watching me and envying me. I felt lucky too in being able to show Rob off to Beep.

He turned his almost grin on her now and asked, "Which is it, Glenda or Beep?"

"Whichever," she answered. "I have this one here to thank for that awful nickname." She jiggled my arm playfully. Anyone would have thought we were the buddiest of sisters.

"Ha!" he said. "That's not so bad. I'll tell you mine sometime."

We chatted a little more—what was I doing, what was he doing, how was school. Then he said he'd better be going. The children kept climbing on and off the bench where Beep and I had been sitting, and I kept turning around and grabbing whichever of them was about to fall or telling them to quit that before they got hurt. It was strange: Once, when I turned back, I caught a glimpse of Beep, but it wasn't Beep, it was some tall, lean, glamorous stranger looking elusively at Rob through half-dropped lids. I felt confused, turned around. Who was this, now?

When he had walked off—no, actually trotted off, whistling, she turned her half-lidded eyes on me, opened them, and said, "Well! Who was that?"

"A student I typed a couple of papers for," I told her. "Last spring." I found myself not wanting to say much. "Weren't you needing to meet what's-his-name before he ran out of patience?"

She let that pass. "He's really cute," she said. "Rob, was that it? What was his last name?"

I had seen that look on her face before. "Wait a minute!" I protested. "Just because you happened to be standing here when I ran into him, that doesn't mean you can just move in and take over."

She laughed. "What do you mean, take over? What do you have to take over? All you did was type something for him, for money!"

An old fury swept over me. Grabbing up the children, I stood openly glaring at her. "You leave him alone!" I yelled. "You always get everything!"

I rushed off a few steps, then turned back. "You always did!"

5

⁓⁓⁓

IT WAS true. Beep had always gotten whatever she wanted, and I had always been jealous of her and envied her and, let's face it, resented her. It all boiled up now, from wherever it had been simmering all those years, and spilled out all over everything, so that while I was driving home I had to keep looking at it, pooled there between me and the windshield: my old grievance. She had been the baby of the family, Mama's pet and Daddy's little girl. Everyone, every adult we ran into—neighbors, Sunday School teachers, every stranger in a store—was always saying how cute she was, what a darling little girl, wasn't I proud to have such a pretty little sister. No one ever asked her if she wasn't proud to have such a pretty big sister. Inside, I knew that I should have had that attention; I should have had that special place. I would have had it if she hadn't been born and taken it away from me.

People were always asking if we resented Sister. I would hear them asking Mama when they thought I wasn't listening. It was because they could tell how much more attention Sister took than any normal child—more than any three or four normal children put together. Apparently they thought that if we did resent her we would do so as a unit, all together, us three against her. No one ever seemed to wonder if there was rivalry among the three of us. They never knew that I had it from both sides, I was caught and pinched between them—the older sister Mama had to take more care of and the younger sister she chose to take more care of. And worse than that, I was pinched by having to keep it hidden. I knew I must never, never let it show that I resented either one of them.

Well, it showed now. It showed to me, at least, in a way that it never had before. Beep got everything she wanted, and I had always felt sorry for myself and maybe even hated her for it. I reached back over the seat and squeezed Gail's sturdy leg as she sat perfectly still, watching out the window. Davey was asleep on the back seat beside her, thumb in mouth. The afternoon had worn him out. I hoped that the two of them would not ever feel that deep-set resentment against each other that I felt against Beep. I hoped they didn't already.

I remembered the trouble about our Easter dresses one year. I think I was ten, Lisbeth eleven, Beep, I guess, five. Sister was always home for a week at Easter, and, of course, we always went to church on Easter Sunday. We always did every Sunday, for that matter. And we always had new Easter clothes. Not Daddy, and maybe not Mitchy, but anyway all us girls and Mama. That was just assumed: If it was Easter, you had a new church outfit. We would have felt really poor if we hadn't had those.

It was always a problem knowing what to get for Lisbeth. She never looked good in anything. Besides the problem of her misshapen face and her misshapen head, which was more or less pointed or anyway not rounded out right, she was thick and shapeless in the body, with no waist at all. Mama tried everything. Dresses without waists were like bags on her; dresses with waists and gathered skirts were just ludicrous, the sashes too high under her arms and the hems either sagging or showing thick trunks of legs above her shambling feet. But she always had an Easter dress anyway. Fair was fair.

That year when I was ten, Mama had made Lisbeth a kind of apricot-colored dress out of voile or something thin like that, with a satin sash. Exactly the kind of thing she shouldn't have had; it looked just awful on her. Mama had made her own dress too—she usually did make her own clothes—but after that I guess she ran out of steam. Penney's advertised a sale and she decided to take me shopping for ready-made.

That didn't seem like near as much fun to me. I loved the slow process of looking over bolt after bolt in the fabric store, watching Mama feel the pieces between her thumb and two fingers, then hanging around while she cut it out and sewed. I would sit on the floor beside her machine and collect little scraps and fit them together like a puzzle. I never liked the trying-on part, but if we bought ready-made I would have to go through that anyway, without any of the fun. But Mama convinced me that buying a store-bought dress would be more special, somehow, and besides, it would save her all that work.

We went on a Saturday, just the two of us, and I immediately found what I wanted, the most beautiful floaty dainty dress of white organdy or whatever, with tiny raised white flowers and tiny dots of yellow at the centers of all the flowers, and yellow taffeta underneath. It was the prettiest dress I had ever seen, the prettiest dress in the world. Of course, it was totally unsuited to the tomboy I was, and I guess that was one reason Mama wouldn't get it for me, but I felt convinced that if I had that dress I wouldn't *be* a tomboy anymore. She mentioned that we were having an early Easter that year, and an organdy dress was too summery, I might be cold in it Easter morning. When I pointed out that Sister's dress, which she had already made, was thin and summery, she said yes, but it had sleeves, this only had ruffles at the shoulders.

So I didn't get the dress I wanted, which hadn't been on the sale rack anyway, but Mama went through the clearance things and picked me out a suit, I guess that's what you'd call it, a skirt with a funny little matching jacket, navy blue, which she said would be very practical, I would get a lot of good out of it. Naturally, after that white froth of a dress, a plain navy skirt and jacket didn't appeal to me much, but then, probably nothing would have. It was made out of what I now know must have been a cheap rayon "linen." Skinny and gawky as I was, and skimpily as it was cut, it hung on me like a limp sack. I looked in the dressing-room mirror and my heart sank. But Mama said it was fine, and started telling me all the different blouses I could wear with it, besides the plain white one that came along, so I said OK. It was the sort of thing that might have been really good on Sister, if it had been better made. But that realization didn't make me feel any better either.

That left Beep still to go. And I don't guess Mama did it on purpose, maybe going shopping with me had just given her ideas, but she wound up making Beep the very dress I had wanted, only better. White dotted swiss or organdy, something spun-sugary, over pink taffeta with a wide pink sash and ruffle sleeves. It looked like something an angel would wear. It would have been simply ridiculous on me, of course; I was past the age of being round and cute, if I had ever been. But at the time I thought I would simply die when I had to get into my practical navy blue while she had the kind of fairy-tale-pretty dress I had wanted. I think if I could have gotten rid of her in some silent and bloodless way that spring, I would have. It had already struck me more than once that having a little sister wasn't such a good deal.

And I had other incidents like that tucked away too. I could remember her getting away with things that would have gotten me spanked. When she was little, she got boxes of forty-eight Crayolas, while I had had only twenty-fours and always wished for the exotic colors in the big box. When she was starting to date, Mama decided eleven-thirty wasn't too late, while for me it had always been ten-thirty. Nothing major, just the kind of petty hurts that people naturally accumulate in families. But seeing her turn on to Rob Brewster that afternoon had brought it all back. Which was really foolish since, as she was so quick to point out, I didn't have any claim on him anyway. I hadn't even thought of such a thing till that minute.

When the children and I got home, and after I gave Davey another aspirin because his temperature was coming back up, I tried to call Mitchy to tell him about seeing Beep and the boyfriend, but didn't get an answer. That was my usual luck when trying to call Mitchy. I also wanted to ask him if he remembered that Easter dress and what a fit I threw about it, and how I hid Beep's new white patent shoes so she had to wear her old brown ones, which spoiled the effect very nicely. But he probably wouldn't have remembered anyway. He probably would have asked me what I was talking about and why it mattered now. And I would have been hard pressed to say why, though I knew it did.

After Daddy left, Mama seemed to think that the great mission in life for all of us was to make up for it to Beep. Why Beep, any more than the rest of us? She seemed to think having your father run out on you was worse for the youngest. Then, after a few years, it was our mission to give Beep the perfect high school experience. Well, that may have been her mission, but it wasn't mine. I had wanted my own perfect high school, but instead I had gotten pimples and no date for the junior-senior prom and an after-school job at the Safeway. Then after I was out of high school I was hoping for a perfect first year in college, and then a perfect second year. But there wasn't any second year. Or not a real one. Because by then I had to get a job and just take a couple of courses at night, and part of what I made went to Mama, who bought perfect jeans and skirts and sweaters for Beep.

At least that was one thing Daddy had never done,

before he left—buy for one and not the others. He didn't buy for us at all, usually, except things like ice cream cones. But then he made sure everybody got the same. He didn't show favoritism of any kind except in very subtle ways, maybe ways I more imagined than actually saw. With us kids he always seemed very detached, very absent. He sort of looked around and blinked as if he was surprised by the fix he had gotten himself into, and hoped to find out it wasn't real after all. He was kind, he was good to us, but he was just sort of uninvolved. Except that it did seem to me that if anyone got an extra pat or an extra wink, it was Beep.

I think Daddy really felt surrounded by children, overwhelmed. Of course, Sister was enough to overwhelm anyone all by herself, so it was no wonder. Mama was different. She threw her whole self into mothering, so there wasn't ever any time left for her to feel like a real, separate person, apart from the mothering, and so she couldn't feel surrounded. Or if she did, she never showed it. Bustle bustle, busy busy, do this, do that. But for Daddy, it seemed, children weren't the whole story. I think he must have felt more or less abandoned, with Mama constantly working, doing, taking care—not of him, but of us. Apparently it never occurred to him to follow her example, and since he didn't, there he was, not a giver but not a receiver either, since nothing was coming his way.

I've thought about this, since I've been older, and I think that even if he had wanted to look elsewhere for that attention he wasn't getting at home, he wouldn't have been able to, because of sheer guilt. Not just ordinary guilt, which would have been bad enough, but a special guilt because of all Mama was constantly having to do for Sister, besides all she was constantly doing for the rest of us, whether she had to or not. He must have felt a great release, or not that exactly but more like a great hope for release, when Sister went away to the state school, thinking that then Mama would have all that leftover time and attention and energy to give to him. But it didn't work that way. She never did have time and attention for Daddy. Partly it was because she let our wants expand to fill the gap, partly because she just switched from constantly coping with Sister to constantly worrying about her and planning her next visit home. So I guess Daddy must have felt more uncherished than ever, because of the letdown.

He never really showed it; certainly he never said anything. Mainly, I'm just guessing. I've never understood Daddy. I still don't. It's the greatest puzzle to me how he could go away like he did, without the least warning, and come back without the least warning and then go away again, and how he could have persuaded Mama to go with him. But what I do know is based on what Mitchy and I saw one summer night through the back window.

We had been playing outside after dinner with an assorted half-dozen of the neighborhood kids. That in itself was a rare occurrence. Usually we kept pretty much to ourselves. So it was already a special and festive night. And to make it even more special, we had been allowed to stay out long after dark, and not with Daddy sitting on the back step and watching us under the floodlight either, but alone, just us with those slightly unfamiliar other kids. I don't know if Mama forgot or was extra tired that night or if she consciously decided for once to allow us that special occasion. But anyway she had taken Beep in for her bath and left us outside. Maybe Daddy spoke up and told her to. I don't know.

All through the prolonged dusk we had played "May I?" and "Red Rover" and "Washing Washington's White Windows White"—wonderful games that I had only overheard other kids playing while Mitchy and I kept to our own private games, but which suddenly seemed to me as natural and inevitable as the muggy night air or the cedar bushes by the house, but with the charm of strangeness too. And then as dusk finally went to dark we switched to Hide and Seek. It was a wonderful, wonderful time to play that great old scary game. We ranged over half a block, front and back, hid in dark places and streaked through the light of front porches and into darkness again for "home." Being It meant venturing not just into shadows but into absolute pitchy recesses of leaves and branches where hidden foes jumped out and ran. Beep would certainly have been too little for this game. That was part of what made it so much fun.

We were all, all six or eight of us, beginning to be tired by the time we started Hide and Seek. Besides, it's a game that invites disorganization. Sometimes you can't tell who has been caught and who hasn't or even who is It. When you get tired of hiding you just run back and forth, for "home" or not. Players go into the darkness to hide and don't come out, but simply go to sleep behind their chosen bush or the bad man gets them or they decide to go home, really home. So after a while we were left with only four players.

We had all flopped down on the grass, panting, when

we heard the accordion. Mitchy and I slipped into our own back yard, followed by the other two, and crouched together on the black grass, well away from the light of the house. All the windows were open, and the room where Mama and Daddy were was bright. We could see them and hear them as clearly as if they were a movie. We could even see the moths bumping against the window screens. Mama sat holding Beep on her lap, and Daddy stood in front of her, moving around a little, playing the old accordion he'd kept in the bedroom closet for as long as I could remember.

One of the neighbor kids whispered, a little louder than I might have wished, "He's serenading your mother!" The other one pointed and laughed with one hand over his mouth. Mitchy and I pointed too, and rolled on the grass, joining them in making fun so we could separate ourselves from the embarrassing tableau in the window. It was only too obviously a romantic moment for them. Or for Daddy, anyway. He was playing some of those old forties love songs. Out in the dark, we made faces and put our hands over our ears. One of the other kids said, "That's weird," and I shushed him. I didn't want to be caught spying. But there was no need for us to be so quiet; they couldn't have heard us over the accordion. In a minute, the neighbor kids got bored and left, leaving Mitchy and me lying on our stomachs in the grass, getting bitten by chiggers, watching and listening.

Mama sat stiffly in the platform rocker, holding Beep, who was in her pajamas and kept wiggling around and burrowing her face into Mama's shoulder until she finally slipped down and went off toward her room, I guess to bed. Usually Mama carried Beep to bed and kissed her and tucked her in, and from the way she looked after her I knew she was wanting to go do that then, but she must have realized that she simply could not get up and leave in the middle of Daddy's serenade. She sat there stiff and uncomfortable-looking, with her hands in her lap, looking at the night against the open window. Daddy kept playing, one song and then another, and sort of smiling at her when he wasn't looking down at the keys. The accordion had a wheezy sound, but it was loud and piercing. I knew Mama hated it. I had heard her say so time and again.

Mitchy asked, hey, did I think they were in love, but it didn't seem possible to me. Later, after Daddy left and we had to listen to Mama's accounts of how she had worshipped that man and given him everything a man could want, I remained unconvinced, partly because of what we saw in the window that night. He wanted so much to tell her something he couldn't say in words. Or maybe what he really wanted was for both of them to feel something he didn't think she felt. And she just looked away and waited for it to be over.

When finally he stopped between songs, waiting for some response—a kiss, something—we heard her say, with a forced emphasis, "Where are those children?" He started to play something else, "Anniversary Waltz" I think, but she got up anyway and came to the back door and called loudly, "Mitchy! Meg! You come on in now." Daddy hit a few wrong notes, but he played it through to the end.

6

WHEN THE kids and I picked Stan up at work, I was expecting him to be still as aggravated as he had been on the phone. I was braced. But instead he came out with a kind of swing in his walk, slid under the steering wheel, and said, "Hey, babe." He gave me a little hello kiss and then reached back and patted the children.

"How's my boy?" he asked. Davey turned away, but Gail told him about having ice cream. She needn't have; her T-shirt bore the chocolate evidence.

"I was right," I told him. "It was the ears." I wanted to get that point established right off.

He said he was afraid of that. Really, you would never have known he had been against taking Davey to the doctor. So then I could ease off too, and admit Davey hadn't seemed as bad as I was afraid he would.

"He seemed to feel pretty good for a while," I said. "I

was beginning to think I shouldn't have taken him in, after all. But then his fever came up again about four-thirty."

"Yeah, that's the way. You took 'em out for ice cream?"

Oh boy, I thought, here it comes. "Yeah," I admitted, "when we left the doctor's office he seemed to be feeling so good, I thought it would be a nice treat."

But he surprised me again. "Sure," he said. "It's nice to do something like that every now and then."

When we got home, he went straight to the bathroom to wash up. He always did, even though he had always scrubbed up already before he left the garage. That was a nice thing about Stan, you never saw him dirty if he could help it. He hated having grime around his fingernails, though of course he could never entirely get rid of it. He knew he was good looking, and he didn't like to have that fact obscured.

I had left spaghetti sauce simmering. While he was washing up I started water heating for the pasta and set the table. But when he came back, sniffing the good oregano and garlic aroma, instead of going to get a beer, he said, "Hey, I have an idea."

I was making garlic toast, but paused in midslice, feeling somewhat wary. Stan's ideas frequently involved work for me.

"I'm not real hungry," he said. "How about feeding the kids now and we'll eat later, after they've gone to bed, hm?"

"Well," I stalled. It really was a nice idea, romantic dinner for two and all that, but, perversely, all I could think of was the extra trouble it would mean for me. I would have to clean the table off and reset it, and I wouldn't finish the dishes till late.

"Come on," he coaxed. "Let's get out of our rut a little. I'll run down and pick us up a bottle of Chianti. OK?"

"Well, OK. That'll be nice." And I knew it really would, even though I did manage to sound grudging about it. What gets into me sometimes?

But this was really his night, he was in a great humor. He didn't even seem to notice that I was being horsey about it. He wrapped his arms around me and kissed the back of my neck and whispered, "I want to see that black negligee too, you hear?"

Why did I have to let that make me feel manipulated? But I did.

I flung my way through the kids' supper, having as little to say to them as I could, and sighed mightily about having to wash the table after they finished. Neither of them ate much anyway. Gail was mystified by eating supper without us, and Davey, though he loved spaghetti, which he ate chopped very small, with a spoon, dawdled. He was cross and whiny, and finally leaned himself way over the side of his high chair and threw his spoon on the floor. That was it. I let him have a butter cookie—he didn't feel too bad to eat that, of course—while I finished cleaning up their mess and took them straight on to the bathtub.

It was while they were soaking in the tub, after I had washed their faces and ears, that I began to feel a little more mellow. It was nice, after all, to be getting them down early and to have our own evening to look forward to. I wished then that I'd had a bath myself. It was too late for that, of course, but I rectified the situation as best I could by undoing my blouse and sponging under my arms with the kids' washcloth. I decided I might get out my black negligee after all, not later on, but now, for dinner.

It worked out great. I deposited the two of them in bed, then headed toward our bedroom to change, and as I passed the door I called in to Stan would he take Davey two baby aspirin. He looked surprised, but if we were getting out of our rut we might as well get out of it in this way too. Of course, he got hung up with them for a while, and when he came out, there I was in my sexy negligee, with the spaghetti water starting to steam. I had even rummaged around and found two candles to put on the table.

He came in saying, "What's this? What's this?" and started exploring the possibilities right then. I told him hold on, let's have supper first. Of course, that's what he wanted to do anyway; he was just showing off. He opened the wine and we started on a glass while the pasta cooked. It was one of those nice bottles with the straw wrapper. We talked about how we could put a candle in it after it was empty and let the wax drip down the sides. Stan said he'd heard there was a special kind that would drip in different colors.

We played knees while we ate, and when we finished he wanted to go on to the bedroom and not bother with dishes, but even though I was half inclined to myself, I told him no, let me get them rinsed and stacked. I've always figured if I ever had to get up in the morning and face dirty dishes from the night before, I mean totally dirty, I'd just run away.

Stan sat there at the table with another glass of wine and watched, and when I had done enough, the bare minimum, I came and sat on his lap and he put his hand up under my gown, and soon we went back to the bedroom clutching each other and getting off balance and laughing.

The next morning he said he had a little bit of a headache, but not too bad, and it was worth it. He teased me a little, saying he might be afraid to come home from work that night, since I'd turned into such a tigress. That was always Stan's way, to make fun of me if I got hot in bed, even though that was what he wanted. He could never just take it and share it and be glad.

But I tried not to let it bother me. And for the next two weeks everything went great. We had no fights, Stan paid a lot of attention to the children, and we had great sex. I even had orgasms. Not every time, but more than usual. It was strange, we hadn't been that turned on to each other since we were first married, and of course then I hadn't really known how, not like I did now. We were making it nearly every day, sometimes more than once. One night when we were sure the kids were asleep we stripped off and tried it on the sofa, me sitting on the edge and Stan on his knees. That was so good we did it twice more at different times before we decided we'd better put that off limits—one of the kids was going to wake up and come in one night and catch us.

Now, looking back on it, I figure the reason Stan was so turned on during that time was that he was excited about what he was getting away with and what a big man he was proving himself to be, fucking two women at the same time, and one of them, at least, getting all she wanted and more than she had ever wanted before, at that. All that sex, and very good sex, didn't solve a one of our problems. The things that had been making trouble for us were still there. But anyone who thinks good sex doesn't go a long way toward making other problems seem less important hasn't been married.

During that couple of weeks in the middle of December, after the question of whether Sister could or could not come to us for her holidays, or when she could come, had been decided and there was nothing else to do but wait, Stan seemed mostly to have forgotten about it. At least, he didn't seem to be still mad at me. He came home from work in the evenings, and he kissed me and tumbled the children, he drank a beer or two and was nice at dinner, not cross or sullen, and he offered sex if I wanted it, with sufficient preliminaries and without talk. The no talking part might sound as though he was doing it mechanically, just for the feel, not really getting himself involved with me, Meg—and as it turned out that was true—but at the time all I knew was, it was a relief. Because before, he used to talk to me a lot, both before and during, but in ways I hated. He made sex sound like a threat. It was always what he was going to *do* *to* me. Or he was at least making it dirty, and not just with the words themselves but the way he said them. And if I objected he would start saying, "Oh, shall we make love?" or something like that, prissy and exaggerated, making fun of me. So instead of feeling disregarded, I was really glad when he started fucking me in silence. Maybe that was one reason I kept getting so aroused.

Anyway, there was plenty to talk about besides sex. It was Christmas shopping time, and nearly every day, for at least two weeks, I went out shopping—looking, pricing, getting ideas. Then in the evenings I would tell him about this thing I'd seen or that idea I'd had or what would be just perfect for the kids and not cost too much. He had done some work on my old car and had it running again; otherwise I don't know how I would have made it through. The whole thing was as complicated as a military campaign as it was. I located two Mother's Day Out programs at churches near us where I could leave the kids one morning a week for a couple of dollars each, and that helped. Mitchy and Beep were to come over for Christmas dinner, so I wanted to have presents for them too, even though I usually didn't. And then Sister, of course, who was simply impossible to buy for in the first place. And I never had good ideas for Stan. This year I was wavering between a sports coat I had found at the menswear discount store, a rod and reel, and a three-record set of music from the fifties and sixties, all of which required multiple trips for checking things out. Of course, money was tight—when wasn't money tight?—so all this took a lot of ingenuity.

For the kids, I had found a whole circus, with elephants and lions and clowns and cages, and acrobats that could actually be made to do tricks, and all of it made out of wood, real sturdy. I always loved wooden toys, even just blocks. I was for buying the circus set for the two of them together, and letting it go at that, but Stan insisted they had to have separate Santa Claus things. Maybe he was remembering his own childhood, when Christmas had been far from a big deal. Even now, his parents couldn't be bothered to send so much as a coloring book to the grandkids. Anyway, Stan wanted to get a bicycle and a tricycle, which not only could we not afford, but the kids were too young for anyway. So, as I say, we had a lot to talk about. There didn't seem to be time for fighting.

About the time things started going so well for us, in fact just a few days after that doctor's appointment of Davey's, when I had run into Rob Brewster and Beep, Stan surprised me by saying he was going to do some Christmas shopping of his own this year. Always before, that had been strictly up to me, just as it had been up to Mama in our family. In a way, it seemed like a nice change. In fact, it made Christmas more fun, since there would be some things I wouldn't know about. But I had mixed feelings about it. Stan was an impulse spender. And spending more than the clerks figured him for always made him feel like a big man. That was a dangerous combination. But also, I think it bothered me not to feel in control anymore. That was really strange to realize, when I finally did realize it, because I had always thought I wasn't in control. I had thought what I wanted was more sharing.

He made several shopping trips, or looking trips, going out right after dinner and coming home when the stores closed, about ten. One time he brought home, besides a little package that he didn't explain, a really nice wooden cutting board. He had found it, he said, at a little shop with all wood things, in a center with some other little shops like that. I knew where he meant, the center where the kids and I had gone that day. I had never bought anything there, and I

had an idea he had paid way too much for the cutting board.
Still, it was nice, and something we would get a lot of use out
of.

One of the times Stan was gone, Rob Brewster called,
not to get any typing done but just to say hello. It turned out,
though, that besides saying hello he wanted to come over—
right then. I guess he thought I was still separated. He
wouldn't say why, just that he wanted to see me. I figured he
had been drinking. Why else would he call *me?* Either that
or he wanted to know how to get hold of Beep. But he could
have asked that on the phone. It was strange. I didn't get it.
Of course, I told him he couldn't come. He said, Oh well,
maybe another time, and hung up.

I was sorry then that I hadn't talked to him more. I
liked Rob. He seemed to go his own way, but at the same
time he was sort of quiet and—gentle, I guess that's the
word. He seemed gentle.

I was afraid I might have hurt his feelings. But in just a
minute the phone rang again and it was him calling back. He
said, Hey, he hadn't meant to come on too strong, he hoped I
hadn't taken offense.

I said, "No, no offense."

"You're sure?" he asked. "No offense?"

"Sure."

Then he wanted to leave his number. "Just in case," he
said.

"In case I want to type something for you?"

He seemed to think that was pretty sharp, and laughed,
but he still wanted to leave his number. He insisted; I might
need to get in touch with him. So I wrote it down on an

envelope flap. I figured if I ever did call him, he wouldn't remember telling me—I still figured he was bombed. But anyway, instead of throwing away the envelope flap, I hid it in the bottom of a little department-store box where I kept junk jewelry.

It occurred to me then what a good thing it was that he hadn't called when Stan was home. I would have had trouble explaining that, for sure, and I didn't want trouble. I was beginning to think again in terms of permanence.

When Stan came home, it was about ten and I was reading in bed. To me, reading in bed is one of the great luxuries of life. I was really looking forward to the time when the kids were a little older so life would be easier and I could read in bed every night. As it was, there were always more things to do than I ever got done during daylight hours, and by ten o'clock I was so tired that if I tried to read I just went right to sleep. Besides, Stan didn't like for me to. So I was enjoying his staying out late. It gave me a chance to indulge myself.

But he seemed to figure he'd better come in apologizing. He had stopped for a beer on the way home, he said. He was just feeling so good about his shopping. Not that he had bought much yet, practically nothing, but he was getting ideas now. Just wait, was I ever going to be surprised.

He went to the bathroom and got undressed and threw his shirt in the corner, the usual routine, and came to bed still talking about it. Just wait, he repeated. I had probably always thought he wasn't any good at this, but just wait and I'd see.

I was getting tired of hearing it. He was right, though. I

had always thought that. Just like Mama, I guess. They say we always turn out like our mothers, even if we don't want to. I can remember her making jokes about what a mess it would be if Daddy took over the shopping.

He turned on his side and began to nuzzle my throat and tease my nipples, first with his fingertips, then with his palms, very lightly. It was nice, but I really didn't want to have sex. I was enjoying just lying there, being languid, reading. But of course I put my book down and pretended to be interested. But then it turned out that he didn't want sex either. He never even got a good erection—I could feel him against my leg, but it wasn't much. What he seemed to want, really, was just to fool around a little and to talk.

He had asked if I had enough light to read there, which I interpreted as meaning he didn't want me to read, and that reminded him of the little light that clipped onto the head-board of his parents' bed, and then he was talking about them and the house he had grown up in. Which surprised me, since he usually didn't want to talk about his parents, or anything remotely connected with his childhood. He told me about the way they did, or mostly didn't do, things at Christmas, about his dad going out and buying presents Christmas Eve afternoon, whatever the drugstore had left, about the time his mother decided it was silly to spend her day off in the kitchen, so they had canned chili for Christmas dinner. Which of course my mother would never have dreamed of doing. It had to be all out, shoot the works: turkey, dressing, fruit salad, pies. Half of that stuff she cooked we didn't even like, but if she thought something was traditional fare she was bound we would have it.

Stan's parents were so different from the way I remembered mine, before Daddy left, that I had always found it an ordeal even to visit them. Fortunately, Stan didn't care to go very often anyway. For one thing, they squabbled all the time, even with us there. They seemed to keep up a running argument that had lasted for years and showed no sign of ever being over.

My parents had never fought at all. That was what made it all the more shocking when Daddy left: There had been no fights, no outward sign. It was strange, now that I thought about it. It was as if all the energy that might have kept them actively engaged with each other—in romance, in fighting, in something at least—had gone into coping with Sister, so they didn't have anything left for each other, not even any real hostility. Just a kind of emotional battening down the hatches, or pulling in of vulnerable parts into the shell, that was all. The great problem of Sister was a kind of vortex, a whirlpool, drawing in all their emotional energy. I had read, in freshman English, an Edgar Allan Poe story about a man going down into a whirlpool, and I remembered the picture printed with it in the book, of some wild-eyed man whirling down the sides of something like a tornado in water, holding onto a barrel for all he was worth. That was what I thought of now. I lay there feeling Stan's cock stir against my leg (but only slightly) and halfway listening to him talk about his folks, and I thought, that's it, that's what Mama and Daddy were like, that picture: just holding on and being sucked down.

But when I ventured, for once, to tell Stan what I was thinking, he rolled over on his back, laced his fingers under his head, and frowned up at the ceiling. "I hope you know what you're doing," he said, "bringing her in on us."

I didn't know what I was doing at all. And anyway, I wasn't *bringing* her in, I was just letting her be sent, because I didn't have the heart not to. I remembered that look of excitement on her face every time she got down off the bus and how we had taken her to the zoo and such, trying to make good times for her, and how tense or just quiet she would get the last day or two before she had to leave to go back. And remembering those things, what else could I do?

7

LISBETH CAME on a Thursday, a week and a day before Christmas, one of those bright, too-warm days that come along in December in Texas but seem so wrong. The calendar says winter, but the weather is stuck in summer.

It occurred to me at the last minute that I should have planned this better. I should have either had the people at the Home put her on an earlier bus, so the kids could be at one of the Mother's Day Out places while I went to meet her, or else asked one of the neighbors to keep them. When I thought about it, I tried phoning the girl next door, then Stan, then Beep and Mitchy, but the neighbor wasn't home, Stan and Beep both said they couldn't possibly leave work in the middle of the afternoon, and I didn't get an answer at Mitchy's. So I wound up dragging the two of them along.

When we went out to the car, Mutt got all distressed

and started barking, and I thought to myself, oh yes, I ought to take the dog and the cat too, no use leaving anybody out.

It had been so long since I'd been to the Greyhound station that I wasn't even sure how to get there, but as we got closer it came back to me. We parked beside the same buckled sidewalk, across from the same weed-tufted, broken-concrete lot where Mama had parked when I was a kid and Sister was coming home from School for the holidays. It might have been the same half-pint bottles, shedding the decent covering of their brown bags, that lay beside the same expired parking meters.

When we got out of the car, I noticed that the sky had taken on a blue-black tinge in the north, and the wind was kicking up plumes of dust. The kids ducked their heads and scrubbed their eyes with the backs of their fists. Great, I thought; that's all we need. I had had my hair done that morning—a rare event, in preparation for Stan's company Christmas party that night—and I couldn't stand to think it was going to waste just because of a dust storm. But it looked like I'd have to stand it. If only I'd had a scarf to hold it down! But of course I didn't.

We had to walk right into it, with dust coating us like breaded cutlets, sticking to the sweat we had built up on the way downtown in our un-air-conditioned car with sunshine glaring through the windows. Finally I picked Davey up and carried him so he, at least, could turn his back to the wind. He wrapped his arms around my neck and his legs around my waist and burrowed his face into my shoulder. That left Gail, who was always quick to protest the slightest favoring of little brother. She made up for his getting the better deal by hurling herself in front of me every quarter of a block and holding on to my legs.

The vast concrete bay where the buses arrived and departed was just how I remembered it—dark, noisy, reeking of exhaust fumes, and littered with papers blowing between the pools of oil. Off to the side stood baggage carts piled with cartons, stacks of newspapers, and cardboard suitcases bound with rope. The whole place was jammed with milling, shoving people. I guess it was always that way near Christmas. One look through the glass doors into the waiting room told me there wasn't anywhere to sit down, either with or without a coin-op TV. But that was just as well because I didn't dare risk not being there when Lisbeth got off her bus.

Figuring out which one her bus was, though, was a problem. The buses kept pulling in every minute or two, and I couldn't always see whether the sign on the front said Austin/Dallas. So I had to keep dashing from lane three to lane one to lane four, holding on to the kids for dear life. While I was checking out one bus, another would come in and start unloading, invariably at the farthest position, and here we'd go again, running across lanes and alongside buses with their engines revving up, getting ready to pull out. I finally found one marked Austin where the driver, standing beside the steps to hand people down, said yes, he had a blind girl on board. We had a minute to catch our breaths while we waited for her, and that was when I noticed that the draft in the bay had turned chilly.

She got off last, groping along the seats with her left hand, the cane dangling uselessly from her right in spite of a decade or more of mobility instruction. When I spoke to her, and the driver handed her over, she put a battered and squeezed lunch bag into my hand and let out a big sigh of relief that said, clear as any words, OK, I've made it this far, now it's up to you.

She didn't have much to say. Which was just as well, since we couldn't hear each other anyway. Mainly she wanted to touch Gail and Davey, to see how big they had grown. She seemed delighted, and doubled over laughing. But when she put her hands on them, they shrank away against me. They had gotten very still, and I was glad, in a way, that she couldn't see how they were staring at her. Gail pointed and piped up, "Mommy, her face is all—" I crimped her mouth shut with my palm and asked Lisbeth how the bus ride had been. I understood, of course; I knew how she looked to them. But they were just going to have to get used to it.

The ride was OK, she said. Mrs. Palmer had given her a lunch to eat on the bus. I knew that already, of course, from her trash and the smears of mustard on her hands and blouse. Just like old times.

Back at the side of the bus, somebody had hinged up the door of the baggage compartment and was slinging suitcases onto a cart. People were gathered around three deep, watching for that familiar bag or box, pulling it off the cart, and fighting their way through the crowd to get out. I tried to worm my way through, hoping I'd remember what Lisbeth's suitcase looked like. I had vague memories of an old yellow castoff that had once been Mama's. But even if that was right and even if I was lucky enough to spot it, I doubted that I could make the kind of quick dash and grab that others were making, not with the three of them hanging onto me. But I certainly couldn't put them off to one side somewhere and tell them to stand there while I got the suitcase. "Oh boy!" I muttered aloud, and the woman at my elbow looked at me and said something in Spanish to the person next to her.

When I saw what I thought was Lisbeth's bag, I asked one of the women shoving forward beside me if she would mind getting it. She looked me up and down and answered, "Fuck you." But a black guy with the standard boom box on his shoulder asked if I meant that old yalla one there, and waded in and got it for me. "Thanks," I said, but he had lidded his eyes and gone back into the music.

Once we got away from the crowd, I could see one reason people had been staring at Lisbeth. The back of her skirt was spotted with two dark red stains. "Oh boy," I moaned again—the ultimate embarrassment. But there was nothing to do about it but march down the sidewalk to the car acting like I either didn't know or didn't care.

The black clouds I had seen earlier on the horizon had now taken over the whole sky, and it felt like the temperature had dropped about twenty degrees. There we were, all of us but Sister, in T-shirts. She at least had on a sweater, but even so she was cold, and hunched her shoulders. I told her it wasn't much farther.

Why on earth hadn't I paid attention to the weather forecast? The wind, coming from our backs now, was cold and strong, a classic norther. Davey's ears would flare up

again for sure. And it was blowing my hairdo all to hell. I
had wanted to look good for the party.

With a block to go, Lisbeth stopped abruptly and
swung her suitcase around, hitting Gail in the mouth with
the corner. "You carry it," she said.

I felt like leaving that suitcase right there on the sidewalk; it was all getting to be too much. But instead I put
Davey down and picked it up. I could understand then why
she had found it heavy. We struggled along, windblown and
cold, both kids practically riding on the suitcase and
Lisbeth dragging on my right arm. I managed to get the two
kids into the back seat, load the suitcase into the trunk, and
spread a newspaper for Lisbeth to sit on in front. Which was
pointless, I guess, since that old car didn't deserve protec-
tion and it had vinyl seats anyway. But it seemed like the
thing to do. Then I went around to the driver's side and got
in and leaned my head on the steering wheel for a minute
before turning the key. Sister had been here just half an
hour.

On the way home, I tried to talk. After all, I hadn't seen
her in nearly a year. But it was frustrating. If my questions
were specific enough, she answered: what she had for breakfast, whether she did her own laundry, how many shoelaces
she could put tips on in an hour. (That was her job—tipping
shoelaces four hours a day.) Otherwise she just sat. Once,
meaning to play with them, I guess, she reached back and
waved her hand all around at Gail and Davey, trying to grab
them. They cowered in the far corner just out of her reach
the rest of the way, taking no chances and totally quiet.

What smart children I had! I hadn't learned the defense of absolute quiet until I was seven or eight.

Back home, the afternoon flew by. I had the feeling that if I stopped to look at the clock I'd actually be able to see the hands circling the face. There were Lisbeth's things to unpack and put away where she could get at them and her supply of medicine to get out where I would notice it three times a day. The first thing, though, was to get a maxi-pad onto her—literally get it on to her, myself: remove the soiled one and fold it and wrap it and press the fresh pad onto her soiled underpants. Persuading her to get out of her spotted skirt and into something else was the hardest part.

"I don't *usually* change clothes," she complained. "I get dressed in the morning, and then I put on pajamas at night." Her brows gathered into a deep frown, and her eyes wavered rapidly back and forth in agitation.

I thought I'd have better luck if I didn't mention the real reason. I told her Davey and Gail and I all had on jeans because the house was drafty, and she might be cold in her skirt. She thought that over for a minute, then started undoing her buttons. What a relief! I had more than half expected her to balk, and for sure I didn't want Stan to see her like that when he came home.

Lisbeth's body always made me uncomfortable. I could never see her without a feeling of revulsion. The thick, disproportioned trunk, the forward left shoulder and humped right, the breasts like little empty coin purses, the pearlike swelling of her big rounded belly and gross buttocks, the singly sprouting pubic hairs. Revulsion wasn't fair, of course. It wasn't her fault she was that way. And then

I felt guilty too just for having seen; I felt like a peeping tom. She could be looked at but could not look. She could be looked at and not know it. I always tried to cover all this up, to sound cheery and casual when she was undressed or dressing. I was determined that if she was going to figure out from someone's reaction that she looked bad, it wasn't going to be from mine. I remember Mama saying once, "It's a blessing she can't see herself." And I guess that was true.

While Lisbeth changed I went in the bathroom and tried to salvage my hairdo. Which was simply impossible. I wound up brushing it out loose, about the way I always wore it but not as good. So the money I'd spent at the beauty shop was just a waste.

When Lisbeth came in with her dirty clothes, she was wearing not only jeans and blouse, but a sweatshirt and a sweater as well. Apparently I had oversold her on the draftiness of the house, but there was no use trying to undo that now. With Sister, what was done was done.

"I'll put those with the rest of the laundry," I told her. I carried them out and put them to soak in cold water in the washer tub. That's where I found the children, in the utility room. Gail had been tearing my whole supply of cling-free sheets into postage stamp-size pieces and throwing them into the dryer. Davey was trying out pooping in the cat's litter box. It put him in an awkward position, though, and he had not quite cleared the backs of his training pants and elastic-waist jeans. So I had to get him out of those with as little smearing as possible before cleaning him up, and not until I had his bottom clean did I smack him soundly. "You mess!" I scolded. Yelled, actually. "Don't you ever do that again!" I gave him a little shake for emphasis. As for the litter box itself, I adopted the cat's own system and simply covered, shielding my fingers with a Kleenex.

I was just starting the washer when Stan came in.

He was unusually nice and cheery, all smiles and sweetness. I would think about that later, how unusually sweet and cheery he was that day. But if his good nature seemed a little forced, I chalked it up, at the time, to his wanting to be as nice as he could about Sister. I appreciated that. Two points for Stan.

After washing up, he came back to the kitchen, gave me a little squeeze, and picked up the children, who seemed glad to have him there as a buffer from my crossness. And he said hello to Lisbeth. She had been more or less hovering around the edges, wanting his notice.

"I'd give you a hug too," he told her, "only my arms are full with these two."

She laughed and clapped her hands. "Arms are full! Oh, gah!"

He asked her if she had a good bus ride.

"Oh yeah," she whooped. "That man with the radio was so funny."

We looked at each other and shrugged. He put the children down and told them to go on and play while he looked at the newspaper a little bit. "We need to leave in about an hour," he reminded me. "Maybe less."

"Right." I had yet to get a shower and do my nails—I was determined to do my nails—besides giving the kids and Lisbeth their supper. Fortunately, the baby-sitter was just across the street, so we didn't have to allow time to go get someone.

As soon as I got their tomato soup and grilled cheese sandwiches onto the table I went back for my shower, leaving Stan there reading the paper. I was just drying when I heard a crash and then another crash and him yelling "Jesus God!" Without waiting to get clothes on, I wrapped a towel around me and went running. Davey was standing up in his high chair looking enormously pleased about it all, prancing a bit and crowing, while Stan held onto his arm to keep him from falling. Two bowls were on the floor, broken into pieces, with a thick pool of tomato soup spreading around the one by the high chair. Lisbeth knew this was no joke. She had pushed her chair back and appeared to be getting ready for a fast getaway, cramming her sandwich down in three bites. Gail, still calmly spooning soup, took it all in.

"What on earth happened?" I asked.

Stan had a told-you-so look. "Oh, Lisbeth knocked her bowl off. She had put it off to one side after she ate her soup, and she knocked it off with her elbow." He gave an imitation of her mealtime sprawl. "So then Davey threw his off, soup and all. I'll tell you, if it's going to be like this every day . . ."

"Well, why didn't you get that bowl out of her way when she was finished?" I demanded. "That was the problem."

"Listen, Meg, don't try to put this mess on me."

"Not me," Lisbeth insisted. "It was Gail. Gail did it. She knocked her bowl off."

Gail looked up from her bowl to see how her name had gotten into this.

"Jesus!" Stan muttered. "I'm going to shower. You better be getting ready."

True, I thought. I'd better. But would someone please tell me how? Lisbeth stood behind her chair, fingering the back with buttery fingers. Absently, my mind still turning over the question of how to clean up both Davey and the floor without letting go of my towel and without letting go of *him* long enough to get a rag, I suggested she go wash her hands.

"They don't *feel* messy," she said.

"No, but they're all greasy. You better wash."

She whined two notes. "They don't *feel* greasy."

Oh, well. I let go of my towel, wiped Davey the best I could with it, then dropped it over the tomato soup pool, broken bowls and all. It seemed a little weird to be cleaning up in the buff, but I didn't present any surprises to the kids, they were used to coming and going while I bathed or dressed, and Lisbeth couldn't see me anyway.

I was just finishing when Stan appeared in the doorway in jockey shorts and shirt, fastening a cuff link, and announced, "Ten minutes." Then he looked up.

"Jesus, Meg! Have you lost your mind?"

"No," I said, "just my towel."

It was all beginning to seem unreal. Ten minutes! I'd never make it! And he said it so absolutely, it was almost as though he was meaning to leave without me if I wasn't ready.

"OK," I told the kids, "you two go play in your room

till Mary Beth gets here. Lisbeth, hadn't you better take some of those clothes off?"

No, she didn't want to take any of those clothes off, she wanted to take my arm and cling to me. So I let her trail along back to the bedroom.

Fortunately, I had laid out my dress earlier. The cat had curled up on it for a nap in the meantime, but it was a slick, shiny material and cat hairs would brush right off. Parking Lisbeth on the side of the bed, I got into my undies and hose in record time and put on my dress, only slightly wrinkled from the cat's lying on it. In the mirror I saw that a little pooch of tummy was showing and tried sucking in. Out in the living room, Stan was talking to the baby-sitter. That meant I needed to be going or he'd get impatient. But it was still three minutes till the time we had said we would leave. If I did a hastier makeup job than I had planned, I might yet be able to put one coat on my nails. Elaborate makeup had never ranked very high on my list anyway, but at the moment my whole expectation of a good time seemed to hang on polished fingernails.

Stan was just starting to pace and look at his watch when I came out from the bedroom, with Sister trailing along behind. He looked me over critically and said, "I thought you were going to get your hair done."

I felt bad enough about it as it was and wished he hadn't found it necessary to comment. "I did," I told him. "Then the wind picked up."

I had already talked to Mary Beth about what to expect and what she needed to do. So all I had to do now was elude the children's possibly sticky hands and make for the door. But Lisbeth wanted to know if I wasn't going to help her with "that thing."

"Oh, hell!" I said, before I could stop myself, then wanted to bite my tongue. With Sister, open disapproval was counterproductive. Sure enough, she stamped her foot and whacked the side of her head with her fist.

Stan pointed to his watch and made faces, but I couldn't see any use trying to leave with her upset. Besides, I remembered the stained skirt earlier. I didn't want to take chances with our sofa cover. So I took her off to the bathroom and got her changed again, and of course in hurrying I messed up my soft fingernail polish. It crumpled on two nails like the wrinkles on top of stale pudding. And when you go to parties at the rate of about one a year, it's a shame to go looking like that.

Stan kept griping on the way. "So this is how it's going to be for two weeks?"

I told him three, it was going to be three weeks. Might as well have it clear at the outset.

"Christ! I told you, remember. I told you not to do this."

The party wasn't too great. In fact, it was pretty much a disaster, and not just because I was worrying about my hair and my fingernails. I didn't really know anybody, though I had met a few of them before; but out of that few there wasn't a single one I honestly liked, and as far as I could tell the feeling was mutual. So I mostly just sat, after the dinner was over, and drank bourbon and 7-Up, and tried to act impervious to the fact that Stan was draping himself over all the girls. Especially one.

She was a sort of square-faced girl with no bust but basically great looking—about twenty-five, tall, with long, blondish hair done up on her head and long, perfectly done fingernails. At the sight of those fingernails, when Stan introduced us, I curled my fingers into my palms. Cindy, her name was. Not a name I particularly liked. She and Stan had already danced three times when I started counting, and I had seen them once, over on the far side of the room, sharing a cigarette while they talked to some other people. Which was funny, since Stan didn't usually smoke. That was when I thought about all those evenings he had been out shopping.

There had been a name drawing, and when the gifts were opened the man sitting right across the table from me got a wooden pepper mill, a really unusual one. It was from this Cindy. As soon as I saw it, I recognized it. I had admired that very pepper mill in the window of Woodpecker's the day the kids and I were at the square and had ice cream, after Davey's last doctor's appointment. Or maybe, I told myself, it had only been one like it. Woodpecker's was where Stan had bought that cutting board, one of the nights he was out.

I told myself that there must be lots of people who shopped there for gifts. It was just a coincidence and didn't mean a thing. But as soon as I thought about that pepper mill, I just knew Stan was fooling around with her. I just knew it. It hit me with an absolute certainty, with no need of evidence, the way you know you're going to have the flu tomorrow. I just sat there feeling that premonitory ache get worse and my stomach start to turn, and drinking more bourbon and 7-Up and then more.

By now Stan had had a good many too many, too, and he was going around with the orange bow tie he'd gotten in the gift exchange as a joke pinned to his fly. And that's why finally I went up to a stranger in a sleazy white suit at the next table and said, "C'mon, let's dance" and then stepped in a wet spot on the floor while trying to pull him up out of his chair and fell backward on my behind.

Stan was really mad. He kept saying on the way home how I had embarrassed him, humiliated him, he would never be able to face those people again. To me, it didn't seem like *that* big a deal; I was more concerned that I might have cracked my tailbone, since it wasn't very comfortable sitting, even on the padded car seat. But he said the man in the white suit was his new boss. You might know, I thought. About my luck!

When I finally said that if what he said was true, that I had humiliated him—which I wasn't conceding for a minute—it was because he had left me sitting there by myself the whole evening while he was running around after that Cindy. Then he *really* started in on me.

"Oh, so it's the 'poor me' bit again, is it?" he mocked. "Poor little Meg. Poor lonesome mistreated Meg. Don't you think if I wanted to run around on you I'd have better sense than to do it right in front of you? Boy, I've heard of dumb ideas! You've got some martyr complex there, you know that? Some goddamn big martyr complex! Let me tell you something, Meg." He kept turning sideways in the seat to glare at me full in the face. I wished he would watch where he was going. "This 'poor me' bit gets old, you hear? It gets old as hell."

"Keep your eye on the road, will you?"

That made him madder than ever, of course, and the madder he got the harder he stomped down on the accelerator. It had been raining a little off and on, and the streets were slick. I was afraid he was going to skid or something. I was even more afraid he was going to get stopped for speeding. Could we both be arrested for DWI? I wasn't driving, but there might be a way, and I thought what a mess it would be in the morning if the kids and Lisbeth woke up and I wasn't there.

For about five minutes he didn't say anything else, just drove like a fool and went on and on muttering under his breath with his teeth showing and throwing these nasty looks over at me. Then just a little before we got home he started in on it again and wound up saying that was what was at the bottom of "this Lisbeth business": my martyr complex. He seemed really proud of having figured that out. "That's it, yeah, that's what it is," nodding like a machine, up and down. "You've just gotta show the world how poor little Meg gets kicked around worse than anybody and goes on doing her good deeds like a goddamn Joan of Arc or something. If it wasn't for that goddamned martyr complex of yours we wouldn't be stuck with a mental defective for two weeks."

"Three," I said. "She'll be here for three weeks. And she's not just *a* mental defective, she's my sister."

If his temper was in fourth gear before, it went into overdrive now. I just tuned him out. I used my window trick and made him real small in my head and thought, Brilliant! Wasn't he just brilliant! He'd heard that phrase "martyr complex" somewhere or other and now he thought he was so smart to be able to come up with it again and use it on me. As if he knew one thing about it! But I kept my mouth shut; I did have that much sense.

When we got home, everybody was asleep, which was good. Even the baby-sitter was asleep on the sofa. But when she got waked up a little, she said, "Oh, yeah, Mrs. Sims, your sister got mad and threw her shoe and broke the glass out of that picture that was on the wall over there."

Stan said "Oh Christ" and went on through toward the bedroom, unbuttoning his shirt.

I told her I hoped she hadn't cut herself picking up the pieces.

"Oh, no," she said brightly. "I left 'em there, I didn't take any chances."

She gathered up her books and said yes, it would be OK if I brought the money over the next day. I didn't want to go back and get it from Stan right then, and I didn't have enough in my purse.

Then at the door she stopped again and said, "Oh, yeah, I don't think I can sit anymore for a while. I talked to my mom tonight and she said to tell you that."

I said I probably wouldn't be needing a sitter again for a while anyway. Which was a laugh. If I was ever going to need one, it was going to be these next few weeks. But I just thanked her for coming and locked the door behind her.

I told myself I ought to pick up the broken glass before I went to bed. I sure didn't want one of the kids stepping on it barefoot in the morning when they first got up. But I just didn't want to. It was pretty well out of the way; I didn't think it would be any problem. Besides, it was 1:30 A.M., and I wasn't in very good shape.

Stan was asleep across the bed with his pants unzipped. He had just fallen down in the middle of taking his clothes off and gone to sleep. I managed to get them off him and get him pulled around where he should be and get the covers back. By then I was feeling worse than ever. I didn't even bother with a nightgown, just crawled in with my half-slip pulled up under my armpits and turned the electric blanket up one notch higher than usual. I lay on my back feeling the bed turn around and around under me and thought what a mess I had gotten myself into.

8

THE NEXT morning was the morning after for sure. I woke up with a headache and an awareness of having slept badly and a taste of something rancid in my mouth. I probably wouldn't have gotten up to fix breakfast for Stan except I figured he would blame it on Lisbeth somehow. I figured there were going to be plenty of things he'd blame on her anyway, no use giving him any extra. So I got out of bed when he did and made coffee and set out cereal and the toaster.

He came in and sat down just like any other morning and stuck out his hand to pick up the coffee mug. He probably would have noticed if there hadn't been anything there to pick up. But he was in pretty bad shape, kind of gray in the face and licking his lips. Didn't say a word. He drank a little coffee and started on a piece of dry toast and then stood up abruptly and rushed out. I could hear him in the bathroom throwing up.

When he came back through on his way out to the car, he pointed at the broken glass in the family room and said, "Thanks to you-know-who." But he felt too bad to get up any real momentum on it. I could at least be glad of that.

I didn't feel so great myself. The headache was throbbing away, of course. That's what you get. But at least I wasn't retching. There was that much to feel smug about. I could feel smug about it while my head boomed every time I bent over picking up the broken glass. After I disposed of the bigger pieces, I got out the vacuum cleaner and went over the whole area to try to get all the little slivers. I couldn't see them, but I knew they were there. I could hear them plinking in the pipe on their way up.

It was while I was vacuuming that I remembered there had been a letter in Lisbeth's suitcase, on top of her clothes. I had stuck it in a drawer so Stan wouldn't see it until I had a chance to read it. Now I almost wished I hadn't remembered. It was sure to be bad news—they don't write to you from places like that to tell you good news. So I poured myself some more coffee and pushed down another piece of toast—being hung over seemed to have made me more hungry than usual instead of less—and steeled myself to read it before the kids got up, while I could still think.

It was neatly typed—a bad sign, I thought, since that implied planning, premeditation. A last-minute note about forgotten laundry or a change in return bus schedule would have been dashed off by hand. It opened very formally, too, with

> *Dear Mrs. Sims:*
> *I am sorry to have to inform you that we do not feel we can allow your sister Lisbeth to return after her Christmas holidays. Her behavior in recent months has been increasingly disruptive and—*

I skipped to the bottom. No use slogging through the details.

> *Best wishes as you make alternative plans for Lisbeth.*
> > *Sincerely,*
> > *Walter Smit, Superintendent*

I sat there and looked at it. Smit seemed like an unlikely name; I wondered if it wasn't supposed to be Smith. But then that seemed like a pretty strange kind of typo, too, and I couldn't say for sure if there was an "h" on the end of the signature or not. It was mostly pretty clear, but it went off into a kind of squiggle at the end. Actually, it didn't look like the signature of a Walter at all. More likely a Charlene or a Marilyn. Probably the secretary had signed for him.

I knew that woman was bad luck the first time I talked to her.

So. There it was. Now I had Sister on my hands not just for three weeks, but for good, maybe, and what was I going to do with her? How was I going to manage? Disruptive, they said. But if she was disruptive there, in a place set up especially for people like her, what was she going to be here? *Disruptive* seemed like a pretty mild word for what this was going to do to us. I put my head in my hands and stared at the tabletop. What was I going to do? What was I going to do? Mama ought to come back and handle this! It was her responsibility, not mine!

Stunned as I was by the news, I was slow to realize that there had already been a couple of faint thuds from the hallway. Just as these registered, I heard shins crack on the coffee table and a stack of magazines slide onto the floor. Lisbeth stood fidgeting in the middle of the room, dancing one-footed. I asked her if she needed to find the bathroom. "Oh yeah," she said, and reached for my arm, for me to lead her.

And so our day started. Diapers, breakfast, trash, dog food, cat food, laundry, spankings. Pick up toys, pay bills— and Lisbeth right at my elbow every time I turned around. Or else she was grabbing my arm, trailing along with me to the closet with clothes, to the bathroom with towels, to the garage with old newspapers. I let the day's clutter take over and tried not to think about the letter in my junk drawer in the kitchen. A couple of times, seeing her eyes roll agitatedly up, her head lean forward and then away, I thought, there's something she wants to say. But whatever it was, she didn't say it; she just hung on to me.

After lunch my headache eased off and I decided to go down to the K Mart before the kids' naps, to pick up something I had thought of for Mitchy, a little electric sandwich-grilling thing, and some gift wraps. I got the kids and Lisbeth into sweaters, got them all out to the car, and went back for my purse. And then the damn car wouldn't start. It was just too much, it was the last straw. I leaned my head on the steering wheel and thought, I give up, God damn it all, God just damn it all to hell. There I sat in the driveway in that old rusted-out Dodge with its battery dead, kaput, with the kids jumping up and down in the back seat and Lisbeth asking me why did I keep talking about that thing for Mitchy but not anything for *her,* wasn't I going to get her a present, and I just kept swearing at that car, but silently, not making a sound, because I didn't talk like that in front of the kids, and not answering Lisbeth a word. I guess we would have sat there the rest of the afternoon, I was that devastated, if Gail hadn't come down on top of Davey's head with the point of her chin and bitten her tongue, so they both started crying at once.

That did it. I flung out of the car and started hauling them out, none too gently, and ranting at them to hush up, they were driving me crazy, and they were going down for naps *right then.* Which of course was not a bad idea; once they've cried themselves down they're more likely to go off to sleep. Only they were still crying, they hadn't quieted down at all when I turned around and there was Rob Brewster with a file folder in his hand and a look on his face that said what am I doing here?

It wasn't one of my better moments. But Rob rose to the occasion beautifully. "You need a ride?" he asked. Just like that, like he had happened to pass me on a street corner or something and it had occurred to him that I might want a lift, like it was the most natural thing in the world.

I was still feeling tied in knots, though, and I was pretty nasty, or sarcastic, in my answer. I said, "Oh no, I just like to come out and sit in the driveway with screaming kids, just for the fun of it."

He wrinkled his forehead in neat ridges that went right up into his hairline, all dismayed looking. It would have served me right if he had just turned around and left right then.

"Oh Lord!" I sighed weakly. "Listen to me! What a bitch!" And I sat down in the driveway and started crying myself. Mystified, the children quieted and crouched on their haunches to peer up into my face. Lisbeth, who had managed to get herself out of the car and around the back end without help, groped around till she found my hand and tried to pull me up.

Rob told her his name and said, "Why don't we just sit down here with your sister—that right? your sister?—and just . . . sit down a minute. Here, you kids go play."

He put them inside the fence and closed the gate. I just sat there crying, but laughing too, the whole thing had gotten so ridiculous.

"Well," he said. "Here we are. And where do you live, Lisbeth—was that it? Lisbeth?"

Unaccustomed to direct questions, she hung fire and began to tie her shoelaces together in knots on top of knots.

"Ah, there you have it!" I laughed, and wiped my eyes. "Where does Lisbeth live? The sixty-four-thousand-dollar question. Or something like that." I pulled my shirttail out and blew my nose on it.

He wrinkled his forehead again, wondering, I'm sure, what the hell, but nodded.

"What are you nodding about?" I snapped. "You don't have the least idea what's going on here."

"No, I guess I don't," he admitted. "Look . . ."

And that's when Lisbeth finally managed to say what she had been working up to all day. "So she's not going to be here, huh?"

"What?" I was blowing my nose again and hadn't quite heard her. Or else I wasn't thinking very quickly. Sometimes you have to think pretty fast around Lisbeth, the way she drags in these things from way out in left field.

"Mama," she said. "So Mama's not going to be here."

I told her no, I guessed not.

"Oh. But she'll . . ." She stopped and rocked her body back and forth.

I turned back to Rob. "So. You really walked into it, didn't you?"

"Look," he said again, in what was surely an effort to get back on firmer ground. "I had this seminar paper I thought you might type for me. I thought maybe you were going back into the business." He paused, noted Lisbeth's rocking, and chose to try to ignore it: I saw him deciding to try. "I thought you might type it for me."

Business: That was a laugh. Big business! Housewife makes a few bucks in spare time, becomes big-business tycoon.

"What made you think that?" I demanded. I couldn't seem to stop being really rude. What I kept thinking was, I was getting into something, all right, but it wasn't business. "I don't know why you just assumed I'd be doing that. I told you I wasn't going to take in typing anymore."

"Well, I saw your sister, and she said—"

"Oh, you saw my sister, did you?"

"Yeah," he said slowly, and he looked at me really closely now. He knew he was stepping on something that was threatening to blow up in his face. "I saw your sister, OK? And she said you might be going into it again."

When Stan moved back, I had told Rob and the others I'd done work for that I wasn't going to do typing anymore. Stan didn't want me to. No wife of his, etc. And I was trying very hard at the time not to do anything Stan didn't like. On the other hand, there was no denying I could use the money, with Christmas right on top of us and all. Even more, I could use the distraction. Rob's papers were full of words like Being and Essence and Time, with capital letters. Capitalized abstractions: I loved them. They had a way of making matters like Davey's potty training seem less all-encompassing. That was one reason I especially liked typing for Rob. One reason.

"I know it's close to Christmas," he said, "and you have your hands full." (Ha!) "But I sure wish you'd do this. I could try to get an extension till New Year's, if that would make a difference."

It was hard to resist; besides the offer of work itself, I liked Rob. I found him very attractive, actually. But I knew I ought to say no. Not to mention the problem of Stan's ego, I did indeed have my hands full. I asked him if he hadn't checked the bulletin board in the student center. There were bound to be other people looking to do this kind of thing.

"Sure there are," he admitted. "But I want you to do it. You can read my handwriting."

Naturally, I gave in and said I would. He looked pleased, and I had an idea he would have liked to stay a while, to come in for a cup of coffee or something, but I didn't ask. I just took the paper and told him to call me in a few days, I'd see what I could do. I got up and dusted off the seat of my pants and called the kids to come on for their naps.

"OK," he said. "Call me if you need me." He started down the driveway, but stopped and turned around. "I mean for anything. Just call." He waved and disappeared around the corner of the house, then reappeared while I was still turning the key in the lock, to say bye to Lisbeth. "Have a nice Christmas, you hear?" he called.

She laughed till she snorted, and flapped her wrists excitedly. He had said the magic word.

I told Stan about the car when he got home that evening. He went out and stuck his head under the hood for a while and then came in saying hell, he'd have to get a new battery for it, and there went Christmas. That didn't bother me too much, since I'd already been trying to get him to cut back on his ideas a little. I was in the kitchen making spaghetti. He stood there in the door with his hands on his hips and said he'd go down after supper and try to get an adjustment on the old battery. I mentioned that maybe we'd go with him, but he had already started back to wash up and didn't seem to hear me.

Dinner that night was one of those times you remember, not because anything so remarkable happens, but because they so perfectly sum up for you, when you look back on them, the Way It Was. Even if they were times when things happened that never happened again, they sum it all up.

The spaghetti was a mistake. We all liked spaghetti, it was always somehow a special dinner, even though a cheap one—and that was important too—but with Sister there it was a mistake. In the first place, it turned out that she didn't like spaghetti, or she said she didn't. That was a possibility I hadn't even thought of. And in the second place, she couldn't manage it. It was too hard to eat.

I had thought I was doing so well. I'd made a fun menu for our first dinner together and had even remembered that she needed bread to use as a "pusher"—that was how the School taught her to manage the problem of getting food onto a fork without getting her left hand into it. So we had garlic bread with our spaghetti. Perfect. Or so I thought.

I put an ordinary amount on her plate to start with, put the sauce and Parmesan on it, and then chopped it up before putting it in front of her, the way I always did Gail's and Davey's, and put a piece of garlic bread in her left hand. She didn't seem to like taking the bread. I guess it felt too buttery. But I just told her that was her pusher, very matter-of-factly, no big deal. I got the kids set up and then remembered the bottle of cheap Chianti I had in the cabinet, so I got that and our glasses and sat down again. I sprinkled Parmesan on my spaghetti and then glanced up, and that was when I saw, by the look on Stan's face, that something was wrong.

In spite of what Lisbeth had said about not liking spaghetti, she was digging in. And she really was managing to get spaghetti from the plate to her mouth—maybe even as much of it as she shoved off the plate onto the table or into her lap. Stan rolled his eyes, grimaced, and put his left hand up to his face so he wouldn't have to look. There was no denying, it was pretty bad. Besides the sauce around her mouth and on her chin and the front of her blouse, she had it on the hand with the fork and all over her left hand too. She had remembered about her pusher all right, and had a firm grip on it with her thumb and forefinger, while with her other fingers she shoveled spaghetti onto the fork. Gail didn't appear to have noticed; she loved 'ghetti and was fully occupied with her own. But Davey had taken it all in and was experimentally dipping his bread and his hand into the bowl of spaghetti in front of him and then holding them up to show Stan.

Trying hard not to let my irritation into my voice, because the last thing we needed was to get her upset, I said, "Remember to use your pusher, Lisbeth."

She frowned, droned one fretful note, and ate faster. With every shove of her fork, a little more spaghetti slid over the left rim of her plate.

It was hard to go on with dinner as usual and just ignore it. We were used to the kids' making noise and spilling their milk or dropping things, and you wouldn't think this would be so very different, really. But when adults make kids' messes, even if you know they're not really adults but only adult-sized and adult-aged, it just bothers you more, that's all.

Lisbeth had finished her first serving before Stan and I were much more than started, and sat there holding her fork and her sauce-soaked bread expectantly. When I asked her if she wanted more, she said gladly, "Oh yeah," then added, "but I don't like spaghetti."

"Wait a minute," Stan said. I guess he felt like he'd had enough. "What do you mean, you don't like spaghetti? This *is* spaghetti, and you like it. Or it looks like you do."

She rocked back and forth on her chair and knitted her brows. I signaled to Stan to let it go. He shrugged and went back to his plate, shielding his eyes again from the spectacle of Lisbeth eating, with her left hand, the pile she had found on her place mat.

It occurred to me then to ask Lisbeth if she wouldn't rather I put her spaghetti in a bowl.

"Why didn't you think of that in the first place?" Stan asked.

I should have; that's how I always gave the kids theirs; but I just hadn't thought.

"No," she said, "just like the first time."

I pointed out that it would be easier to eat.

"I ate it all right," she insisted.

"Right," I said, "but it kept going off your plate." I was careful not to sound cross—I'm sure I didn't sound cross.

She pushed back from the table and stood up, stood poised there a minute, then slammed her chair in and started more or less toward the family room, grazing her cheek on the door facing as she went through.

"OK," I said, "but let's wash your hands anyway."

Through clenched teeth, she droned that one fretting note, then a higher one.

"There's dessert."

That stopped her. She came back, yanked her chair out, and flopped back down. Now the chair back would need washing in two places instead of just one.

Gail caught that right away. She repeated, "Got sert" and pushed her plate away. Stan slapped her face and roared, "Eat that spaghetti!" Which, of course, started her crying.

"Oh, great!" I spat. "Just great!"

Stan shook his fist at me and left the room.

So much for our first dinner together. I cleared the plates and got the kids' pudding. The kids' and Lisbeth's.

When Stan came back through, in a fresh shirt and with his hair combed, I asked where he was going. "I told you," he snapped. "To Sears. To get you a battery."

I reminded him that I had wanted to go too, but he acted like that was a big surprise. And maybe it was; I hadn't really been sure he heard me in the first place. Anyway, whether he had or hadn't, he sure didn't want to wait for us now. He had things to do, he said; he didn't want to wait around for them to finish eating and get cleaned up to go. I had meant to clean them up, hadn't I? Lisbeth, anyway? I hadn't meant to take them to the shopping center like that, had I? Not if I expected him to go along!

He was right, of course. Lisbeth certainly was a mess.

But I was sure I could have them ready to go soon, maybe ten minutes.

"It won't hurt you to wait up for ten minutes," I insisted. "I need to do some Christmas shopping. It's less than a week now."

He stopped in the doorway, looking thoroughly put out. His mouth was a thin line. I should have known not to push him. But instead I snatched Davey out of his high chair and starting swiping his face and hands with a damp cloth, harder than I needed to, making a great show of rushing to get ready. And that was like a red flag to Stan. Wham! He hit the door facing with his fist, bellowed that he wasn't waiting, damn it, he had no intention of dragging this whole mob along, he'd be back later. He slammed the door on his way out.

I don't know why it hit me so. It wasn't that important for me to go shopping right then anyway. I didn't even know for sure what I wanted to shop for, except that thing for Mitchy and the records for Stan, which I couldn't buy with him along anyway. But good reason or no good reason, I felt thwarted and mistreated, as though he was deliberately keeping me from doing what I simply had to do. What it was, of course, was the way he had acted—like the kids' not being ready was only an excuse, like he had already had his mind made up to go out, and to go alone, before he had even heard about the dead battery or Sister's not liking spaghetti or anything. And I didn't want to think about that.

So it was a relief when Lisbeth broke in and stopped me from running compulsively down those greased mental tracks and I could think about her urgent question instead. She tugged my arm and pushed her face right up into mine to ask, "You going to buy me a Christmas present, Meg? You going to get me something and wrap it up?"

"Sure," I told her. "Sure I'll get you a present." God knows what it will be! I thought. But I'd think of something. I'd have to.

Two days: She had been with us two days. Or not even that long; just one and a little over. And already Stan was having fits and Lisbeth was getting wound up tighter and tighter and I was—what was I? Reeling, that was it; reeling from the blows. I was ready to duck my head, curl into a ball, and try to protect the soft spots.

I read the kids a story, a fifty-cent Santa Claus something I'd picked up at the grocery store, and we each colored a picture in their Santa Claus coloring book. By then it was late enough that I could start their baths.

I liked sitting on the side of the tub or on the commode lid and watching them play in the water, all sleek and rosy, and then wrapping them in a big towel, first one and then the other, and pulling them close between my knees to rub them and cuddle them. Bath time was one of my favorite times of day. But it was a chore, too. All that bending over the tub to wash knees and ears, hauling them out, getting them into pajamas, picking up the dirty clothes scattered on the floor—all that on top of everything else I had done all day—left me done in, ready to sit down in front of the TV and put my feet up.

But now when I had finished all that I still wasn't through, because Lisbeth still needed her shower. I don't know how they managed at the Home; maybe they knew how to teach her a routine and where everything was and she was able to do it all for herself. Or maybe, to judge by the dirt caked behind her ears, they didn't manage at all, just let people do the best they could on their own and didn't worry about it. Anyway, however it was there, here I had to show her where to leave her shoes beside her bed and where to get her pajamas and then lead her to the bathroom and show her where to put her dirty clothes and where to get a washcloth. Then when she stepped into the tub I had to get the water temperature adjusted and reach past the mildewed curtain to turn the water dial to spray, then watch to see that she found the soap dish and call instructions when she didn't— "No, down a little, a little to the right, now down some more, there it is"—and hand her the shampoo bottle and take it back after she got some, turn the water off when she was through, help her find the towel, help her hang up the towel, remind her where she had laid the pajamas. It would have been easier, I thought, to strip off and get in with her. But that wouldn't do. The point was to show her enough times and maybe she'd get the routine down and be able to do for herself the rest of the time.

The rest of the time. However long that turned out to be.

I took her to the kitchen for her medication, then helped her find her way to bed. She settled in with a bounce and a sigh and pulled the cover up to her nose, but sat up again just as I started into the hall.

"Yes, Lisbeth," I said. Probably she could hear in my voice that I was reaching my limit by then. "What is it?"

"It's good you're going to give me a present," she said. A crooked sort of grin spread over her face. She looked really pleased. "Will I get one from Mama too?"

It was hard to know how to answer that. I just told her I didn't know about that but I hoped she'd like what I got her.

Whatever that was going to be.

She settled back into bed, content.

By then it was five after nine. Stan had left at seven-twenty-five. It didn't take an hour and forty minutes to buy a battery. Not when the store was maybe a ten-minute drive. Better not think about it. Better not blow up over it. Better not find out what he was doing and *have* to blow up over it. What would I be able to do about it if I did? If I was going to have to take Sister over for good, for all the time. If I couldn't leave her during the day, to take a job, to support the kids and myself. Better not know what he was doing.

Call Mitchy: That was the thing to do.

But Mitchy was at work. All I got was the recording: "Hi, this is Mitchell Taylor. I can't . . ." I hung up and went to the bathroom. Then on second thought I dialed Mitchy's number again and left a message. "This is Meg. Sister's here. I need to know when you can take her. I haven't talked to Beep yet, but—" My time was up; it switched off.

I gathered up a load of clothes and put them in to wash. It was nine-twenty; still no Stan. I decided to try Beep, and got an answer OK, but it was the roommate, and she didn't know when Beep would be in.

Probably, I thought, it was that girl from the party last night. Stan had arranged to meet her somewhere, and this battery business just gave him a good cover. The way they were hanging on to each other, the way they passed that cigarette back and forth—it had to be her.

And only four months ago he had moved back and we had said we were going to make it this time.

I dialed Mitchy's number again and left another message: "Listen, Mitchy, it's not just the Christmas holidays, it's worse, now you've got to call me and help me figure out what to do, I don't care what time it is when you get this, you've got to—" End of message.

Later, trying to read in bed, trying to stay awake till Stan came in, I got out an old spiral notebook left from when I was in school and made out a shopping list. Beside each name I wrote in what I wanted to buy, and if I had bought it already I put a big check mark. For Beep I had bought this terrific beige-tone slip, really great looking, with lots of lace. For Gail a little nightgown, her first nightgown, white with red dots and a red bow and little slippers to match. For Davey a plastic bat and ball. Tomorrow I would go shopping again and get Stan's records, Mitchy's sandwich cooker, the wooden zoo for the kids. By Lisbeth's name there was still only a question mark. After thinking for a while I gave up and tried again to read.

In a couple of pages, though, it came to me, the very thing for Lisbeth. I would get her one of those stuffed animals with a radio in its stomach. A cocker spaniel, maybe, with dangly, fuzzy ears, or a poodle, it didn't matter what, just so it was furry and cuddly and I could tell her it was a something or other. That was the best I could possibly do for $14 or $15. Maybe that and a couple of pairs of underpants; hers were looking pretty far gone. I wrote those ideas in my notebook. Tomorrow I would go out and finish my shopping. I would make Stan put in the new battery before he went to work so I could do that.

Later, I couldn't tell how much later, I woke from a doze and looked at the clock: 1:00 A.M. I had been dreaming that Mama and Daddy were back. Or not so much that they were back as that they had never gone. We were all back at home and Beep and Mitchy were little again, but Gail and Davey were there too, and I kept calling Gail "Beep." They were both there. I decided I might as well turn off the light so it wouldn't shine in my eyes while I went back to sleep. But first I went to make sure the family-room lamp was on.

Getting back in bed, I thought maybe my dream was a premonition. Maybe they really would come back. Maybe they would be there for Christmas, and Mama could help me cook the turkey and make yeast rolls and a pie.

After a while Stan was getting into bed. I heard him easing the waistband on his shorts before he slid under the cover, that was what woke me up. But he didn't say a word and neither did I.

9

⌒⌒⌒⌒

THAT WEEKEND was a wreck, simply a wreck. Or anyway, I was a wreck. I was convinced Stan was having an affair. Twice on Saturday he was gone for an hour or two at a time with flimsy excuses. Sunday afternoon he took his golf clubs and shag bag and said he was going to hit practice balls at the park—it was about forty degrees and damp and the wind was blowing twigs out of the trees.

I was sure he was off with that girl, that Cindy, but then again I didn't really *know* it, and I kept trying to think I didn't believe it. I tried to think I wasn't even thinking it. And while I tried to think that, I got edgier and edgier, thoroughly bitchy in every way. Both of the kids had colds and kept whining all afternoon. Lisbeth was cranky and fretful; the Christmas excitement was once again proving too much for her. As it always had. As it always, I thought, would. Always, every December for the rest of my life, up into old age, I would have to contend with this creature who rocked on her chair and whined and grimaced and clawed the palms of her hands until they bled, all on the chance that Santa would, or maybe wouldn't, bring her a box of candy.

I tried getting out Rob Brewster's paper to type, but couldn't settle down to it. By the time it occurred to me that we could pass the time making Christmas cookies, the afternoon was so far gone I didn't feel like fooling with that either.

When Stan came in, he was all loud and hearty, covering up. He was hitting the ball pretty well, he said. Yes sirree, he was really hitting the ball. And I kept on pretending not to see through it. I kept on not wanting to see through it, wanting not to. Then after dinner he got cleaned up and left again, without even bothering to give an excuse. So I went to bed by myself again and finally, several hours later, also went to sleep by myself.

All the next day, Monday, from the time I got up till about the middle of the afternoon, I kept thinking I would confront him with it. I kept running over in my mind exactly what I would say to him, as soon as he got home, and how I would say it. I hugged my wrongs and promised myself an end to them and snapped at the kids. Because couldn't they see I was trying to think? Only I wasn't thinking, not really, not in any practical way. I was just imagining my big scene.

But by three o'clock I knew I wasn't going to be able to carry it through. I just felt the venom, or not the venom so much as the juice, the actual power to do it, drain right out of me, as if someone had punched holes in the soles of my feet and it was all running out and soaking into the carpet. I had set a chicken out to thaw and was thinking maybe I'd get a shower and change into something decent when the phone rang. I just knew it was Stan calling to say he wouldn't be home. I just knew it. So of course I snapped a hello that would have bitten the words right off at his lips, if it had been him.

There was a little silence at the other end, and then it wasn't Stan who said hello back at me but Beep. She asked what was wrong, but I didn't want to get into reasons and causes. Ignoring the question, I managed to exclaim, "This is a surprise! Really, I'm surprised you remembered how to look up my number."

"Ah, that's my big sister," she said. "Sweet as ever! Listen, how's it going with Lisbeth?"

"So-so." I didn't want any idle words, when I knew from way back how much she was going to do about it. About anything. So I changed the subject. How come, I asked, she had told Rob Brewster I was doing typing again?

There was another silence. Finally she said she just figured I might. But still I wanted to know why. Why had she figured that? She knew I had told Stan I wouldn't.

"That's a good one!" she mocked. "So you told Stan. Big deal!"

I waited, and after a minute she went on. She had just had an idea, she said, that whatever I had told Stan might not matter so much anymore.

"Why wouldn't it?" I demanded. I was really pushing it.

The silence was longer this time. She just thought, she

said, that maybe things weren't going so well for us after all, so it wouldn't hurt if I got a little work. "A dollar or two here and there" was how she put it.

I asked her why she had thought that.

"Jesus, Meg! What do you want me to say?" She took a big breath and then there it was: She had seen Stan the other night over at that shopping place where she and I had run into each other that day. He wasn't alone.

So she had said it. It wasn't as though I hadn't known, of course. I had it all figured out, actually. But I hadn't wanted to hear it, even while, in a way, yes, I had wanted to. As long as I didn't hear it, I could ignore it. And even after she told me, I still tried to explain it away. I made up a whole story about someone retiring at work and they took up a collection and Stan and this other person were selecting the gift. It sounded so plausible I almost believed it myself.

"O-kay," she sighed, humoring me. "Have it your way."

It wasn't "my way," I insisted, it was just the way it was. Everything was fine with Stan and me. Just fine.

"OK," she repeated, and this time she was the one who changed the subject. What she had called about, she said, was Christmas. Mitchy had mentioned that he thought I was expecting both of them over at my place, and she was wondering what were the plans.

Of course, we had talked about it ages ago. She couldn't have forgotten. Or anyway, I thought we had talked about it. I wasn't absolutely sure. But it was self-evident; we didn't even need to have talked about it. Since Mama was gone, I would make Christmas, and they would be at my house. But she had a different idea.

"Look," she said, "I may not stay around for the whole day. In fact, I'm not sure I'll be there for dinner."

That was about like Beep, I thought, you couldn't count on her for a thing. I gave her an icy, "Oh?"

"I knew you'd be that way!" she complained. "Just don't start in on me like that! I'm going skiing."

"Oh, you just decided to go skiing on Christmas Day."

"No, I didn't just decide to go skiing," she pouted. "I was asked."

I wanted to ask, *Why*, Beep? Why do you do these things? I thought about that operator I'd seen her with at the shopping center and I thought, how can she let that sleazebag touch her? But when I asked, she was amazed. Him? Oh God, no, not him! She had met this terrific guy. She would tell me all about him sometime. Anyway, he had these friends, see, who had this condo at Steamboat Springs. They might be flying up Christmas Day. Or the next day. But then there was packing, too, so she'd be busy.

"Right," I said. "You wouldn't want to miss packing."

"All right, Meg, enough already. Look," her voice easing off, going smooth again, "what else I wanted to say was, Mitchy said you were figuring on both of us taking Sister off your hands some of the time while she's here, but since this has come up I won't be able to."

"How long are you going to be gone, for God's sake? I mean, here I am stuck with Lisbeth for three weeks—"

And that was when I saw her, standing in the doorway, listening to every word. We had always been so careful what we said when she was around. There had always been this conspiracy of kindness, all of us maintaining this fiction of the loved and wanted Lisbeth, and now I had broken it. But having broken it, I set it aside and went on. "Actually, it's worse than that. She's—"

Beep didn't wait to hear it. "It's not I'm going to be gone so long." She raised her voice, just a shade, just enough. "I do have a job, you know. I'm taking vacation days for this trip, and I won't be able to take off any more. So what I'm saying is, that lets me out for keeping her for you.

"Besides," she added, "I'd like for this to work out with this guy. She wouldn't exactly be any help."

Oh, wouldn't she really? But I let that go. There was too much going on here, I couldn't hang on to all of it. What really got me was what came before that: for me? keeping her for *me?* I didn't bother answering; I just hung up. When she called back—I had known she would; being Beep, she would have to explain why I shouldn't have expected it in the first place—I just took the phone off the hook and laid it on the counter and went to put in a load of wash.

By then, of course, it was too late to freshen up before Stan got home. I had to settle for putting on a clean blouse and some lipstick. He probably wouldn't look very close anyway; that was part of the problem.

Then the kids were waking up from their naps, and for once Davey was dry, so I took him to the potty. It was while I was sitting there on the side of the tub, waiting for him to perform, that Lisbeth came to the door and stood, just stood there with her eyes rolled up toward eleven o'clock, stacking and twisting and untwisting her fingers. She didn't say anything, just waited for me to notice her and ask what she wanted. And when I did, she asked me, "What did you mean while ago when you said stuck with me?"

Oh God, I thought, what am I going to say? Even though I had known as soon as I said it that she must have heard me, and had wanted to bite my tongue, still I had let myself hope she didn't really notice. Why hadn't I thought before I opened my mouth? I should have known she was listening; she listened to everything. All those years, all my life, we had watched every word when she was around. We had never let her know how we felt, that the problem of her, of her life, was wearing on us, in all kinds of ways, big and little, and wearing us out. She had never known she wasn't totally wanted. And now I had done it; I had broken the great taboo.

She stood there waiting for my answer, her eyes rolled up and wavering back and forth. I was afraid she was going to cry, and thought, Oh my God, what'll I do?

"I didn't mean it like that," I told her. "I was mad about something else. That's why I said it. Sometimes when people are mad they say things they don't really mean."

"You shouldn't say things you don't mean. That's telling a—you know; I don't want to say it."

I tried kidding her out of it. "Oh, come on now, you don't have to be afraid to say—"

Davey had started climbing down while we talked and now stopped partway and peed against the side of the toilet. I broke off to yell at him and slap his bottom, though of course that accomplished simply nothing. All it did was to make him cry. I still had to clean it up, while he hurled himself on the floor and bawled, and the thing was, he wouldn't be any more likely to use the toilet next time. When he stopped to catch his breath, Lisbeth asked doubtfully, "Oh, so you like for me to be here, huh?"

"Sure I do!" I said. "We're glad you could come. It just wouldn't be right if you weren't here for Christmas." And I meant it. It wouldn't be right. I'd be carrying around a load of guilt too big to see over.

She turned away with a twist of smile and started down the hall, then reappeared in the doorway while I was diapering Davey on the bath mat. I could see her listen, with her head cocked, for some sound to indicate I was still there. For a moment I had an impulse to hold very, very still, the way we had when we were kids. But I resisted that and patted Davey on the stomach, making a gentle smacking sound. "Oh," she said, "so you like me here at Christmas but not any other time."

I pretended I hadn't heard that. It was too much for me.

When Stan got home, I was in the kitchen looking as perky and sweet as I could manage, with the radio turned low and the kids scrubbed up, happily playing cars on a fold-out plastic town in their room. An aroma of frying chicken was in the air. How much wifelier can you get?

All that evening I made up to him in the most shit-eating ways. I practically carried him his slippers in my mouth and begged for a pat on the head. I practically licked his hand. I've asked myself how I could have done that, how I could have been such a shit-eater. And I think I was just afraid to face up to what the consequences might be otherwise. Or not even that so much as afraid to face the first step in starting toward those consequences—the Big Scene.

Stan must have been expecting the Big Scene too. All evening he kept a kind of pleased but puzzled look on his face, as if he wondered what was going on but was glad to fall in with it. Or maybe what he was expecting was the Big Nag, and when that didn't come he more or less sat back and said, Well, let's see how *this* develops.

Probably Stan had always wanted more than he got from me—more understanding, more admiration, maybe just more dynamics. God knows, I had wanted more than I ever got from him! It had seemed to me that marriage was strictly a one-way street in Stan's book, he took and I gave. But let's say he felt the same, like I didn't care enough or anyway didn't give enough. That one night, at least, he got it, all the sweetness and attention and catering-to that he could want. I said, in every way but words, Please please oh please don't leave me for that other woman! Please don't fool around with her on the side and make me feel like shit! If you just won't do that I'll make things so nice for you here you won't believe it, you'll wonder why you ever even thought of leaving!

There's something wrong with a proposition like that. But I made it anyway. I practically knocked myself out making it. And he knew; he was bound to have known. Right up to the minute dinner was ready—fried chicken and hot homemade biscuits and I don't know what all—I managed to keep Sister back in her room with the door closed. I figured the less he had to look at her, the better, even if it meant I had to run back and forth every few minutes. I had her pacified with a radio and a bag of Chee-tos, and I kept running back and sticking my head in and asking what was that song they were playing, had she heard the time, anything, just to keep her interested so she'd stay there. I kept the kids playing with their car set the same way. The last time I checked, though, one of them—Gail said it was Davey—had gotten out their box of crayons and drawn something on the wall. It was all I could do to keep from blowing up, but I just shook my head at them and hurried back to make the gravy.

After dinner I kept them all in the kitchen with me while I did the dishes. Stan could lounge on the sofa undisturbed. He was poring over the NFL playoff matchups and who had home field advantage, all that, and he wouldn't have been very happy to be interrupted. I read them a Little Golden Book, or actually recited it, while I put food away and rinsed and washed. Gail turned the pages at the right times to keep the pictures with the words. By the time I finished I was pooped. One thing for sure, I couldn't live like that every day.

I had a sense, though, that it wouldn't have to be every day. Even though there was no end in sight for Sister's visit, so I couldn't think of that as the hump to be gotten over, I still had this feeling that it was a make-it or break-it time, that if I could just get us through the next few days without a fracture it would all be OK, I wouldn't have to keep on carrying the whole weight of it all. Because that's how I felt, that I was the one who was carrying it. Who knows what load Stan may have felt like he was carrying? To me, he didn't seem to be carrying anything. To me, he was part of the load. But I tried not to look at that, even though it was plain as day.

When I finished in the kitchen it was still too early to put the kids to bed, but I didn't want them bothering Stan, so I had them "help" me wrap Mitchy's present. We made a big, fancy bow and stuck seals all over—bells and wreaths and sleighs and Don't Open Till Christmas—anything to take time. After that they sat on my lap and looked at the pictures while I read "'Twas the Night before Christmas." What a picture we must have made! American motherhood at its most appealing! How could he resist? But if he ever looked up, I didn't know it. Lisbeth sat on the sofa at the end nearest my chair, Stan having sat up to make room when we came in. That was his contribution to the evening. She laughed at everything: "a bowl full of jelly, oh sure"; "happy Christmas to all, it's supposed to be merry Christmas, everybody knows that." She was into it every bit as much as Gail and Davey.

After I finally got the kids to bed and persuaded Lisbeth to turn in early (on grounds that she'd better rest up so she could help get ready for Christmas), I put on some cologne and some fresh underpants, partly because I had this fear of smelling stale and partly because I had just remembered these black bikinis Stan had bought me once. They had been a big turn-on for him the only time I had worn them, so I decided to go dig them out of the back of the drawer. And they did make me feel sexy, in a way. Then I went back in the family room and came up behind him and put my arms around him. He was watching TV. He asked me what was up.

I sat down with him and watched for a while. I was feeling wound up tight inside, but I had to make my move, whether I felt like it or not. It was now or never. So I sidled up and wormed in under his arm. If he was surprised, he must have decided not to show it. His eyes stayed fastened on the screen. But with the hand that dangled over my shoulder he fiddled with my left breast. Long experience told me it didn't mean a thing; he probably didn't even know what he was doing. But I chose to act as if he did. I slipped my fingers inside his shirt, between the buttons, and pulled the hairs on his belly. In response, he squeezed. I blew on his neck a little and whispered that I'd been missing him. I could tell that surprised him, because his shoulders tensed. Otherwise, he didn't give the least indication at all except that after a minute he gave my breast another squeeze.

We sat there like that through the rest of the movie. Fortunately, there wasn't much to go—my neck was getting a kink. The movie was pretty good, Chevy Chase, I think, but I didn't pay much attention. I was busy thinking how I was going to give this my best shot.

When it was over, he squeezed again as an excuse-me and got up and turned off the set. Before the news, that is. So I knew I'd made an impact. I trailed him back to the bedroom, locked the door just in case one of the kids got up, and said, "Let me show you what I've got on."

I was down to the black bikinis before he had his shoes and jeans off, and it looked as though they were going to be just as big a turn-on as they had been the first time. Then instead of waiting, as he expected, I went down on my knees to him where he was standing unbuttoning his shirt. He wound his fingers in my hair and shoved in.

When he sagged over onto the bed I climbed up and lay against him. My knees felt scored by the carpet. After a while, he whispered, "Baby, you give head like nobody else."

It wasn't exactly what I most wanted to hear, not my highest aspiration, you might say, but I whispered back, "So you don't need anybody else, do you?"

We lay there for a long time. He seemed to go to sleep, but I wasn't sure. Maybe he just wanted me to think so, so he wouldn't have to talk. A norther was coming in; I could hear the wind pick up and begin to sing around the house. The furnace began to come on. We hadn't turned it down for the night, but I felt chilled anyway and finally shoved him around so we could get under the cover. I felt swollen and blocked between the legs and thought of doing something about it myself, but it seemed like too much trouble. Slipping into sleep, I dreamed about Dr. Krawitz and his wonderful brown eyes. It seemed he was putting his stethoscope on my breasts and apologizing for its being cold, but it wasn't, it was warm, and then I saw he didn't have anything on under his lab coat. He had a big erection, I could see it, and then it was just suddenly in me, not that he made a move, it was just there, so I didn't have any choice in the matter, I wasn't responsible. I woke up in a hard, pinching orgasm.

That was when I realized that what I had been thinking was my own moaning in the dream was really a wailing cry from down the hall. I pulled on a nightgown, pulling the black panties off as the gown came down, and went to see what was wrong. I was half asleep, of course, all disoriented. I thought at first it was one of the children crying or even sick and throwing up in bed, even though I knew it was coming from Lisbeth's room. But then I knew it was her.

She lay flat on her back, her face twisting and pulling like one of those fish with the donut mouths that stretch and wobble in the wavering of the water behind the thick glass. Tears ran along furrows that shifted with the working of her face. I asked her what was wrong, what was the matter. But I think I knew before she told me.

Her mouth stretched, she gulped, her eyes wavered up behind the welling-up tears. "You said you were stuck with me," she wailed. "Stuck with me! Stuck with me!" Her voice rose and rose like a siren. She heaved up from the bed and crouched there on her knees, beating her fists on the mattress in front of her and bellowing over and over, "Stuck with me! Stuck with me!"

Stan appeared in the doorway, naked, his hair and his eyes wild, and the kids pressed in to look, not even noticing his nakedness. Davey started to cry, in sympathy maybe, or maybe just scared. Reaching down automatically, Stan picked him up. "Holy shit!" he yelled above them both. "What is going on? Can't you stop her?"

I pushed them out the door and told him to take the kids back to bed, then closed it after him and went to sit beside her. She was still beating the mattress with her fists, but not so hard now, and her shrieks were wearing down.

Taking care to avoid her fists, I caught her by the shoulders. I practically had to shout to get her to hear. I kept telling her over and over to listen to me, listen to me, I hadn't meant that, listen, I didn't mean it. Of course, the truth was that I had meant it. At that moment, I had. But not in the way she heard it. Or I didn't think I had meant it that way, as if I didn't care about her. You could love someone and still feel stuck, couldn't you? But how could I explain that to her? So I kept telling her I didn't mean that, I didn't mean it, and maybe she believed me. Anyway, after a while she lay down, and I lay down beside her. She was all in a sweat and shaking, worn out.

It was after she settled down, so I wasn't struggling with her anymore, that it really hit me: God! To be blind and have everything else wrong that Lisbeth had and to be unwanted besides! And to know it—that was the worst part! If she had had a little less intelligence than the little she had, she at least wouldn't have had to know it.

I felt low, low; I had really hit bottom. Why on earth had I let myself say I was stuck with her? All the time we were growing up, whatever happened, however bad it got with her, we had never let her know that.

After a while she sat up again, abruptly, as if she had just thought of something else, and said, "Mama wouldn't have said that."

"I know she wouldn't." And it was true; no matter what, she wouldn't have. "I didn't mean it, Lisbeth. I was bothered about some other things and . . . it just came out, that's all. I didn't mean it. I'm sorry."

She lay back down.

I stayed there with her all night, till I heard Stan up getting ready for work and then going and the house was quiet again. The roll-away bed Lisbeth had been sleeping on wasn't very big, and, as I now realized, wasn't very good either. But I stayed with her and slept or dozed off and on and thought about things.

All this time I had been thinking how bad it was to be stuck—with her, with everything; just how bad to be stuck. That was me, of course; I was the one who was stuck. Now I thougnt how bad it was to be the one somebody was stuck with, how bad a place that was to have to be in. I felt like I didn't have any options—she *really* didn't have any options. And apparently she knew it. But the thing was that knowing that, seeing it now after not seeing it before, didn't seem to make it any easier to be stuck with her. I felt sorry for her and I realized now how much she could hurt inside, but I was still just as stuck myself. That was the hell of it. And I couldn't figure any way out of that, for either of us.

10

ல௳௳ல

THAT WAS a Christmas to remember. Not that I *want* to remember it. I wish I could have wadded it up and thrown it away with the torn wrapping paper. But I keep coming across it, even now, in there among my nicer things, the mental keepsakes I keep around on purpose. It's there like some piece of trash I should have taken out long ago but somehow never could.

I've always been a sucker for Christmas. I always hope it's going to be like a Christmas in a magazine, all fireplaces and snow and jinglebells. I guess I'm that much like Mama. And of course it's never that way. It never was. Growing up in Dallas and pinning my hopes on "White Christmas"— what else could I expect but letdown? Only letdown may be too mild a word for the way our Christmases used to go.

I remember one Christmas when Sister got a talking Bugs Bunny. She had always been a big problem to buy for, of course, because what could you get her that she could manage to have fun with? But this was the Christmas present to end all Christmas presents. Something even she couldn't mess up and have a tantrum about. It was this terrific gray-and-white Bugs Bunny with an orange carrot in one hand and a string with a ring on it coming out from his middle. You put your finger through the ring and pulled, and Bugs said, "Hiya, toots" or "What's up, doc?" Smart-aleck things like that. We all had to try it out the day Mama brought it home from the store, early, before Thanksgiving even. And we all agreed it was perfect.

Mama felt so good about finding that thing for her. It was like finding the magic happiness charm at last. For once, Christmas was going to live up to its reputation instead of tumbling down around our ears. I really think she had some vague, unreasonable notion that if she could only make a perfect Christmas, just once, it would be like weaving a magic spell: Sister would be normal, everything would be OK. Well, everything wasn't.

Not that the Bugs Bunny wasn't a hit. It was. There couldn't have been a bigger hit. Mama helped Lisbeth get it out of the package and showed her the ring and helped her pull it, and when that rabbit said, "What's up, doc?" just like Bugs Bunny in the cartoons, Lisbeth absolutely cracked up. We all did. I have never seen anyone look so tickled. And I know the rest of us were all thinking the same thing, that at last we had made her happy, this once we were having a good Christmas.

It was a wonderful moment. But that was just the trouble: It was *a* moment. But she couldn't let it go at that.

She had to go on and on, like a needle on a scratched record, pulling the ring, pulling the ring, pulling the ring. The rabbit kept yakking and Lisbeth kept laughing, but not quite so much, gradually less and less. But still she kept it up. And we knew, of course, from long experience with this kind of behavior, what was happening. But what to do about it we didn't know.

Lisbeth wasn't made for excitement; she couldn't handle it. That's one reason our Christmases were always such a disaster. And the Bugs Bunny meant just that much more excitement for her not to be able to handle. What was on all our minds, I think, maybe even Beep's in a way, was, when would something go wrong, when would she go off into screaming fits, like she always did?

For a while it looked like that wouldn't happen, we would escape for once. Mama served up our big Christmas breakfast and then got started baking pies and making candied yams and doing all the rest that has to be done for Christmas dinner. The rest of us scattered to enjoy our presents. But Lisbeth kept at it, pulling that string, pulling it again, not even really listening anymore to what the rabbit said. By noon she'd had about all she could take. Or we'd had about all we could take, between Bugs's yakking and the suspense of wondering when it was all going to crash. She had been pulling that string for about three hours solid. We hadn't been able to distract her for more than a minute. By this time she looked tired, she looked like she wanted to stop, but she still kept at it.

She pulled the string and the rabbit yakked, and she pulled it some more and the rabbit yakked some more, and all the time her shoulders got more hunched and her face got more twisted. And still she pulled the string. Mama kept coming to the door with her dish towel to look in at her, and Daddy brought in a cup of eggnog with a little whiskey in it, to relax her, but it didn't work. She drank down the eggnog like water and groped around in a panic till she found Bugs Bunny, and started pulling that string again. And by then she was droning a constant little fretful tune.

Then it happened. She gave a big jerk on the ring, and the string broke and the stub flew up inside the rabbit, stopping it in mid "What's up—". I looked up from my card game to see a look of absolute outrage on her face. For maybe ten seconds she just sat there. Then she let out a bellow like you never heard, a bellow that rose like a wave and gathered and rolled over us.

Daddy yelled to Mama, "Great God in heaven, Margaret, can't you do something?" But of course she couldn't. She fluttered and clucked and soothed, but nothing did any good. Finally, whether in the hope of shocking her into silence or just as a natural outburst of frustration, she stiffened and drew back and slapped Sister's face.

Lisbeth sucked in her breath with a rush, and for a minute we were all caught in the silence it left behind. Mama stood up, her hand caught between reaching and drawing back. She had never done that before. In all those years, I honestly believe, she had never once hit Lisbeth. Some power, some absolute determination, had held back her hand who knows how many times. Now that determination had broken, and she looked as hard hit as Sister did.

Then her breath came back, all our breaths came back, and Mama hadn't hushed her after all. She roared louder than ever.

If we thought she had thrown temper fits before, we just didn't know what a temper fit was. It went on and on. Beep and Mitchy went outside and made a big show of playing Frisbee, in spite of the cold. I stayed in the kitchen to try to keep things going along while Mama tried to do something with her.

And still it went on. She was red in the face and sweating and looked tired enough to drop, but still she screamed and hit her fists on the couch, or now and then hit herself, on the sides of the head. Once she unclenched her fingers and raked her fingernails down both cheeks, leaving red lines on each side that slowly filled.

Finally Daddy took hold of her and dragged her off to the back bedroom, shut her in, and barricaded the door. And still she went on bellowing. We ate our Christmas dinner with that in our ears. Mama insisted on a blessing, I remember, wouldn't do without it, and there she was, thanking the Lord over that miserable racket.

We tried to eat. We tried to keep up a good front. But after a bite or two Mama threw down her fork and pushed back from the table, put her hands over her face, and cried and cried. I had never seen her cry like that. Lisbeth was getting a little quieter by then, but it had been too much. Mama kept crying and crying until Daddy finally got out the bottle and poured her a shot glass full and then another one. And Mama wasn't a drinking person, either. But there are times when everybody needs a little something to get through. Mitchy and I did the dishes while Mama lay on the sofa and Daddy got a little food into Lisbeth. And about six o'clock he gave Mama another shot of whiskey and put her and Lisbeth both to bed.

That's how it was when Sister came home for Christmas, when I was a kid. I know it wasn't always that bad; it couldn't have been. I wouldn't remember that time so well if it wasn't a standout. But when I think about our Christmases back then, that one seems to sum them up.

So is it any wonder I have all this tension about holidays? And yet, getting ready for our Christmas with the kids and Lisbeth, I fussed and overdid and helped the tension build up, just the way Mama always did. I hadn't learned a thing. I did all the real Christmas things, made fudge dropped by the spoonful onto waxed paper and cookies in the shapes of stars and bells and a date cake that fell. Nobody liked date cake anyway, but it smelled like Christmas; it was what we should have liked, if we had been the people I was wanting us to be, who kept Christmas right and kept it all together. At the last minute I even bought some red felt and silver braid and glitter, and sat up half the night making fancy stockings for the kids to hang up and even one for Lisbeth, because she was a kind of kid. None of those ninety-eight-cent bought stockings for us, no sir-ree.

I don't know what I was trying to prove. That we were wholesome and home-centered, I guess. That I hadn't lied when I told Lisbeth to go to bed early because we had a lot to do getting ready for Christmas. That at least I hadn't lied about that.

And I did involve her, I got her in on everything. I saw

to it that she had plenty to do. That was one reason I was so worn-out by the time the big day came. I had her in the kitchen with me stirring and cutting out and molding. I had her spreading glue to stick the glitter on and stringing popcorn and tacking up a red ribbon clothesline to hang our cards on. I took her hands and put them through the motions and then we could say that she had done it. It was a great time for her. It was the big buildup to the great climax. You would almost have thought Monday night hadn't happened.

The trouble, of course, was that Sister's buildups never came to anything but a crash. They never had. I should have remembered that.

And all through those last few days while I was busy keeping Lisbeth busy, Stan more or less stood back and watched. He stayed pretty close to home for those few days. I think of him as leaning against a door facing, hands in pockets and head on one side, watching. Puzzling it out. Like he was trying to figure out what I was trying to do. And for a while it was as if that last weekend and his "involvement," his screwing around with whoever she was, hadn't happened at all. I was able to act like it hadn't, at least, and he let me act that way. But of course it had happened, that was the thing. I was really setting myself up.

On Christmas Eve he got off at noon and hung around the house for a while. Then about four he took off without a word and was gone for a couple of hours. But when he came back he had presents, all wrapped up, so we could act as though that explained it and made it all right. We were doing a lot of acting those days. And it worked, we made it through without incident, filled the stockings, went to bed and fucked grimly, without a word. Settling into sleep, I felt relieved that nothing worse had happened.

Then we were waking up again, and, sure enough, it was just like old times. Sister bolted up from her pillow looking alarmed and unrested; probably she hadn't slept more than an hour or two all night, lying there waiting for Christmas to come. She refused to dress or drink her orange juice or even go to the bathroom before she got her stocking. And then Gail and Davey ran in and got into everything at once. And I had that old feeling of not enough time, not enough attention to spread over everyone, too much happening at once. I was showing Gail how you pressed on the bottom of the wooden Mickey Mouse and he went limp and then straightened up again when you let go—she had picked that out as the star of her stocking loot—when I glanced over at Lisbeth and saw that clenched look on her face, the frown and the set teeth, just like in the year of the Bugs Bunny, and I knew what was coming. Just like old times.

We hadn't planned to let the kids open their presents then. We were going to wait until Mitchy and Beep came. But after the stockings it got out of hand, I guess you'd say, and we thought oh what the hell and let them go. When I asked Lisbeth if she wanted to wait and open hers with the adults, her answer was to reach out with both hands and sweep the empty air in front of her until she encountered a package there and tore into it.

"Christ!" Stan muttered, and turned away. He was good at being disgusted, he had that down pat.

What she had was her dog radio, of course, her one big

gift. And she did like it. She was carried away with it. She clutched it and chortled, treating it like a great joke—"Dog radio, who ever heard of a dog radio?" Holding it to her ear, she began to run through the stations. Christmas choirs merged into newscasts into country Christmas blues into Latin rhythms and church services and more choirs. Across the dial, back across the dial, across the dial again. After the kids had opened everything and had time to mix it all up together, and after I had made coffee and heated packaged sweet rolls and gotten everyone else into the kitchen for breakfast, she was still sweeping the dial with the radio up to her ear. I had to practically pry it out of her fingers to get her to come eat, even though she wanted to do that too. She always wanted to eat. And after she bolted down her food the only way I could get her to brush her teeth and get clothes on was to say I wasn't going to tell her where her radio was until she did.

Stan said, For Christ's sake you'd think she had never heard a radio before. But I told him maybe the fuzzy dog fur felt good against her face and I was just glad we had gotten her something she liked.

"Oh yes," he said, "that's the way, be Miss Goody-Good. You never miss a lick with that routine, do you?"

I went to start on our Christmas dinner.

We were planning to eat about two, the idea being that it was one of those meals you need the rest of the day to recover from. I was cooking turkey and dressing and candied yams and two pies, the works, just like we used to have. I guess it was a way of summoning up those times again, or even of summoning up Mama and Daddy again, to take care of things. I kept going to the front window to look for Mitchy and Beep—they should have been there already—and I think I wouldn't have been half surprised to see Mama and Daddy drive up too. Stan kept coming out to the kitchen and telling me I was going to have to do something about Lisbeth, but that wasn't bothering me too much, not yet. It was just part of Christmas.

By one o'clock, I was getting worried. I tried Mitchy's number but didn't get an answer, only the answering machine. I figured he must be on his way. But after another ten minutes I was back looking out the window again, and that time I stopped to notice how bad Sister really was. There she sat on the sofa, right where she had been all day, turning that radio dial like it was an assignment she didn't dare slack off on. She was strung tight as a guitar string, I could see that at a glance. Her eyes were bloodshot and rolling up, and she had that clenched, grinding look around the mouth that I knew so well.

When I came through, Stan looked up from what he was doing, winding line onto a new fishing reel he had turned up with, and said, "This isn't good for the kids, you know that."

Of course I knew it, I'd been a kid too once.

They were playing in their room with their little cars, having admired the new circus for maybe half an hour, and they kept coming to the door and looking solemnly in at her, then checking each other with a glance and fading away to their room again. They knew something was wrong.

Poor Lisbeth. I tried to persuade her to come set the table—she could do that, if I made every move with her—

but she wouldn't budge. When I reminded her how she had enjoyed getting ready for Christmas, she fretted and pulled away from my hand. "That was getting ready," she insisted. "Now it's here." She changed stations and sang along with a few notes of what she found playing.

Stan looked up from his reel with a disgusted shake of the head. "Coming any minute, are they? That's that reliable family of yours for you!"

I hurried away to the kitchen. If I tried to answer him, I'd only say more than I should and start crying, I knew that. Besides, what was there to argue about?

By then I had let the pecan pie get black on one side, and I burned my finger on the rack hurrying to get it out. Two dollars and fifty cents' worth of pecans, and I had to go and burn them! Of course, it was partly the stove's fault, a cheap one that baked everything unevenly, about what you'd expect in a rent house.

"Damn crappy oven!" I muttered, and flung the pot holders, and just then I heard Beep's car in the drive.

She bustled in with a present and an off-target kiss for everybody. Big deal! I thought. Where were you, Beep, when I needed you? Of course, she looked terrific, just terrific—clothes I wouldn't know how to pick out even if I had the money, makeup like a magazine ad, and thinner than I'd ever even hoped to be, let alone been. She made a big to-do about sitting by Lisbeth and talking to her, fairly dripping sweetness, and of course Lisbeth ate it up. She fastened on to Beep like the long-lost princess. Isn't it always the way? Stan would hardly even look at her, though, even when he opened the liter—not fifth, but liter—of Jack

Daniel's she had brought him. It puzzled me at first; no matter how he might talk about my family, he had always thawed when she came around. But this time there was something going on between them. I could feel it, only I couldn't figure out what it was, until much later. It was while I was washing dishes that it came to me: She knew, and Stan knew she knew.

Right off, Beep announced that she couldn't stay long. She hadn't even meant to stay for dinner but she figured out, I guess, how mad I'd be if she didn't, with Mitchy not there either, and she slipped back to the bedroom to make a phone call and didn't say anything else about leaving for at least a half hour. Then she asked when I was planning for us to sit down to eat, and since everything was actually ready, or nearly so, I said I guessed there wasn't any use waiting anymore for Mitchy, so we might as well go ahead. So she went to the kitchen with me, and in the middle of helping set the food out stopped to give me a hug and say she was sorry everything seemed so bad for me now and she wished there was some way she could help. I could have told her she could take Lisbeth off my hands for a while or help me decide what to do about her or even just come over and talk to me once in a while, but what was the use? So of course I said there wasn't a thing she could do but I appreciated her thinking of it anyway. And we acted like everything was fine between us, and maybe it was, as fine as it gets anyway.

While I was mashing the potatoes—real ones, not packaged—the phone rang and Beep answered. It was Mitchy. She mouthed his name to me before handing me the receiver. I propped it between my shoulder and chin and kept on mashing. I started by asking him why he wasn't here yet, and as soon as he said a word I knew why—not in an ultimate sense, but practically speaking. He was drunk. I never got out of him where he was. When I tried to, and let it become obvious that I wasn't any too happy about all this, he started crying, blubbered out, "Fuck it, just fuck it all," and hung up.

I had never heard Mitchy drunk before, and it really bothered me. My little brother—what was wrong with him that he would do this?

We went ahead with getting things ready, though, and sat down to eat, and it was right after that that the disaster happened, putting an end to all pretense. I had tried so hard to make it a happy day, and it had already been such a bad one, that this just seemed like the last straw. I felt like giving up, only I didn't know how.

Beep had made a big show of helping, now after all the real work was done. Or maybe she did want to help or even thought she was helping. Anyway, when we came to the table she asked Lisbeth sweetly, "Do you want me to fix your plate for you, or do you want Meg to do it?" And of course Lisbeth said, "I want you to." That was fine with me; I was fixing the kids' plates anyway. Only I knew what Lisbeth liked and didn't like better than Beep did; or at least I knew to ask her if she wanted this or wanted that, I wouldn't have just put it on her plate. So, logically enough— and I wouldn't deny that for a minute; it was a reasonable thing to do—Beep piled a big heap of dressing on Lisbeth's plate and put her turkey beside it and dribbled giblet gravy over the whole thing. Also, she helped her to a big spoonful of candied yams, which I would have known she wouldn't eat for the world, though as it turned out that didn't come into play at all, she never even knew they were there.

Stan had just said stiffly, as if making it a point to do his duty, "This looks terrific, Meg," and he had taken a bite of turkey with a respectable semblance of enthusiasm, when Lisbeth let out a squawk. "What's this stuff?"

At first I didn't know what stuff she meant. Whatever had been on her fork was gone now. But her paddling in the gravied dressing with her fingers, combined with the revolted look on her face, made it clear what was the offender.

Beep told her what it was. "And didn't Meg do a good—"

The rest was lost in the uproar. Lisbeth bellowed that she didn't like that stuff, slung her chair back from the table, and stood up with a stamp of her foot. For a minute she seemed to tower over us as we sat there immobilized. Then she reached down, picked up her plate, threw it against the wall behind her, and went yelling and stamping off into the family room.

Stan charged after her, roaring "Goddamned cretin!" and grabbed her by the shoulder. He would have hit her for sure if I hadn't gotten there first, so the blow went off target onto my face instead, splitting my lip. It wasn't entirely his fault. He hadn't meant to hit me. He was trying to catch his hand back, I think, but the momentum carried it through, and it just happened that my lip caught the edge of a tooth. The blood started welling up, all warm and salty, and I turned away and rushed back into the kitchen for a towel.

Davey was crying, and Gail knocked her milk off

getting down to run away to her room. Lisbeth was still bellowing away, doubling up her fists, putting her whole body into it.

Stan yelled over it all, "I have had it! This does it!" and walked right out. He just got in the car and left.

Beep and I were left facing each other across the big Christmas dinner that nobody wanted to eat.

"I'll help you clean up this mess," she said, looking halfheartedly at the food and the pieces of broken plate in a vomited-looking mass against the baseboard. Fragments of sweet potato and a couple of green beans still clung to the wall, slowly sliding down. She checked her watch. "Oh, gosh! I'll have to make it quick! I've got a plane to catch."

Later on, Mama and Daddy called. But by then I was too worn-out to be surprised or glad at anything. They were in Louisville, Kentucky, they said. When I asked what they were doing there, they said, oh, living in a trailer park, a nice one, and they had some nice neighbors. That wasn't what I had meant, of course—not what they were *doing* there, but what they were doing *there.* Mostly, though, all I could do was cry. I just sat beside the table with the receiver in my left hand and cried. Mama said they missed me too, but she didn't mention coming back. And after she hung up I realized I hadn't gotten their phone number or anything.

11

STAN CAME back after an hour or two, but not for long. He wanted to take the kids to see someone, he said. He changed Davey and washed their faces and got them into their jackets and left again. Seeing them go was, I don't know, sort of familiar in a way. It was as if I'd always known it would be that way, or would have known if I had thought about it.

I was still in the kitchen washing my way through all those dishes, and I think it was right then, seeing them drive off, that it all got to me. Beep gone to catch her plane, Mitchy self-destructing, Mama and Daddy, Sister—it was too much. Everything had gone wrong. But the more I thought about it all, or really the more I thought about Stan and his putting the kids in the car and driving off, the more I felt not just wiped out, but mad. His taking the kids like that, taking them over to some girl's apartment who had probably never had to wash dishes or change diapers or deal with any real, dirty problem, gave me something to focus on. I don't mean that all of a sudden I just bucked up. I was still crying and wiping my nose on my sleeve. But now I was muttering things like "You son of a bitch, you bastard, I'll show you," and it was therapeutic.

One thing was clear—I had to take care of Lisbeth, I couldn't just dump her. What dumping her would mean, anyway, I didn't know. But whatever it would mean, I couldn't. She didn't have anyone but me. Mitchy and Beep, and certainly Mama and Daddy, had made that clear enough. But as soon as it became clear to me that I had to, and was going to, do that, it became clear that the only way I could do it was to be finished with Stan.

It wasn't so much that I had to choose between them. That's what it amounted to, I guess, but that wasn't how it felt. Stan was a whole other matter—a whole separate problem, really. His being the way he was about Lisbeth was only part of it. If he hadn't been that way, or if we hadn't been the way we were together, I would have been able to talk to him about her. I wouldn't have had to play up to him with food and with sex, I wouldn't have had to crawl, in order to break the news that I was going to do what I ought to.

That was what made me sick: thinking how I'd crawled all this time. I stood there Brillo-ing burned-on casserole crust and turkey grease and mashed potato crud till the dishwater was thick with it, and I saw what a cocksucking slavey I'd been, and the one made me want to puke as much as the other. I let the dishwater out and drew up some fresh and went on with it. But I wasn't going to go on crawling for Stan, I promised myself that much right then.

While I was waiting for the sink to fill, I stopped to blow my nose. Lisbeth seemed to take that as a signal that she could come in. I hadn't heard anything out of her for a while. I guess she had been standing there waiting for some sign from me and she decided that was the only one she was going to get. Not that she came in all sweet to make up to me, oh no. With every step, planting her heel and slapping her foot down, she showed me she was still mad and I need not think she was apologizing. Her hair was all clumped and wild, and her face puffy and red. She stomped her way across the kitchen till she encountered my elbow, and then stood there, sullen, not saying a word, but reaching out with her hand rounded around the shape of a glass. I asked if she wanted some water.

"And ice in it," she said.

She drank, thrust the glass back at me, and stomped her way out. It was rich. It was vintage Lisbeth. And I thought, as many times as she's made life miserable, she's also made it funny. As far back as I could remember, she had been doing these funny things, not being funny on purpose, but just countering the world as she found it with her own little quirks. And I thought, if I had to get through life with all she has to get through it with, I'd do a lot worse.

Break with Stan, then; that was decided. It had to be done anyway, and it would clear the deck so I could deal with Lisbeth. The awkward thing was, I couldn't leave, I didn't have anyplace to go. But he, apparently, did. So it would be a matter of telling him to go. Actually, it was good that he did have a place to go, since that meant he wouldn't have to pay rent for a while. Because I couldn't pay our rent on the house if he didn't send money, and he couldn't send it, or he couldn't send enough, if he had to pay for a place of his own. It was funny, how part of the problem became part of the solution.

Even at that, when I started adding things up in my head I didn't see how I could make it. I would have the kids to feed, and Lisbeth, and for that very reason there would be no way I could go out and work so I *could* feed us. I was trapped! Utterly trapped! For a minute it all seemed hopeless. I felt like running away while Stan was gone with the kids. He would come back and I would be gone, and then he would have to deal with the kids—and Lisbeth—himself.

Then she was back. "You're crying some more," she said.

I said I guessed I was.

"I don't like it when you cry."

She waited, I guess for me to say OK then, I wouldn't. But I couldn't say that.

"Mama used to cry," she said, finally. "She used to cry a lot. I didn't like that either."

Then, more than ever, I didn't know what to say. It surprised me that she would tell me that. I wondered if she had thought out a parallel: Mama cried, Mama left; Meg cries, Meg's going to leave. It was almost as if she had heard what I was thinking. And I wondered, if she had thought of that, was she also feeling threatened? It was so hard to know what Lisbeth felt.

I was saved from having to make up an answer that might be wrong and set her off again by the phone ringing.

Stan, I thought, calling to say he was, or wasn't, ready to bring the kids back and why hadn't I reminded him to take diapers. I figured that would be my fault too.

But it wasn't Stan after all. It was Rob Brewster. He gave me a Santa Claus ho-ho-ho and then said, seriously though, how was I? Beep had called and told him things weren't going too great for me. Could he come over?

My first impulse was to cover up, to tell him I was fine and it was none of his business anyway. My second was to wonder what Beep was doing with his phone number. Instead, I only said I wondered why Beep had done that and what he expected to do if he came over. It must have sounded pretty unfriendly. I'm lucky he didn't take that as my final word. He said, "Let's just say I want to check on my paper, okay? So is it all right if I come over?"

What could I say? I told him OK, then blurted out that I wished he would, and hung up.

So Beep had given me a Christmas present, after all, a real one, besides the useless frilly nightgown lying under the tree in its white box and tissue. She had given me what I would never have expected from her, a sign of caring, and I was touched by it. It wasn't so much, I guess; it hadn't cost her anything. But what it amounted to was tossing me a lifeline, and I was grateful for the chance to grab and hold on.

I had barely hung up when Stan came in with the kids, both of them tired and sleepy and whining. When I saw them, I started crying again—partly from relief, I guess, not that I had thought he wasn't going to bring them back, but partly from being so mad at him. It's always been a disadvantage to me to have the kind of anger that wells up in tears instead of words.

He growled, "Christ!" and went on through to the bedroom without another word. I started running water into the tub while I got the kids out of their clothes. Get them to bed early, I thought, and then have it out with Stan.

And I really think I would have. I don't think I would have buckled and decided oh well, what's the use. But I didn't have to find out because Stan beat me to it.

He came to the bathroom door and stood there massively looking in, filling the doorway from side to side, with his jaw thrust out and his eyes shooting fire. His old blue bag was in his hand.

"All right," he said. "Now you listen. I'm leaving this goddamn place and I'm not coming back till you get that . . . moron out of here. If I ever come back at all. So you just make up your mind when it's going to be."

Lisbeth was standing in the hall behind him, and all I could think was, oh no, not again—for her, that is; not oh no, he's going, or oh no, can I stand up to him, what'll I say. I did stand up, and when I did I fair yelled. He had already turned around to go, thinking he had had the last word, no contest, and it absolutely jerked him up short.

I told him I didn't have to think, not for a minute, I already knew, my mind was made up. "You're not telling me anything," I yelled, "I'm telling you. You get out and stay out. Don't you ever set foot in this house again unless it's to get your clothes. I mean it. Get out! Get out!"

I rushed at him and would have, I don't know, clawed, I guess, hit—something. But right then I heard a slip and a clonk in the tub and at the same time the doorbell ringing. The clonk was Davey's head—he had stood up or maybe even tried to climb the side, anyway he'd slipped and hit his head. When I snatched him up I saw that he'd cut his lip too. I sat down on the commode lid, hugging him and patting him, wet as he was, and rubbing the bump that was coming up on his head. Stan went to the door. Later, when I saw another head silhouetted in the car as he drove off, I realized he must have thought he knew who was there. Only it wasn't her, it was Rob.

When I heard Rob's voice, I went out to the family room still holding Davey dripping and crying in my arms. In all the turmoil I had forgotten Rob was coming. All I could think was, how embarrassing for him to see Stan like this.

Of course, Stan put on a big show of righteous indignation. That was quick! Just let him leave for an hour and I had someone lined up to pinch-hit! Or had he already been pinch-hitting, on a regular basis? Oh, he was really nasty about it, started calling us both names, all of them utterly predictable, but no less ugly and hateful for being what you'd expect. But I didn't have time to stay and hear him out anyway, because then I remembered that Gail was still in the tub by herself. I handed Davey over to Rob and ran back to check on her. She had climbed out and was making puddles by squeezing out her washcloth onto the floor and then splashing her feet in the water. Rob followed after me, and when I heard the front door slam, I turned Gail over to him too and went to the darkened kitchen window to watch Stan drive off.

That was when I caught a glimpse of the figure in the car and knew he'd brought his girlfriend with him. After the way he'd acted about Rob coming in, it seemed pretty rich. I actually laughed. But not for long. I was exhausted—physically exhausted and emotionally more so. I went to lie down on the sofa while Rob, by some magic, got the kids to bed.

I lay there and looked at the ceiling and didn't even go check to see whether he had Davey's diaper on right. If he wet the bed till he floated it away, so be it. Then Rob went back out to his car and brought in a bottle of bourbon and a carton of eggnog mix. He turned on the Christmas-tree lights and mixed us up a cup and came to sit on the coffee table so I could tell him all about it. After the second cup, I took a nap.

When I woke up, he was teaching Sister to play rock-scissors-paper and had managed to get her to hold down the laughter so I could sleep. They had both had turkey sandwiches, he said, and he would make me one, if I wanted it, while I helped her get set for bed.

Later, we played gin rummy and had a little more eggnog, and I typed for a couple of hours on his paper. About midnight he went home, on the condition that I call him up if I wanted someone around to talk to. I said I'd finish typing his paper the next day. I had an idea he would have been glad to stay over, but I didn't encourage him. Right then I needed to make things simpler, not more complicated.

12

ഗഗ

FOR A couple of days I felt, emotionally, the way your legs feel when you've gone out and run three miles after sitting in the house all winter—sore. It was a relief just to go through the necessary routine, to make our breakfasts and lunches and dinners, and in between to sit at the kitchen table and look out the window. Even the kids seemed subdued, and the dog slept all day in the sun. When Stan phoned, I hung up.

Then we ran out of milk. No problem—I had $14 and some odd in my purse, and there was a couple of hundred in the checking account. I loaded the kids into the wagon, Lisbeth held my arm, and we walked down to the store. Naturally, while we were there I picked up a few other things we needed—coffee, peanut butter, bananas. By the time we got to the checkout counter it all came to $9.50, and I was down to less than $5. It was right then, putting my change away and seeing what was left, that I knew my short respite was over, and I was going to have to start thinking what to do.

We pulled the groceries home, Lisbeth riding the last half-block and Gail and Davey pulling. This time, no Mitchy waited in front of the house for us. We pulled Lisbeth up the driveway, got her out, and went in for lunch. No bread. Or at least, not enough bread. I had forgotten to buy any. That would mean another 89¢ from the $4.92 left in my wallet. The only solution was to use both heels. Naturally, that set off an argument—first no one wanted heels, then they all did. My patience was wearing thin. Fortunately, the kids went to sleep right after lunch, and I could use their nap time to get back to typing Rob's paper.

During lunch I had calculated it in my head. Thirty-five pages at $1.75 equalled $61.25. Not that the money was the only reason to finish the job; he needed to get it turned in. Then too, I would be glad to have him come in and sit down and talk a while when he came to pick it up. There was no denying it, no reason to deny it. But the money was the main thing. The sum of $61.25 looked pretty big at the moment. Probably, I thought, Rob was already telling his friends about me, and they would come in droves, bringing their papers, their master's theses, their books, even. I saw a long succession of philosophical writings, stretching away one after the other into the distance, all typed by me at $1.75 a page. Our future was assured. I flexed my fingers and got at it.

It seemed as though I had barely gotten started when the kids woke up. But actually I had typed several pages. So

I was happy enough to quit and hold them in my lap in the rocking chair. Breathing heavily, they sucked their thumbs and stared into space. After a little while, Gail slipped down and trotted off to their room. In a minute she was back with *Color Kittens,* an old favorite, for me to read. Lisbeth came and stood against the arm of the chair, listening intently, her eyes moving back and forth as she mouthed the words after me—pink, purple, orange. She must have been wondering, she must have wondered all her life, what secret code those words represented.

I wished Gail had chosen a different book. I always hated it when things like that happened and reminded me how much Lisbeth was missing. I always wanted to make it up to her some way. But how are you going to make up to someone for pink and purple and orange?

Before I knew it, the afternoon was gone, and the paper still not finished. I could have worked on it while the kids played in the back yard and just checked on them after every page or something. But that would have left Lisbeth just sitting again, the same as she had during their nap, and that didn't seem right, so I persuaded her to go outside, if I went too. At first she was going to refuse, but when I asked if she remembered how we used to go outside while Mama washed the dishes or ironed or something, she popped up from the sofa and held out her hand for me to take her.

We found the kids scooping up handfuls of dirt from the flower bed and carrying them to sift over Mutt, where he lay in the sun. Except to twitch his hide now and then, he ignored them. Their hands and the fronts of their clothes were already grimy. My first impulse was to scold them, but instead I merely redirected their attention to the kickball, once brightly speckled with color, now faded from staying day-in day-out in the back yard. Lisbeth and I sat on the swings, our legs folded under us. Whenever the ball whumped against her, as it did more often than you would have expected something like that to happen just by accident, she doubled over laughing. After a while, when that wore out, we walked back to the store for the bread we had forgotten earlier. On the way home, Davey wet his pants. When he climbed out of the wagon in the driveway he walked spraddle-legged but seemed otherwise unconcerned. That's what did it. I swatted him on the bottom and told him Bad boy! Bad boy! He cried the whole time I was changing him, so then I needed to love him out of it, and by then it was time to make dinner, and of course no more typing had been done.

That night, when Stan called, I didn't hang up. I said, "All right, we need to talk."

"Maybe we do, maybe we don't," he answered. Just as I figured, as soon as I seemed to give in the least bit, he got cocky. "I'm coming over to get some stuff."

"Come ahead then," I told him.

I hung up and went back to typing. The kids were playing cars, and Lisbeth was listening to a basketball game on television.

Stan came strutting in after about half an hour. I was supposed to be impressed, I guess, because he was coming from someone's apartment. I was determined not to be. I rolled a piece of paper into my typewriter and kept at it: ". . . the difference between *esse* and *posse* being so basic a concept that one . . ." I was so glad, I kept thinking, to be through with that walking-on-eggs period when we were giving it another try, so glad to be started, at last, on getting things going for myself.

He went through without a word, not even answering when Lisbeth turned her head and asked who was that. I heard him go down the hall to the kids' room, then in a minute go back the other way and bang drawers and closet doors for a while. After a bit he came back through with a bunch of hanger things in one hand and a pair of boots in the other. I thought, my God, boots! What am I doing married to a man who thinks his cowboy boots are a priority item? On the second trip, though, he took out a pillowcase stuffed with what appeared to be the basics—underwear, socks. I reminded him that there might be some work socks on the dryer. He stopped and checked on his way out.

Then he was back and sitting across the table from me, with his chair turned away at an angle, looking prepared not to give an inch. "You wanted to talk?" he asked. "So talk."

At that point, after seeing how he walked and sat and how snarly his face looked, I wasn't sure I wanted to. I wished I could put it off. I was glad when Sister appeared in the doorway, giving me an excuse to stall. I told her to tell Stan good night and took her back to the bedroom to find her pajamas. That gave me the minute I needed. When I came back to the kitchen I was ready to talk money. He had gotten himself a beer, and he sat there drinking it and looking at me in a kind of sarcastic, amused way.

I told him I needed to know how much money I could count on a month.

Probably I should have known what he was going to say, but I didn't, so it came as a shock when he said it. Money? What made me think he was giving me a dime? He had his own expenses now, or had I forgotten that? And it was his money, remember. He made it. He'd do what he pleased with it.

Of course, I knew he couldn't get away with that. No judge was going to let him off without child support. But it hit me anyway. I wanted to grab him, shake him, yell in his face that they were still his kids and he had to support them. But I held myself steady and simply pointed out that if he wasn't willing to work something out I could get a court order and he knew it. Secretly, I wondered how long that would take.

"A hundred and fifty a week," I said, "deposited in the checking account. At least a hundred and fifty. And you won't draw on that account."

He stood up, tossed his empty can more or less in the direction of the trash, and said, "What checking account?"

There wasn't a word I could say to that. I sat there feeling chilled and numb and trying not to show it. All I could think was, thank God the January rent was paid, thank God I'd sent that early, when he got his Christmas bonus.

He started toward the back door, then turned around and went back to the bedroom again. This time when he came by he had the sports coat and records I had bought him for Christmas and a pair of good slacks. I turned my face away as he passed. But he surprised me again.

In a completely different voice, emptied of all the

sarcasm, he said, "I didn't get a chance to tell you, thanks for the Christmas things. They're real nice." He pulled out his wallet and tossed a twenty and a five and a couple of ones onto the table in front of me. "I'll send another hundred or so when I get paid. I'll try to make it a hundred a week."

I didn't move a muscle, not a hair. I just sat there and looked at the money there on the table and waited for him to go.

He let out a deep, sighing breath, like he'd been waiting for something that hadn't come. "Listen," he said, "all you'd have to do is get rid of that half-wit and I'd come back tomorrow." When he finally turned away, I stared him out the door.

That said it all; that really said it all. There wasn't anything left to say after that. "Get rid of that half-wit." How could he say such a thing? How could he even think it? Sure, I knew life would be easier without her here. But how could I just "get rid of" her? Even if I wanted to, even if I was willing to put it to myself in those terms, how could I actually do it? *Where* would I? He should have seen that. He should have understood how hard it was for me. He should have known you don't just "get rid of" someone. He should have known that most of all.

It was impossible; the whole thing was impossible.

When I heard his car start, I was already rolling another sheet of paper into the typewriter. I finished that page and was starting on the next when I remembered the kids: I hadn't put them to bed. I raced back to their room and, sure enough, found Davey curled up on the throw rug, thumb in mouth, sound asleep. Contentedly stepping over him, Gail was going back and forth scattering little cut-out bits of coloring-book pages all over the room. A snowstorm of paper! But it was too late to fuss at her, and too much trouble. I picked Davey up, diapered him, and tucked him in without his so much as opening an eye. Gail continued her paper snowfall, watching me out of one eye, wondering, probably, why I wasn't stopping her. I did stop her, of course, when I finished with Davey, and got her ready for bed too. I pulled her clothes off—what a wonderful little stocky body she had, with that round little bottom and neat cleft in front! I gave her a big bare-skinned hug before pulling her new nightie over her head. When she emerged, she said solemnly, "Daddy gone to bed."

I didn't stop to explore what that meant—that she was denying what she didn't want to know by insisting that he really was there in the next room?—but just gave her the usual good-night kiss and went back to my typing. It was time for me to be doing what I could.

It didn't take much longer; I was nearly to the end. When I finished the last page, I decided to call Rob and tell him it was done. It was much too late, nearly 1:00 A.M., but I told myself that students stayed up late anyway, so it didn't matter. But when he answered I could tell he had been asleep.

"Nothing urgent," I said, "just wanted to tell you your paper's ready and you can pick it up in the morning." How I wished I hadn't called! He yawned and had me say it again. I felt like a fool. What I had to say was obviously not worth calling about at that time of night.

When I started to hang up, though, he said wait a minute, how was I doing?

"All right," I said. "So-so."

"I mean really," he said.

And what was I to say? I'd had a few days' peace and quiet, and that was good. But the way I was feeling now wasn't all right at all. I was scared. I wondered what was going to happen next week or next month, how we were going to make it. I felt tears coming and covered the receiver.

He said at once, "How about if I come on over?"

I still couldn't answer. I just nodded and hung up.

When he got there, ten or fifteen minutes later, I had a pot of coffee ready. I had heard his car and was standing at the counter pouring two cups when he came in the door. He walked right up to me, took the pot out of my hand and set it back on the stove, and put his arms around me in a long hug, a friendly sort of hug. Then we sat down and drank black coffee and talked till after three. He had brought a yellow pad and a pen, and whenever we resolved some little point, anything, he wrote it down. When we were talked out and falling asleep over our empty cups, we went back to the bedroom and lay down, clothes and all, on top of the bedspread.

That was the time, of course, when you'd expect he might want something for his trouble. He hadn't acted like he was thinking that, but I wouldn't have been surprised. It would be only natural. But he didn't make a move. He only tossed his arm over me, patted me a couple of times, and went to sleep.

When the kids woke me up the next morning, I was still on top of the bedspread, Rob was gone, and the afghan from the family-room sofa had been spread over me. I found a note on the kitchen table, on top of the yellow pad with its list of ideas: "Figured I better go turn in my paper before my professor's patience wears out. Here's your check. Thanks."

13

ⲉⲟⲉⲟⲉⲟ

ONE OF the things Rob had said was, I should have gotten to the bank sooner. I went to the bank the next day to check. He was right. Stan had taken out all but $50.

I sat at the drive-through teller machine and heard the girl in the glass box two lanes over ask twice if she could help me and tried to deal with it. Finally I shook my head at the machine, gunned the motor, and got out of there. She couldn't help me at all.

After a couple of blocks I turned off onto a side street and pulled over, to let it sink in. He had grabbed all our money, or nearly all of it. That was money for groceries, for the telephone bill, the electric bill. I tried to think what I was going to do, but it was hard, with the kids bouncing on the back seat and Lisbeth reaching back to grab at them, making them squeal. When I couldn't take it anymore, I turned around and yelled *Be quiet*—which of course accomplished nothing but to make me feel like shit, a familiar feeling, and set Lisbeth off. Davey primped his lip, and Gail put her fingers in her ears.

I did decide one thing, that I'd better go back and get that last $50 before Stan did. It seemed sad to think we'd gotten to that, but I guessed we had. I circled the block and pulled into the drive-through again. But then, while I was sitting there waiting to pull up, I realized that if I was going to have a typing business I was going to need a way to cash personal checks like Rob's, and that meant a bank account. So I drove on past the teller machine a second time and parked in the lot.

I hadn't meant to go in; anything like that was such an ordeal, what with holding Gail's hand, carrying Davey, and leading Lisbeth on one arm. And for sure we weren't dressed for it. To make matters worse, Lisbeth was still stewing because I had yelled at them in the car, and she stamped her right foot every step from the parking lot to the New Accounts desk. People kept staring at us. But I didn't have much choice.

I closed out the joint account—luckily, it was the kind I *could* close out on my own—and opened one in my own name, Margaret Taylor. I also deposited Rob's check, holding out $10 cash. The whole process took over an hour, with the kids having to be corralled and settled down about every two minutes. By the time we got back to the car I felt beat. But at least I had done it; I had taken the first step. When we got back to the house, I actually checked it off on the list Rob and I had made. Clearly, that was how I was going to have to approach my life for a while, as a problem to be approached in separate little steps.

I was so elated by making that first check mark on the sheet that I decided to tackle the impossible. I grabbed Davey and marched him off to the bathroom, and for once, standing on the tops of my feet to reach, he peed in the toilet. Things were looking up indeed.

Step Two in my own mind, though it didn't appear on Rob's list, was to find some way of increasing the clientele for my typing service. But that one was too complicated; it was a whole problem-cluster in itself. So I deferred it till later and went back to the sheet. In big letters, underlined, Rob had entered, GET HELP FROM M & D. What he and I had arrived at, sitting there drinking coffee in the middle of the night, was that if I was going to assume primary responsibility for Lisbeth, Mama and Daddy ought to help. But if that was Rob's idea of Step Two, it was too complicated too. The first problem was that I didn't know how to reach them. I had been so overcome when they called on Christmas Day that all I could do was cry. I had heard "trailer park" and "Louisville," but I hadn't thought to ask any more till it was too late, they had already hung up.

No, what was higher on my own list, and a whole lot easier, was to get in touch with Mitchy. I still hadn't heard a word from him since he had failed to show up for Christmas, and I had been too mad about that to call him. But now it was time. Too much had happened for me not to tell Mitchy, and besides, I needed him.

This time, for a change, I was almost glad when I got

the answering machine. It was easier that way; I could break my news gradually. After the tone, instead of hanging up as I usually did, I said, "This is me. I have Sister here, and I need you to call me. There's a lot going on." I wanted to add, "Where were you, anyway?" But I decided to let that go.

For the next hour or so, it was as if all my problems were being taken care of. Of course, that was pretty silly. Mitchy was not one to come riding to the rescue like the U.S. Cavalry. But at least I had called him; I was starting to get things straightened out. I felt so good I decided we ought to go outside before lunch. Lisbeth, of course, refused to go. It was as if she had taken root on the sofa. But then, on inspiration, I told her we would have a picnic. We would pack our lunch in a bag and eat in the back yard, after Gail and Davey had a little play time. That did it. She popped up, ready to go. So we packed up our peanut butter sandwiches and a jar of milk and paper cups and went on a backyard picnic. It was a nice day for it, bright enough and just warm enough, with sweaters on, one of those springlike days you sometimes get in Texas in January.

I left Lisbeth standing beside one pole of the swing set while I went to put our bag on a high windowsill, so Mutt couldn't get it. Which reminded me that in my rush to the bank that morning I had forgotten to feed him. I popped into the house for just a second to fill the old bent pan that served as a dog dish and came back out just in time to see Lisbeth's right foot slide through a fresh dog mess as she tried to pursue Gail and Davey across the yard. And it was my fault, of course, because for the last week, or more than a week, I had been too mired in my big crisis to think about things like shoveling the backyard.

So that was what I was doing when Rob Brewster came up the driveway, shoveling dog messes. I came, shovel in hand, from around behind the garage, where I was depositing it under the same bush where Gail had deposited her own that day back in December, to find him just walking up to the back gate. "Hi," he said. "I heard all the fun, so I just came around."

"Oh, lots of fun!" I said. I didn't particularly like being caught that way, with a shitty shovel in my hand and my hair stringing down.

But I got over that and made another peanut butter sandwich, and we all sat on the grass in a spot of sunshine—there was still some sun, though it was beginning to cloud over—and had our picnic. I chained Mutt up to keep him out of our food, and he sat at its full length and turned his head from side to side, watching every bite. I guess he had never seen his humans eat in the yard before. Rob kept the kids and Lisbeth giggling so much they could hardly eat by saying all the time what good chicken, what good scrambled eggs, while they roared at him, "No! peana-bura!"

Once, while I was gathering up our things, I caught Rob looking at me with a particular kind of expression, a susceptible expression, you might say. We both looked away, and after that, when we went in, we were brisk and formal. He asked if I had some coffee made—we seemed to be drinking a lot of coffee, I thought. Anyway, I put the percolator on while I went to change Davey and get the two of them down for naps. I put Gail on my bed, partly to

separate them, but partly, too, to keep it from being unoc-
cupied. Not that Rob had ever shown any interest, but when
you've been asleep on the same bed with someone, you have
an idea it may seem like an option.

I turned on the TV to an audience participation show
for Lisbeth to listen to, and we sat down, as we would many
times over the next weeks, to talk about what I was going to
do. Rob wasn't at all surprised about the bank account, of
course; he had only been surprised, earlier, that I hadn't
thought about getting there first. He thought that was
standard procedure, he said. But I was new at this sort of
thing. None of it was standard procedure to me. He said I
was too good for my own good—giving me more credit than
I deserved, but that was fine with me.

Now, he asked, what was I going to do?

Take in typing, of course. At least, that was the only
thing I had thought of. And I was hoping he could give me
some suggestions on how to get business. He said he would
tack up some 3×5 cards around campus if I wanted to make
them up, and he'd take an ad to the campus newspaper. But
he didn't sound very encouraging. He didn't exactly tell me
that there wasn't enough work to go around for the number
of people already trying to do it, and even if there had been,
the work wasn't steady enough to serve as my only income;
and he didn't tell me that most of the people who did that
sort of thing had word processors, not typewriters. He left
those things for me to find out later. But I could tell he had
his doubts.

Shifting the conversation over to my parents, Rob
asked what I might expect from them in the way of help.

After all, if I was going to keep Lisbeth, I was in a sense doing their job; they ought to help with expenses. I couldn't disagree; I just didn't think it would happen, even if I could find them. If they had left without telling anybody where they were going and had scarcely said hello or kiss my foot since, why would they send money? But I didn't know where they were anyway, so it didn't matter. I was going to have to manage on my own.

He bit his lip and looked thoughtful. What was it they had said when they called? Louisville? And a trailer park, just that? "Shame you didn't get a phone number or an address," he remarked.

I pointed out that you'd think you wouldn't have to, with parents. You'd think they would want to keep in touch.

He agreed—you would think.

But of course I knew why they didn't. They had had years of trying to take care of Lisbeth and cope with her and of wondering what they were ever going to do with her. It had just gotten to be too much. I knew that. So why would they want to keep in touch now, when everything was falling apart?

About two o'clock Rob said he had to go. He was working four to ten at a drugstore over across town, and he needed to stop by the library for a while first. He rapped his knuckles twice on the table and got up to go. "Thanks for lunch," he said. "And for the coffee."

He went. The rest of the day was quiet, routine. Nothing else remarkable happened. I didn't go on to Step Two or Three or any other steps. And yet I remember that day so well. It was the last day Sister was even approximately cooperative.

From that day on, it all went downhill. She had been glad to come see us and to sit from one meal to the next with no one making demands on her, not being made to do anything. But she couldn't go on that way forever, with her time so unstructured. I tried to think of things for her to do, of course, but whatever I started her on always ended in frustration and screaming fits—if I could even get her to try. She inhabited the middle of our sofa like gloom solidified, only stirring herself once in a while to stick a foot out and trip one of the kids or pinch or scratch if they came too close. But that was later. It didn't get that bad all at once, just little by little.

Another reason I remember that day is it ended the good nights' sleep I'd been enjoying. I had absolutely reveled in having the bed to myself. I could turn over all I wanted, throw my arms any way I wanted, sleep catty-cornered if I wanted to, there was room. I had enjoyed being left alone, not being bothered if I was tired and wanted to lie flat on my back and let my muscles settle out. I didn't have to be afraid my body was going to be invaded in some way I didn't want.

That night, though, for the first time, I had trouble going to sleep. I lay there for the longest, looking up into the dark against the ceiling or over at the window, and thinking about the bank account business that morning, not knowing where Mama and Daddy were—all the things I would rather not have thought about. Then, when I did go to sleep,

I dreamed about sex. Not about Stan, but about sex, so vividly it woke me up. After that, even if I didn't have the sex dream and even if I dropped right off to sleep, I never again luxuriated in lying there by myself, easy and unbothered, the way I had at first.

All through those early weeks when I didn't know what to do, Rob was my mainstay. And God knows, I needed him! Mitchy didn't call and didn't call. And when I finally did get hold of him he didn't sound right. I had an idea he was drinking a lot. It worried me, but I didn't know what to do about it. Beep didn't do much better. After she'd been back from her ski trip a few days, she called and said she was going to come over and get Sister that next Saturday so I could have a little time out from under her. As it turned out, she didn't do it. Saturday came, and she didn't show up. But at least she had thought about it; that was something.

It was Rob who really helped. He came by practically every day, not at lunchtime any more—I think he figured I couldn't afford to be giving out extra lunches, even extra peanut butter sandwiches—but some time in the afternoon, between classes and work.

When he came that next day, the day after our little backyard picnic, he acted very casual, sort of deliberately casual. I could tell something was up. Thought he'd talk me out of a cup of coffee, he said, before he went to work. Oh, and by the way, he had found a Louisville phone directory in the library and looked up trailer parks and jotted down some names and numbers. Also addresses, just in case I wanted them. He figured I might get a line on my folks if I tried calling up trailer parks and asking to speak to them, not like I was looking for them, but like I already knew they would be there. He had looked up the zip codes too, in case I wound up writing. Oh, and something else, no big deal, but I'd be getting calls from a couple of people he knew who had papers they needed to get typed. Not that he didn't want to stick up notices for me, like he said; he'd do that whenever. But he had just thought he would mention it to a couple of people in the meantime. I ought to be hearing from them soon.

I was as excited as a child getting roller skates. I squealed and ran around to his side of the table and hugged him—I practically knocked the cup out of his hand. But he only passed his hand over his hair a couple of times and took a slow sip of his coffee before saying he hoped I wasn't expecting too much out of this. He doubted a person could make a living by typing papers for college students.

I doubted it too, but I didn't have anything else in the works, so I had to hope for the best. Anyway, I knew he had taken a lot of time on this, on both of these things. It really touched me that he would do that.

While we were talking, Lisbeth had been standing in the doorway clenching and unclenching her hands and looking generally miserable, her eyes red-rimmed. I knew she was slipping into the grip of her old demon, tension or depression or whatever it was, but that, too, I was trying to ignore, because I didn't know what to do about it. But when I squealed and clapped my hands over the prospect of the typing jobs, she shrieked and stamped her foot. It was hard to ignore that.

But Rob went right on talking, just as though he hadn't

noticed a thing. It's a wonder he didn't run out the door! When he finished what he was telling me, about the typing business and how I shouldn't get my hopes up, he turned around and asked her if she would like to go down to the Baskin-Robbins and get an ice cream cone.

She quieted and stood rolling her eyes. I knew she wanted to go, of course; she loved ice cream, or for that matter anything sweet. But I also knew that when she was like this she wasn't going to agree to anything, even if it was something she wanted. She just stood there, tight as a spring, and when he asked her again she said, *"No!"* and stamped back into the family room. I knew, of course, how she'd be for the rest of the day. She'd beat herself over the head for not going, and fret and carry on and generally throw a fit, when even if she was given another chance to go she'd turn it down again, the same as the first time. That was Lisbeth. I had seen it too many times. But it wasn't Rob's fault; he didn't know.

He shrugged and said maybe next time. I couldn't help thinking how different that was from Stan, who wouldn't have been seen taking Lisbeth somewhere on a bet.

On his way out, he asked if there was anything I needed. I told him he had already done too much—which was true, though as he pointed out it didn't answer the question. He shrugged again and passed his hand over his hair. "I don't see how you're going to be able to do this," he said.

I didn't either. But that was one of those things I wasn't

thinking about if I could help it. There seemed to be several things like that.

That evening, after the long-distance rates had gone down, I started on Rob's list of trailer parks in Louisville. Sure enough, his idea worked beautifully. The third number I called, I got a crabby old guy who said he didn't give a hang whether the Taylors were in or not, he wasn't going to walk clear down there to get 'em, and this wasn't a public telephone anyway. I told him he was a doll, and hung up. If he thought I was being sarcastic, he was only half right. He had told me what I needed to know.

So I had found them, easy as that! I felt so good I put off writing the letter and made us some popcorn. Gail caught on right away that it was a celebration of some sort, and she and Davey pranced around the room singing "Party, party." Only, Davey looked puzzled; I believe he thought what they were saying was potty, potty—a word he had never celebrated with before. It all seemed very jolly until Lisbeth, who had been protesting the whole time that no, it couldn't be a party, it wasn't anybody's birthday, abruptly decided she'd had enough, clenched her fists, and screamed. The children cried and ran to me, and the rest of the evening they kept their distance and looked at her distrustfully. They didn't want to go to bed either. In my same old way that always irritated Stan so, I had let them sleep too long at their naps, and they weren't sleepy now. So it was nearly ten o'clock when I got them to bed and sat down with pen and paper.

Even the first words were hard to write. How do you

address a mother and a father who have run out on you, first one and then both? What do you call them? I settled on "Dear Folks"—a bit cozier than I intended, but the best I could do.

It was good talking with them on Christmas Day, I said. I had been so surprised I probably hadn't made much sense. "You'll probably," I wrote, then crossed it out. I was going to say they would probably be surprised I had found them, but that was like accusing them of deliberately hiding out, and besides, it would involve too much explaining. There was going to be enough of that already.

Stan and I were separated, I wrote. Actually, we were separated for the second time now, and I guessed I'd file for divorce soon. I saw my own words on the page almost with surprise; it was right then, I guess, that I first realized that of course that was what I had to do next.

They may not have understood when we talked that Lisbeth wasn't just here for Christmas, but permanently, or anyway indefinitely, since the place where she had been was saying they wouldn't take her back and I didn't know anywhere else for her to go. I really didn't know what to do, I went on, because I needed to get a job but I didn't have anyone to stay with her while I worked. So if I was going to take responsibility for her, I needed help with money.

I had been trying to decide how much to ask for, but since I didn't know what their finances were, or for that matter what my own were going to be, I decided against mentioning any particular amount. Instead, I just pointed out that whatever they sent, it would surely be much less than they would have to pay for her to be in an institution, and after all, it was—I was going to say it was their responsibility, but instead I wrote that that was one thing that might be expected.

I had signed "Love, Meg" and was about to fold it up when I heard a crash. The whole time I had been writing, there had been rising and falling waves of lament from Lisbeth's room. I had blocked them out. Now, when I went to check on the noise, I found her sitting up in bed, wild-eyed. Her pillow lay across the room, in the pieces of a broken lamp. Just a cheap lamp, and I hadn't been using it anyway, but it seemed like the last straw. I yelled at her—something, I don't know what—in response to which she shrieked and raked her face on both sides, from temple to jaw, with her fingernails.

"No ice cream!" she yelled. "I didn't get any ice cream! You didn't let me go!"

I picked up her pillow, brushed it off, and put it back on her bed. "Good night, Lisbeth," I said, as steadily as I could. "He'll take you to get ice cream tomorrow."

"He will?" Miraculously, that did it. She lay quietly down. The scratches on her face were oozing red, but I tried not to see them. Might as well leave something for in the morning.

I went back and, reopening my letter, drew a line through the whole last page and wrote at the bottom, "I don't think I can do this. She's your daughter. Come and get her."

14

czczcz

I HAD not been brought up to take adultery lightly. On my
mother's list of sins, where everything was put down for
exactly what it was worth, guilt-wise, adultery was at the
top. How I knew that is not clear. I'm sure there was never
anything said on the subject. Still, there it was; I knew. And
no matter how much rebelling and rejecting and redefining
you do, upbringing sticks. Which means there was no way I
could go to bed with Rob and not feel guilty about it.

Stan and I were still married, though in only the most
technical way. I didn't *feel* married to him anymore. I felt less
married every day. So why couldn't I enjoy Rob and not feel
guilty about it? I couldn't, that's all.

And there was every reason to enjoy him. He was good
and helpful and sometimes funny. He read and he
thought—he represented that whole world of books and
ideas and dean's lists that I had turned my back on when I

married Stan, and had missed ever since. Besides, he was great looking and sexy, in a wonderfully unthreatening way, tall, with a loose-slung thinness, almost too thin, light haired, brown eyed, straight nosed. He had long fingers that started to point when he was saying what he thought about something and then curled themselves apologetically back into his palms, or tapped against their opposites in front of his chin. He looked up hesitantly from under blond eyebrows, but then wasn't at all evasive, but friendly and open. How much nicer could a man be? So of course I enjoyed him. I enjoyed his company, and I enjoyed coming to count on him to help me out, and now I started enjoying him in bed.

How it came about, when it did, was funny in a way, very much in character and also very much tied up with money and with how we were getting by—with the whole way everything was then.

I had managed to keep us going, but just barely. Stan had been as good as his word, so far, sending us $200 a payday. And there had been help from other quarters. Mitchy had shown up one day late in January, just walked in one afternoon when I was trying out a recipe for cookies made with stale bread crumbs, so you used up old bread you would have thrown away—a moneysaver, in other words—and had sat down and talked for a while and left me $50. Even Beep came by and took us out to eat once, to a cafeteria, where she wouldn't be in danger of running into anyone she knew, and once sent a check for $30 that didn't even bounce. Not that it was her place, or Mitchy's either, to support us, but then, it was their sister too that I was feeding and looking after and dealing with, with all that meant, every day. So I took it. And what with all the bits and pieces together, I was able to pay the February rent. But just barely. We were just barely getting by. One month of it was bad enough; I couldn't go on month after month this way, counting on Stan's better self and Mitchy's and Beep's occasional charity.

I had to make us a living, but without getting a job—a good trick if you can do it.

The two things I had pinned my hopes on, that kept me going, were what Mama and Daddy might do and what I might be able to make typing. They were both jobs, in a way. If the folks settled on a certain amount each month that I could count on, it would be like they had hired me for so much a month to take care of Lisbeth for them. She was their daughter, their responsibility. She couldn't take care of herself, that was for sure. So if they weren't going to take care of her, and if the state wasn't, then they naturally had to pay someone to do it for them—me. As for the typing, it wasn't amounting to much so far, certainly it wasn't making us a living, but it was bringing in enough to keep up my hopes that it might amount to a living one of these days, if I kept at it. Thanks to Rob. Because it was clear that whatever good I was going to do would be due to him. I had sent notices to T.C.U. and S.M.U. too—to all the schools in the area—and if I started getting any calls from those places it wouldn't be because Rob was twisting people's arms. But it was his idea that I try sending the notices, and he was the one who "drove by" and tacked up my 3×5 cards. So if

anything came of it, it would still be, once again, thanks to
Rob.

One of the people he had rounded up at Arlington to
bring me typing was a girl named Patti Nesbitt who was in
one of his seminars. Actually, the name I typed on the title
page of her seminar papers and, later, her M.A. thesis was
Patricia H. Nesbitt. But she went by Patti.

The first thing I thought of when I saw her, when she
came over to leave that first paper to type, was how good-
looking she was and how Rob must have something going
with her, or if he didn't he must be wanting to. It was that,
just that, hearing myself think that about Rob, that first
alerted me to the fact that I was wanting him for myself. I
honestly hadn't realized it till then. But once I did, I really
did. I went around miserable and envious and certain that
he was bound to like her better, of course he did. How could
he not, how could he possibly be attracted to a cow like me?
Cow, because after my second pregnancy and breast feeding, I had stayed heavier than before all over, but especially
in the bust. Having big breasts had pleased me for a while,
since I had never had any to speak of before. But now they
seemed like twin single-nippled udders.

Patti wasn't one of those conspicuously good-looking
girls who attract attention just walking down the street. She
wasn't showy. Beep, whose standards are very high as well as
very narrowly defined, involving up-to-the minute styles
and makeup done just so, would have bumped into her in a
crowd and never seen her. If you didn't look close, she was
rather ordinary. Hair an even mousier brown than mine and

too lean, too narrow hipped and flat chested to have any figure. Her over-large, heavy-lidded eyes, a kind of greenish hazel color, loomed at you from behind thick glasses, and her clothes ran to tight, faded jeans and resale shop men's sweaters, or else to full, full skirts whose uneven hems brushed her anklebones. But she had something special, some magnetism, I don't know what. I thought she was terrific, and not only good-looking but good, one of the world's really good people. I was convinced of that. Even jealousy didn't put me off.

We took to each other right away. I hadn't made a new friend, a new woman friend, in years. I almost think I hadn't *had* a friend in years. And now I had Patti and Rob—though he was threatening to turn into something more than a friend—both. It was great.

The children seemed to stand back and look her over with noncommittal eyes, but Lisbeth latched onto her immediately. And Patti seemed to know instinctively how to talk to Lisbeth, how to deal with her. She seemed to take one look around and understand the whole situation. Maybe Rob had told her a little about us. Probably he had. But I had a feeling, right off, that she was interested, personally interested. Like Rob, she took time to look at me and to care what happened. When she said, "You mean you're letting that son of a bitch get by with four hundred dollars a month for two kids while you scrape and scrimp and do everything?" I knew she wasn't just being a man-hater, but really caring that I wasn't getting a fair shake.

So when Rob mentioned in an offhand way, a couple of weeks after I had typed the first paper for Patti, that she was volunteering to stay with Lisbeth and the kids the next night so he and I could go out—we had never "gone out"; the idea had never even been mentioned before—my only surprise was that he wasn't going out with *her.* That time, it didn't work out. Her parents, who lived in Shreveport, I think it was, developed some problem, medical or financial, I don't remember which, and she had to leave unexpectedly. But Rob came over anyway, with a bottle of wine and two gourmet-type frozen entrées and a salad, and we had a nice dinner, late, after Gail and Davey were in bed, and then watched a TV movie, with only minimal interference from Lisbeth, who joined us on the sofa. And if there wasn't sex that night, it was only because I was having my period; it was obvious that there would be soon. We kissed and fooled around some, and he didn't seem to think my breasts were udderish at all.

Patti called a couple of days later, when I was in the middle of somebody's bibliography, to apologize for having cancelled out. Of course I told her not to worry about it, I had appreciated the idea anyway. But she insisted that we would pick another time as soon as she got caught up from the two days she'd missed. "I've thought how I'd be," she added, "if I were shut up in the house with two kids and an impaired person all day every day, and I'd go crazy. I would, I'd turn into a monster. You need to get out."

She was right, of course; I did need to get out. There were times when I thought I already had turned into a monster. I had talked to Mitchy and Beep about their alternating taking Lisbeth for a day or two every so often, and they had agreed in principle, but something always came up. The most relief I ever got was when Rob took her to get ice cream or to run errands with him, or once when Beep took Lisbeth over to her place for a couple of hours on Saturday and gave her lunch. While Lisbeth was gone that day, even Gail and Davey seemed to relax and to understand that we needed to use our precious free time wisely, every minute of it. We took a walk, we played ball, we made no-bake cookies with peanut butter and dry milk and honey. When Sister got back, a little after 1:30, the two of them got quiet, drew together, and retired to their room.

Except for those odd little intervals, it was all the time, all the time, never any relief. I had thought it would get easier in time, that we would get used to her and fall into a comfortable routine. But it only got worse as the novelty of being with us wore off for her and she became more and more restless and irritable. I saw now that what I had taken for her typical unreasonableness had really been her best behavior.

She took over our lives. Not only did she need help with the simplest everyday activities, so that I was always on call for every little thing, but she overreacted to the least frustration or the least thwarting of what she wanted, even to the least tone of impatience in my voice—and I had never been able to control that, with the kids, with my own work at jobs or at school. I got impatient and burst out and it was over. The kids knew it; they were used to it. But Lisbeth couldn't take it, not at all. She would pull her hair and stamp and scream. Try living with that! My life became a perpetual walking on eggshells.

Typing, especially, was becoming a problem. Lisbeth

didn't want me to type. She was like a little child who doesn't
want you to read the newspaper because it takes your attention, and climbs on your lap to get in between you and the
paper. I made it a point, after every page, to say something
to her or to get up and go check on the kids, anything to
keep from seeming totally preoccupied, but still she hated
it. At first, she said things like, "Are you going to do that
again?" Or, "Gah, don't you get enough of that?" Then she
would come and stand beside me when I typed, touching
my shoulder and making discontented, whining sounds.
Lately, she grabbed at my hands, pulling them away from
the keyboard.

What could I do? It was the only way I had of making
any money, and I could see the time coming when I couldn't
do it, physically couldn't, while she was awake. I tried
staying up late to type after she was in bed. Once I even set
my alarm and got up for a couple of hours in the middle of
the night. But I couldn't get much done that way, and if I
started getting more work, which God knows I needed, it
was going to be impossible. I couldn't type all night and take
care of them all day.

I was into something I couldn't handle, and I was
getting crabbier by the day. Patti was right. I needed time
out. I needed a whole *way* out, but time out would help.

Sure enough, a few days later, Patti called and asked if I
had any plans that night. Plans! As if I ever had plans!
Actually, I was planning to get everyone to bed early and
work on a thirty-page history paper that was due in two
days. But I chose not to count that. She said good, then she
was going to bring over dinner, nothing fancy, and Rob and

I could go out to a movie. It seemed funny that he hadn't called me about it himself. But after all, I'd been out of the dating game for a few years, how did I know how people did it now? Anyway, maybe graduate students had always done things differently. So I said great and tried to thank her, but she brushed it off. "I hope somebody'd do the same for me if I was in your situation," she said. "Anyway, Rob's one of the all-time nice people. You two are good for each other."

So we had our dinner, all beans and sprouts and things the kids had never seen. But they took it philosophically, the way they always seemed to take Patti herself. If Rob and Patti noticed Lisbeth's scooping her food with her fingers and her open-mouthed chewing, or if they were offended by it, they made no sign. Afterward, they cleared away while I changed into my trusty brown slacks and orange sweater, and we did indeed go to a movie.

It was the strangest feeling, to be out with someone who was not Stan. But Rob made it easier than it might have been by walking along, hands in pockets in his loose, easy way, talking about school, about work, about what he hoped to do when he finished his degree. If he had turned chivalrous and opened the car door for me, or if he had wanted to walk with his arm around me, or with even the least touching of arms or hands, I would have felt like a Jezebel. He seemed to understand that. When we sat down in the theater, he patted my knee a couple of times, briskly, as if to say, "Now, it's OK, see?" And that was all, I could relax.

Afterward we stopped at a Denny's for coffee, and he told me a little about his parents and how he practically never saw them, because they had more or less disowned him a few years ago when he was smoking a lot of pot and they found out. They were wrong, he said, to react that way, but he guessed they were right in a way too. Right to be concerned. Anyway, he didn't smoke anymore. But he didn't tell them that, because they had been wrong to react the way they did.

Talking like that made me feel closer to him than I ever had before, even when he was coming by every day and listening to me moan and groan about everything. Then when we were back in front of the house, and he turned off the ignition and said he was hoping to sleep with me that night, I was able to say I was hoping he would too, and not even feel awkward about it. He had brought rubbers, he said, in case I wasn't on the pill, since we hadn't talked about that.

Who would have thought I could look a man in the face and listen to him say, in a perfectly ordinary tone, that he had brought rubbers, and not be embarrassed!

Thinking back on it later, after I found out that he and Patti had lived together some time before, it seemed really strange to me how we said good-bye that night and hugged all around and she went on home with a bless-you kind of smile on her face. If I thought about it in the abstract, without the difference that they made by being themselves, it seemed almost corrupt, almost as if we had been sharing three ways. And maybe there was something of that in it. If I hadn't been so crazy about Patti, I might not have found it so easy to go to bed with Rob and not label it, for even one minute, adultery, the way everything in my upbringing had prepared me to do. But she had said we were good for each other, and I accepted that and believed it.

The more I thought about it, though, the more I thought there wasn't anything strange in it at all. She hugged us both and kissed us good night and left all smiles because she was glad we were going to enjoy each other, that's all. I decided she had a much, much greater capacity for disengagement than I had. It would never have occurred to me to help somebody be good for Stan or to tell another woman what a nice guy he was. But then, I couldn't have said that anyway, because Stan wasn't a nice guy. There was that difference.

We didn't have great sex that night. Good, but not great. It was exciting, naturally, being the first time—the first time to look at each other (there was a good moon out, besides light seeping over from the neighbor's yard lights), the first time to hesitate at the brink before shoving together, the first time to see how the two of us could move together to make it best. But it honestly wasn't great. We fumbled out of our clothes and fell against each other, uncertain what to do first. He came too quickly, and I didn't at all, and then later when we did it again, it was the same story. Besides, I never liked rubbers. I don't like the way they sound when they're unrolling on or the way the little puckered bag droops at the end afterward, and most of all I don't like the idea of them. I want skin against my skin, not rubber or Saran Wrap, whatever it is.

Even so, even if it wasn't great, it was good enough. Mostly it was good just being up against another body again, being close, feeling another person's excitement. I enjoyed looking at him, and I enjoyed touching him, and if we didn't yet know how to do spectacular things together, we would surely learn.

The next morning he left without breakfast, without even coffee, before the kids were up. He didn't want to upset them, he said, by being around at a time they didn't expect him. He wanted to let them get used to him gradually.

I was a little sore between the legs, because of doing it twice, but wonder of wonders, I felt only the least twinge of guilt, just that minimum that was built into me and came up involuntarily. With my mind, consciously, I didn't feel any. And after that I never felt guilty at all, not at all. (Not even when Stan's lawyer mentioned the presence of a male visitor at my house overnight and showed a couple of pictures and implied that I was not so deserving of child support as I might have been otherwise. Though what that had to do with rent and groceries I wasn't sure.)

This was about a week into February, and thanks to Rob's ingenuity I was thinking I might hear back from Mama and Daddy any day and they might help with our support, even if it was only a little. And then it was the tenth of February and I was still waiting, and then the twentieth. But then finally one day, when I heard the lid on the mailbox flap and went to check, there was a letter with Daddy's familiar handwriting that I hadn't seen in so long.

He had written, for some reason, on graph paper. The printed lines crisscrossed through his words like window screening, making them hard to read. But even with lines there to guide him, his writing sloped away down the page, getting smaller and more sloping as it went, as if the impulse to write was dwindling and might not carry him through to the end.

They were glad to hear from me, he wrote. What a nice surprise. Sorry to hear I was having rough times, but those things happen. Yes, they knew what a problem Lisbeth was. There was no good answer. But they couldn't take her just now, that just wasn't the place, not room enough and not the right situation. She wouldn't be happy there. Maybe I could get the Home to take her back. Or maybe another place. The state ought to help. But he and Mama had done it for years, and that was enough. They were out of it now.

I read that over several times: "We did all we could for her and struggled with it all we could, year after year, and we have had it. We are out of it now."

So. They were out of it, and I was into it. She wasn't mine, and yet she was mine. At least, she was mine to the extent that I couldn't walk out on her. So there I was.

I had gone back to putting the laundry in and wondering what I was going to do, with March rent coming up and not enough money in the bank and no divorce decree yet so no child support, when it dawned on me, he hadn't said a word about money. Certainly he would have said something if they hadn't been meaning to send anything. There must be a check in the envelope. I had pulled the letter out and not seen it. He didn't say anything because he didn't need to, the check was self-explanatory.

I pulled the knob to start the washer and went back to look, to see how much they had sent. That was probably how much they would send every month. But there wasn't any check, there was nothing at all in the envelope, nothing had fallen out on the table, nothing on the floor, nothing was going to come, nothing at all. And nothing Rob could think of was going to help this time.

15

FEBRUARY HAD been cold and wet, the whole month, and March started out the same—depressing weather, and I was depressed enough as it was. It wasn't so much that we had northers blowing through, ice storms, that kind of thing; the cold just settled over us and stayed, with once in a while a weak front to reinforce it without clearing out the clouds. It was nice when Rob was sleeping over and I could snuggle up against him and be warm all night, but the rest of the time I felt chilly, constantly, all day and all night. I had really forgotten how drafty that house was. Or maybe I hadn't noticed it the other winter we had lived there.

Besides everything else, Davey kept having trouble with his ears. I guess it was all the cold and damp and wind, or maybe it was just his age or something about the way his inner ears were made and he would have been sick in any weather, I don't know. But no sooner would I think he was over it than he would get up whining and pulling his ear again. His nose ran a thick yellow, and his temperature seemed stuck at 101.

Naturally, I tried to keep from taking him to the doctor. Stan had shorted me by $50 early in the month, and even if he hadn't, I hadn't thought about doctor bills when I named a figure. There was a sign on the reception desk at the doctor's office, PAYMENT DUE WHEN SERVICES ARE RENDERED. I had had to stand at the desk facing that sign once and say I couldn't pay, and I didn't want to do it again.

So when the ears flared up again, I tried to wait and believe he would get better. I put drops, left over from an old prescription, in his ears and I held him on my lap by the hour with a hot-water bottle against his head, while Gail got into everything and Lisbeth refused to do anything. She seemed to be just waiting for something to happen that she could have a temper fit about. But finally, when the earache and the drainage and fever kept on, in spite of anything I knew to do, I gave in and called for an appointment. And that was what turned things around, for more than Davey's ears.

I had known I had to do something, but I couldn't think what. We were all perched over a chasm and about to fall, but I couldn't see which way to jump for safety. I didn't even know if I *could* jump, with three of them clinging to me. So I froze and waited for us to go over, or for our crumbling perch to fall completely away under my feet.

When we had gone in the last time, Dr. Krawitz took one look at Lisbeth and got the whole picture, diagnostically speaking. He didn't say anything, but I could tell that he had taken it all in. He said, with that professional pleasantness doctors have, "And is this your sister you have with you?" I had said it was, that she was living with us now. He had nodded.

This time, when he came in, his black eyes flicked over to Lisbeth and flicked back again without expression. He washed his hands, glanced at the chart, and said, "Hey, big boy, what are we going to do with those ears? Mama, you stand over here and let's have a look."

Off in the corner on the one chair, Lisbeth chortled. "Big boy! Aw!"

Dr. Krawitz kidded with her a little. "Oh, so you don't think he's big, huh?" She giggled. "Looks pretty big to me."

Davey wasn't falling for any of it; he stayed tensed up, ready for a good cry.

They laid him down, and the nurse held his arms flat to the table above his head. Into the first ear went the little chrome tip of the thing with the light, and the doctor gave the usual um-hms that never tell you anything. Then they turned his head to the other side and in went the chrome tip again. And while he was peering into that ear, taking a good long look, he said, "You don't look any too good yourself, you know that?"

Later, after he had drawn fluid out of one ear—a pretty ghastly process, to judge by the way Davey screamed—and after the nurse had given a penicillin shot, he had me come down to his office. I had never been in his private office before. It might have been pretty nice if it hadn't been so piled up with books and medical journals and sample boxes. Dr. Krawitz was rummaging through some of them when I came in and stood by the door. It occurred to me then, for the first time, that I hadn't dressed for this visit. And this was the man I used to go wet between the legs for, just thinking about!

He gave me some sample antibiotics to give Davey for a week and a supply of multivitamins with iron for myself. "I'm not supposed to do this," he admitted. "A pediatrician is supposed to practice on kids, not their mothers." He asked me a couple of questions about Lisbeth and what was going on, then shook his head. "You can't go on like this." He looked at me intently, as if he was trying to see in my face whether I understood him. "You hear? You can't go on like this. You're going to have to get her placed."

It wasn't until later that I thought, easy enough for him to say. At the moment I only felt flustered. Even after all my erotic imaginings, I wasn't prepared for him to speak to me so personally. I dropped into a chair and moaned in a wavery voice, "Oh, Dr. Krawitz, I can't even pay you!"

Realizing I was about to cry, he became very brisk and busy, getting me a Kleenex and assuring me that we weren't going to worry about that. Then he added, as if he thought he'd better clarify that a bit, that he knew I would pay him when I could.

It's funny, but that minute or two in Dr. Krawitz's private office got me going. Not the part about getting Lisbeth placed, I brushed that aside. "Placed" where? What did he know? But the way he told me I couldn't go on the way I was. I kept hearing that, while I was driving us home, while I was heating up soup for lunch, all afternoon. It was the way he had said it, like a simple statement of fact. You can't get around facts; they just *are*.

All this time I had been trying to think what to do, and when I couldn't think of anything, I had just more or less done nothing, I had stayed the way I was. But now I saw that staying the way I was was the one thing I really couldn't do. I was going to have to do something different. It wasn't a matter anymore of deciding whether I could think of anything else to do; it was just a matter of deciding what the something else was going to be.

I let it ride for a day or two. Now that it was clear I was going to make a move, I could afford not to rush things. Besides, the weather was still nasty—blustery and wet and cold. If I hadn't felt as though I absolutely had to get Davey to the doctor, I wouldn't have taken him out in it. We spent two long afternoons just doing nothing in particular, giving Davey his medicine and letting his ears get better. To try to keep everybody cheered up, I made big bowls of popcorn both afternoons, and hot chocolate. We sat over our warm snacks and felt cozy, listening to the utterly cold-sounding wind and gusts of rain. I got some typing done during Lisbeth's favorite TV shows, a $34 job due the end of the week, and Rob and I drank coffee and played a couple of games of backgammon when he dropped by between classes and work. That night we made love to the sound of sleet against the window.

The next day, though, by midmorning, the weather broke. The wind fell off and the sun came out, and I knew it was time.

I got everybody bundled into sweaters and told them

we were going to see Uncle Mitchy. Of course, they were all crazy about Mitchy, so they shouted and jumped. Except Lisbeth had to correct me: "Uncle! You mean brother!" And when the children insisted, "Unca Mitchy! Unca Mitchy!" she tried to grab them and cover their mouths.

I had been to Mitchy's only a couple of times, and I made several wrong turns getting there, but it was easy to be sure of the house once we found it because the garage apartment in back had a big rainbow painted on the side toward the street. It was that kind of neighborhood, mostly run-down but with a slight flavor of the artistic. That was why it appealed to Mitchy, I guess, as well as why he taught most of his piano lessons at the pupils' homes but a few at his place. There are always some, I guess, who go for that sort of thing—a fairly good baby grand in an otherwise bare room with wallpaper coming off the walls in strips, in an area of derelict cars and curbless streets dead-ending at railroad tracks and freeway overpasses.

Sitting in the car in front of the house, hoping Mitchy would show up some time soon (because I hadn't called him first; I hadn't wanted to tip my hand), I figured out, I thought, the appeal it all had for him. It was about as far as he could get from the way we had grown up. That had to be it. And I could understand that. But I also thought it was bad for him, it reinforced his natural tendency toward drifting and disorder. And the point was that the rest of him wasn't happy with that part of himself. So he was always divided and dissatisfied. Or maybe it was only that my own inbred conventionality made me want to think he was dissatisfied. Anyway, sitting there in front of that ratty old unpainted house (the rainbow was the best part, actually) with its sagging porch and an accumulation of shopper papers in the yard, I was convinced it was true. Given my mission, I had to be.

We had been there maybe three-quarters of an hour, and I was thinking of giving up, when Mitchy's car turned the corner. He pulled right up into the yard. To judge by the ruts, that was where he always parked. Then he got out and stood beside the open driver's-side door for a minute with his eyes cast up to the heavens as if this was all the biggest drag.

After a minute he came sort of lounging over to my car window. "So," he said, "Meg's come calling."

I told him I had to talk to him and asked if we could come in.

He shrugged. "Sure, why not? Of course, you may not like it. I haven't taken the trash out in a while."

He turned away and lunged up to the front door and into the house, leaving me to follow with my troop. Sure enough, as soon as I hit the door I could tell that part about the trash wasn't just talk. The smell seemed to be mainly stale beer, but maybe that was only because the cans sitting around the room we were in, on window sills, on the floor, everywhere but on the piano, covered up the more distant sources. Through a door off a short hall I could see piles of dirty clothes.

Mitchy sat down on the piano bench with his back to the keys and regarded us more or less belligerently. But when the kids ran and hurled themselves at him, he seemed glad to take them up onto his lap, one on each leg. And when he said, "Hey, Lisbeth, how're things?" she snorted with pleasure and made her way over to shove onto the bench beside him.

I felt like a cross mother persecuting her defenseless kiddies. But God knows, I was feeling pretty defenseless myself! It wasn't fair.

I started explaining that our situation wasn't working. Financially, emotionally, any way, it just wasn't. I told him that I couldn't pay the rent, that I needed someone to trade off with me on this. "This" meaning, of course, the care of Lisbeth. Also, I added, I was worried about him, about his health—meaning mainly his mental health and his liver, but I left that unsaid. It wouldn't hurt him, I said, to live in a more healthy environment, with regular meals and clean laundry.

So what I had decided—I didn't say I was suggesting it, I very deliberately said "decided"—was that he would move in with us. He could pay half the rent and half the utilities and help with family responsibilities. "Family responsibilities" meaning Lisbeth. I would buy the food and do the cooking. Also, I added on impulse, do his laundry along with ours, at least as long as I didn't have a regular job. It would be good for all of us, and he would save money besides.

"I don't know about that last," he said. "You probably won't believe this, from the looks of it, but I get this place pretty cheap."

"Sure you would," I insisted, with somewhat more assurance than I actually felt. "Even if you wound up paying more rent, you'd still save. You wouldn't be buying meals out all the time. And I'll bet more of your piano pupils would come to the house, so you'd save on gasoline. Not to mention all that time driving."

The part about the piano pupils had just come to me on the spot. I had forgotten all about the piano, which would certainly have to come with him. It was his one valuable possession, and the one thing he cared about. Luckily, the house we were renting had one of those useless dinky living rooms set off to one side of an entry hall. I had been expecting to use it as a fourth bedroom, probably Mitchy's, but the piano could go there and it could be the music room. I didn't know where that left us on bedrooms. But we would just have to figure all that out later. This was the thing to do, and I was determined to get it done.

He looked dubious—not definitely negative, as I had figured he would, just dubious. He shook his head in an amazed sort of way and looked down at the scuffed bare floor under his feet with a little sideways grin. I wondered what he was thinking—of me, of my idea. He seemed way off somewhere, though he continued automatically to deal with the kids bouncing on his lap and Lisbeth's ploys for attention.

"You need to be around people more," I urged, "and have more regular hours. You've got to get out of this depression."

If he heard me, he gave no sign of it.

But when he finally looked up, the mockery had dwindled to only a self-protective hint. When, he asked, was the rent due?

I told him the first. It was nearly three weeks away.

"I don't know if I could pay as much as half this time," he said. "Maybe only a fourth. I'm behind here, plus other things."

"What happens to your money?"

He shrugged. "It goes. Maybe you can do that for me too. Give me an allowance and bank the rest."

"A third, then. A third the first of April, then half after that."

He shrugged again, set the kids on their feet, and stood up, with Lisbeth hanging onto his arm. "Oh, well," he said. "Why not?"

16

~~~~~~

When we were kids, Mitchy was always the privileged character. Beep was the pet, and Mitchy was the privileged character. Or that's how it seemed to me. The first time I ever heard the phrase I thought of him, and I used to taunt him with it: "Privileged character, you think you're such a privileged character." He hated it. So then I always had a way to get at him if I wanted to.

Actually, I don't know that he got any more privileges than you'd expect—the only boy in a family of girls, it was inevitable. But that was enough. Just seeing him pee was enough, by itself. Oh, to stripe the side of the garage like that! But there were other things too. Like his tent and his sleeping bag, bought for weekend Scout trips and used maybe twice. I didn't have things like that; even Beep didn't. Or like his room. Naturally, the only boy, he had a room by himself, while we had to share.

Having him move in with us brought all that back. Even though it had been my own idea, even though he was bailing us out by paying half the rent (or a third), I found myself thinking again, "privileged character." Once again we would be crowded in a house of three bedrooms, and once again he would have his own. Naturally enough; it was only reasonable. I had my own too, of course. So it didn't make sense to resent it. And yet I did. That's how it is—childhood keeps coming back.

I guess it was the work of shifting around to make room for him that did it. Or even, before that, the effort of figuring out how to shift around. I had been thinking of putting the children in separate rooms, but that was out now. Instead, I decided to move them both into the middle bedroom, where Lisbeth had been sleeping, so Mitchy could have the one farthest from mine. That way we'd both have the most privacy. But we had used that middle bedroom as a storeroom the whole time we had lived there, and all that stuff had to be moved out to the garage. There were wedding presents still in their boxes, bowling trophies, high school annuals and old bank statements, maternity clothes, baby things—the typical junk people accumulate. I started going through the boxes and throwing things away, but after half a day I gave that up and just carted it out. Most of it was Stan's anyway.

The only place I could think of to put Lisbeth—because I wasn't going to put her in with me, I was determined not to do that—was in the family room. It was a fairly long and narrow room, so I thought we could improvise a kind of bedroom area at one end. By "we" I don't mean

Mitchy and me. Mitchy took no part in it. It was Rob who helped. He had never once commented on Mitchy's moving in except on practical details; I had no idea what he was thinking about it. But he kept coming by every afternoon and staying over a couple of nights a week, sometimes two or three nights in a row, and just somehow making himself available without seeming to feel that he had to pass a verdict. He was the one who carried the heavier boxes out to the garage from the middle bedroom after I gave up on deciding what to throw away.

When everything else was out of there, we moved the roll-away bed out to one corner of the family room, at the end nearer the hall, with a bookcase as a room divider, leaving just enough space in between for her to get in and out and for me to make up the bed. I was a little worried that she might somehow pull the bookcase over on top of herself, so Rob bracketed it to the floor at one end and to the wall at the other. Later we hung curtains from the ceiling directly above the bookshelf, and then her little corner was almost like a separate room. Even so, she still seemed to be always *there,* always right in the middle of things. We went back and forth past her bed area and there she was, sitting on the bed and rocking back and forth, or undressing, or naked, or putting on clothes I had laid out for her.

She complained about the change, of course. She could never accommodate change. When I told her we were moving her bed, she ground her teeth and bopped the side of her head with her fist. And she never got over having trouble with the bookcase. She was always running into it or groping for her bed on the wrong side. But she liked the idea that Mitchy was going to live with us, and that helped reconcile her to the new arrangement. After a few days she seemed happy enough with that narrow strip of space and would retreat to it at odd moments during the day to sit on the bed with her dog radio, rolling her eyes and droning along with the tunes she picked up as she swept the dial.

At the last minute, I decided to give Mitchy my room, the room that had been Stan's and mine, and take the one that had been the kids' for myself. That meant giving him the best room, of course, because besides being the biggest and having the most closet space it had its own bathroom. But I thought I, or Rob and I, could share a bathroom with the kids and Lisbeth better than Mitchy could.

So Mitchy was still a privileged character. And in fact the bedroom wasn't the only room he would have to himself, because there was also the living room—his studio. I had never had any furniture for that room anyway, so it would be no trouble to put his piano there. With one chair and a peeling old cabinet for music books, it would practically fill the room, wall to wall, that's how dinky a living room it was.

The night before Mitchy was to move in, I had gotten the kids to bed and Lisbeth bathed and was getting started on some typing when Stan just appeared. I hadn't seen him in quite a while; he had missed getting the children the last two weekends he was supposed to. It was funny, he seemed almost like a stranger in the house. "You could knock," I said. "Or call first."

"This is still my place too, remember. For two more weeks."

It was two weeks till our hearing.

I rolled a sheet of paper in, and he went on through toward our bedroom, or what had been our bedroom. I knew he'd be right back. There was nothing in there except a few clothes—his—on one rod in the closet. I typed the title.

Then he was standing over me again, demanding to know what was going on. Demanding, demanding, he was always demanding things. I wanted to tell him it was none of his business, but I just said that Mitchy was moving in, so we had to switch around.

"Mitchy!" he snorted. "What's he moving in for? So you can bring him a pan to barf in whenever he has a hangover?"

I should have taken note of that—he seemed to know more on that subject than I did—but I was too set on scoring my own points. "I had to find *some* way to pay the rent since you don't send enough to keep a roof over our heads."

"Yeah, there it comes, the old money routine. God, am I tired of listening to that!"

And to do him justice, I'm sure he was. But I couldn't stop to consider that then. I was too busy being righteously indignant.

"They are your responsibility, you know. How do you expect me to support two kids on four hundred dollars a month?"

"Did you ever think of getting a job? People do that, you know. They go to work in the morning and they get paid. Or do you still think you can make big money typing papers for school kids? Christ!"

"How can I get a job, with . . ." I heard my own voice going on with all the reasons it was different for me, why I couldn't do that, all my hardships—it was like a scratchy record. And I thought, do I really sound like that now? How did I get to be like this?

Lisbeth came out of the bathroom in her pajamas, her head cocked toward that voice she hadn't been hearing in a while. She made her way past the bookcase and around the coffee table, and clutched Stan's arm.

He shook her off and snapped, "Can't you learn not to grab people?"

She clenched her fists and let out a shriek, then stamped and shrieked her way back across the room, bumped against the bookcase, and groped her way around it to her bed. There was a rummaging sound, and sheets started flying out into the room.

Roused out of their sleep, Gail and Davey appeared in the doorway, rolling their eyes from Lisbeth to Stan. They seemed to find one as startling as the other.

I brayed at him, "Now see what you've done!" He turned away with a gesture of disgust and went back toward the other part of the house. From the hall he yelled back, "Fuck it!"

For a while I was too taken up with getting the kids back to bed to wonder what he was doing. Lisbeth was sitting bunched on the side of her bed, sporadically hitting the mattress with her fists. She refused to move when I suggested she let me put her sheets back on. Feeling weak and trembly all over, I went back to my typing table and tried to start the first sentence.

In a minute Stan came back through carrying folded sheets and some towels and a pillow. It occurred to me that he might have taken other things while I wasn't noticing. When I heard him rummaging around in the kitchen cabinets, I went out and told him to leave those things alone. He glared at me and pulled out a skillet. I went back to the family room.

I had already thought it was funny for him to be still in dirty work clothes. Usually he changed as soon as he got home. And now, with this sudden interest in household things—did that mean his girlfriend had kicked him out? I wouldn't ask; I typed.

When he had taken out some last clothes and shoes, he stopped to ask where something was, an old sweater or something. I said how should I know, maybe in one of those boxes that used to be in the middle bedroom. Probably, I added, he ought to go through all those boxes some time in the next week or two; they were out in the garage.

Something about that hit him. He pulled one of those sudden about-faces that had always kept me so off balance. So I couldn't even wait another two weeks to get rid of him! All his old stuff—I had to get every reminder of him out of sight! He dropped down beside me and started begging me not to do it, not to go through with this thing. It wasn't too late, he said, we could still call it off and get back together. He kept rooting around on my breasts and the side of my face, and then I realized he was actually crying.

I was so caught off guard that I couldn't think what to do. I felt sorry, I didn't like seeing him unhappy, but my whole body went stiff, shrinking away from him. It was over, that was all. But there was nowhere to shrink to; he was all over me. I tried to tell him to let me go, there was no use in this, but he kept going on about how I was killing him, I had to give him another chance, we could make it this time. Until finally I managed to make him hear me: "No!" I practically yelled it—"No! Stop this!"

It was as if he thought and chose not to hear me at all. He heard, but he refused to react; or he did react, but in a very indirect way. His crying and pleading went on, but in a different way, aggressively. Now he was not so much begging me as forcing me to hear him beg, taking me over and making me listen to him. Then he was pulling me to my feet and across the room, still going on about how he was so miserable he was going crazy, he didn't have anything to live for, maybe he wouldn't even try, maybe he would kill himself, I had to help him through this, I had to give him something to show I still cared about him.

What can you say when someone starts talking about killing himself? Even if you don't believe it, you can't just shrug. He hadn't been like this the first time—maybe because it had been his idea that time, and now it was mine. I tried to tell him yes and no at once, to soothe him and resist him both. And in the middle of it, as he shoved me first one way in the hall and then the other way, I realized what he was getting at.

"Oh, no!" I said. "No way!" But he had tight hold of me, his grip was beginning to hurt my arms, and he was twisting them, not very hard, just enough.

He kept saying, "One last time, come on, Meg, just once for old times' sake." I was telling him no, no, I wouldn't, but he kept begging and insisting, both at once, and giving little twists to my arms to move me along. And then he was forcing me back on the bed and I thought, what was the use of fighting, when we had done it so many times before anyway?

He couldn't get hard. He kept fumbling and shoving, trying to get it in, and by then I had started crying. He didn't even seem to notice, just kept saying it was going to be all right in a minute and it was just this once more for old times. He kept trying to put my hand on it, but I wouldn't, so finally he just forced it in like it was. I was so dry it hurt, but I didn't want to get wet. That would mean I was participating, and I didn't want to. I didn't want any of this to be happening. But when he did get hard, suddenly I was lubricating after all, in spite of myself—as if that part of my body had gotten out of control and was going through the old motions all by itself. But I kept still, absolutely still. I could do that. He went on and on; I thought he would never come. And I just lay there under him and cried the whole time.

As soon as he finished I shoved him off and started getting my clothes back on right. I was so mad I was shaking—mad at him, mostly, but also mad at myself, for having let it happen. I could tell myself I had been afraid of him, and it was true, but I should have found a way to stop him. "Get out of here," I told him, "and don't ever come back unless you phone and ask first. Don't you ever barge in on me like this again."

He was still weak and dull from sex and just lay there looking at me with his khakis down around his shins and his penis lying spent and wrinkled on his leg, with a thread of semen trailing from it. Two little globs shone whitely in his pubic hair. I noted the grime around the nail of his right middle finger and felt sick thinking of it shoving up inside me.

"Oh, baby," he begged, "don't be like that. You know how much you and the kids mean to me."

He waited for a response, which I didn't give. "Well," he said, "I'm damn sure not going to beg you," and started pulling up his pants.

I stood in the doorway, trying to hurry him, then followed him down the hall, driving him out. So he was the first to see Rob, just coming in from the back door.

Rob had been there the night before, and I hadn't really expected him back. I guess if I had I would have been even more tensed up, wanting Stan out of there before he came. I don't know why, but it had seemed terribly important to me to keep them apart, as if that would keep things from being even more tangled up than they already were.

Stan stopped, with a little "hah," and then said nastily, "Well, so look who's here, if it isn't the stud."

Rob told him, "Back off." I knew how much he must be hating this and wishing he could back off himself, just back off and leave. But he didn't, and I loved him for it, for the way he stayed for me but without belligerence.

Stan turned back to me with an ugly sort of almost grin. "So he's quite a stud, huh? Doesn't look like it, but I guess he must be, that's what you'd be after all right, a real stud."

"Oh, Stan," I said. "Just go."

Rob seemed to notice, then, for the first time, Lisbeth's bed things wadded and trailing on the floor. He picked up one sheet, then the other one, then the pillowcase and pillow, and went around Stan to the end of her bed, where she sat, rigid, her pajama buttons torn off, twisting and re-twisting her face.

"What's happened here, Bethy?" he asked her. I had never heard him call her that before, and wondered if it had been his pet name for her for some time or if he just used it then for the first time. I doubt she had ever had a pet name before. "Here, let me get these back on for you, so you can get a little shut-eye."

"Shut-eye!" she scoffed, as if it was a great joke, and stood up.

Before I went to bed, I wiped and wiped myself with toilet paper, even shoving it up inside to wipe there, to get every bit. If I had had a douche, I would have used it. It seemed to me that it would be disgusting for Rob to paddle in what Stan had left. It would be the messiest tangle yet. So I had to get rid of it, every slimy trace, because I knew if Rob wanted to have sex I wouldn't resist. That would mean explaining, and I didn't want to explain. So I wiped till I was so dry the paper rasped on me, and I went to bed feeling as raw as an open sore.

But he didn't start anything. Maybe he had seen the rumpled bedspread and guessed something of what had happened. We lay close and talked about the next day and about Mitchy's moving in and how things would be. After a while, when I thought he had gone to sleep, I started to turn away to my side of the bed. But then, in a voice that sounded completely awake, he asked me, "Meg, why do you let things like this happen?"

As if I had an answer for that.

17

の/の/の/の

THE NEXT day Mitchy moved in. Patti came over to help
carry stuff, and with four of us working it didn't take long.
Then while we all stood in the front yard waiting for the
movers to bring the piano and his bed and dresser, he filled
me in on his lesson schedule, how late he needed to sleep in
the mornings, when he would need coffee ready, when he
needed dinner. It was like he was lining up a catering
service. I saw Rob and Patti look at each other, and I knew
what they had to be thinking, that he was a real jerk. I
wanted to tell them, but you don't know him like I do. He
just didn't know what to do, that was all. He was tense about
the move, tense about his whole life probably, and he didn't
know what to make of Rob or Patti either, so he was taking
refuge in assholeness. That was Mitchy all over.

    They left pretty soon, and the rest of his stuff came,
and Lisbeth knocked Davey into the edge of the door and

raised a knot on his forehead and bellowed longer and louder than he did about it, and there we were, settled in together.

We got along pretty well, for a while. Mitchy complained all the time, but I felt like underneath he was glad to be in a real home again, with regular meals and people to talk to who didn't expect him to be interesting just because he was a musician. And for a while there he was sober.

After a couple of weeks we put some folding doors across the opening to the living room, partly to contain the sound but mainly to keep Lisbeth out. Before that, unless I devised a trip to the store or some other way to get her away from the house, she went in and stood at the end of the keyboard all through every lesson. Nothing could induce her to leave. There she would stand, and Mitchy's pupils, unnerved by the sight of her and by her loud reactions to their playing, would falter through their lessons. Two quit. So we put up the folding doors, with a hook on the inside so they could lock her out, and after that she stood in the entry hall through every lesson, her ear pressed against the crack. The pupils would open the door and run smack into her when they started to leave, every time.

One side benefit of Lisbeth's interest in Mitchy's lessons, though, was that she became more tolerant of my typing. There was another sound-producing activity she was interested in now. So I was able to go back to working a little during the day.

It was a relief, having Mitchy there. He helped a lot— for a while, at least a couple of months. He spelled me with Lisbeth from time to time so I could get out a little, for lunch with Patti, to wander around and window-shop, any-thing. I actually got to go see my lawyer for the last session before we went to court without dragging the kids along, so I could concentrate on what he was telling me. What a difference! But it was more than that. It was really great, he was good company, it was like being a family again.

The weather warmed up for a few days and we went to the zoo, all of us, a big family outing. It was like going back and being kids again. There had always been something special between the two of us. We could look at each other and laugh when nobody else saw anything funny. We no-ticed the same things. Now, the day we went to the zoo, it was like that again. People we saw standing in front of cages, a favorite flavor listed on the weathering sign of the closed Sno-Cone stand, anything could set us off. The slightest tilt of a head in the direction of something one of us had noticed, and the other would know what association it was bringing back. We were just that way. After years of having gone wrong, not of becoming strangers to each other ex-actly but almost, it was good recovering that closeness.

And I don't mean the kids and Lisbeth were left out. It was a good time for them too. I mean that whole time, those first few weeks after Mitchy moved in. The kids had always been crazy about Unca Mitchy, of course, and now he was there all the time for them to tackle and climb on. But besides the fun he provided—and there was a lot of that there at first; he seemed to get a kick out of it himself—I think they felt reassured by having another adult in resi-dence. They liked Rob-Rob, and he was good with them, better than Mitchy, really. But they knew the difference between a visitor and a regular member of the household. Mitchy was around every day. He shaved in the afternoons and pulled them in their wagon. He devised games they could play with Lisbeth. He talked to her about things she heard on the radio, on TV, game shows, hit songs, anything. And he was a buffer—between them and Lisbeth, or if I was having a bad day between them and me, or between Lisbeth and me. Kids need a buffer.

That day we went to the zoo was a high point for all of us. We walked through the front gate and conferred about which direction to go first as if we didn't have another worry in the world. I kept wanting to keep a firm hold on the kids' hands—I was always one to be afraid they were going to wander off and get lost—but Mitchy persuaded me to let them go and he'd be sure they didn't get away. They seemed not to know what to make of all that freedom. They looked thoughtfully from our faces to each other and walked along timidly beside us, looking at tropical birds, leopards, whatever. But after a while they got bolder, dashing ahead and stopping and running back shrieking. Fortunately, there weren't many other visitors in the zoo that day. A weekday afternoon in March, unseasonably warm but with skies starting to cloud over and a stiff breeze turning cooler, it wasn't prime time. So they weren't bothering anyone. And sure enough, if they got too far ahead Mitchy would shift Lisbeth's hand from his arm to mine and dash after them, with lots of laughs and horseplay every time.

We got so carried away that we even paid and went into the children's zoo, where the kids could pet small animals. In the goat pen the goats came crowding around and butting into us the way they always do, and Davey got knocked over in the dirt, but he didn't cry. He was so carried away with petting those unfamiliar gentle beasts his own size or bigger that he only primped his lip and got back up.

Lisbeth was scared and eager both; she managed to reach out and back off at the same time. "What's the matter," Mitchy kidded her, "those ferocious wild goats getting you?" But it didn't bother her. She knew he was kidding, and for once she could take it.

In a small fenced area there was a baby elephant that we all got a special kick out of looking at—or all but Lisbeth. I kept wishing the little fellow would come over to the fence so she could touch him, but he never did, and there was no keeper around. And it was while I was wishing for that to happen that I remembered being here once before, a long time ago, with Sister and Mitchy. That baby elephant might have been just waiting for us to come back, all those years, without growing an inch. I asked Mitchy if he remembered, but he didn't. For once I had him.

Mama had taken us all to the zoo for somebody's birthday treat and had bought tickets to the children's zoo and the goats had been pushy, just the same. And there had been a baby elephant, probably in this same pen, but lying down asleep on its side on a kind of grassy slope. That time, there had been a keeper in the pen with it, just sitting on the grass beside the sleeping elephant and chatting with the people at the fence. So when Mama saw how everyone else was oohing and ahing over the cute little elephant, and saw the keeper there, she spoke right up and told him that here was a little girl who couldn't see the elephant and could he bring it over to the fence so she could touch it. And he did. He slapped the little fellow on his flank a couple of times and got him roused and onto his feet, just like waking a baby from a nap, and led him over to where we were. And Lisbeth got to put her hands on his bristly hide and feel his ears and trunk. Actually, I don't think she was as excited as we were; we thought it was the most wonderful thing for her to get to do. We always liked to think we were doing special things for her.

I think that was the day someone standing close to us said something rude about Lisbeth's appearance, how she ought to be put in with the baboons or something like that. We weren't sure if she heard it or not. She gave no sign. But it ruined the day for the rest of us. Mama marched us right out to the car and took us home.

Naturally, after I told about it, not about the rude remark but about the keeper and the elephant, Mitchy remembered. But Lisbeth wouldn't believe it. No, no, she said; she had never touched an elephant. An elephant is too big; you can't touch an elephant, it would eat you. Gail and Davey shrieked, a bit uncertainly, "Elefa eat you, elefa eat you."

"Well, I'll tell you," Mitchy said, "I want everyone to get to see this baby elephant. This is one fine baby elephant." And before I knew it his foot was on the fence and he was going over.

He didn't have the least trouble with the elephant. It just peaceably came along with him right up to the fence. Gail and Davey were dancing all around with excitement. When I put Lisbeth's hands on the elephant's side, her mouth gaped wide and she absolutely cackled. "Oh gah," she said. "Those hairs." I guided her hand along the trunk and showed her the funny triangular lower lip. She was having a great time. When the end of the trunk went snuffling up her arm she jumped a foot.

Unfortunately, that's when a guard saw Mitchy in the pen and came running, and we were kicked out with a stern lecture about setting an irresponsible example for kids. But Lisbeth had had her elephant. We all felt good. It was a wonderful day.

Things didn't immediately go downhill after that day. We got along pretty well for a while. But there were problems, and the situation started coming apart.

For one thing, there was Rob. He pretty much made himself scarce for a while after Mitchy moved in, giving us a chance to settle in, I guess. And that was nice. But I hadn't by any means thought of this as a trade, Rob for Mitchy. So I was glad when he started coming around again, though I knew that if Mitchy hadn't realized before that we were sleeping together—and I didn't think he had—he was bound to figure it out before long. Even if they did keep very different hours. And sure enough, when he did, he didn't like it. A couple of times I had a feeling he was listening at our door. Maybe not; I wasn't sure. But I felt like it, and froze up. Then one night Rob got up to go to the bathroom and ran into Mitchy in the hall just as he was coming in from playing, in his rumpled tuxedo, and words were said on both sides. I never knew what; I didn't want to know. I kept thinking if I hadn't given up the room with the private bath this wouldn't have happened. If we had been sleeping back there and Rob had needed to go, he wouldn't have had to go down the hall.

The next morning, while Rob and I were having our toast and coffee along with the kids' breakfast, Mitchy came in, all grungy, shoeless, shirtless, in cutoffs so short the pockets showed underneath. Of course, he never got up at such an early hour; this was strictly a planned gesture, appearance and all. He stalked in, poured himself the last of the coffee, looked at us a minute, and said, "Well. Guess I moved into a bigger household than I thought."

Rob got up and left without a word.

I thought about our zoo day. How someone who could be so sweet could be so horsey was beyond me. I tried to talk to him, but he insisted there was nothing to discuss. Obviously, I was a grown woman, I could sleep with whomever I wanted to. I could sleep with every man who drove down the street if I wanted to, for all he had to say about it. Of course, he assumed I wouldn't try to run *his* private life either. If he was paying equal rent here, he assumed he had equal privileges. It was only fair, after all. "What's sauce for the goose is sauce for the gander, right? Isn't that what Mama always used to say? So you have your company, and I'll have mine." And from then on, he did. As he said, it was only fair.

As it turned out, though, his sleepovers were other men. I hadn't expected that.

I should have expected it. I should have known. That day we went over to his place, the day we talked about him moving in with us, there was a guy there, a good-looking guy in an open tuxedo shirt, barefooted, needing a shave, who came strolling in from the back of the house and asked Mitchy if he had any money for cigarettes. So I should have known then. But some things you don't want to understand.

I knew I shouldn't let it bother me, but it was something I just wasn't used to. I tried talking to Patti about it, but she only shrugged and told me I wasn't taking a very enlightened attitude about this. Which was true but didn't help much.

There were other problems too. Money. Mitchy kept saying he was going to pay half the utilities, which was our agreement, but somehow he could never come up with the money. I kept thinking I would get more work, but the work didn't come. We were barely getting by. I kept thinking, what *would* I have done if Mitchy hadn't moved in?

And there was Sister, of course. Always Sister. There had been a brief honeymoon period at first. With both of us there, she could get more attention, and attention was what she thrived on. But it didn't last long. We ran out of family reminiscences to talk to her about. We ran out of patience. She was just always so insistently *there*. Wedging herself between us when we tried to go over bills. Interrupting conversations, any conversation. Any time we tried to get away from her for a minute to talk, there she was, pushing in and drowning us out, talking about anything, nothing, eyes wobbling back and forth. Or stamping her foot and screeching if we tried to go on talking around her. It got old. We would look at each other and shake our heads. But what can you do when you're dealing with a one-hundred-and-forty-pound two-year-old? Oh, I can see now that we were shutting her out, that's why she had to be always pushing in. I didn't think so at the time, but we must have been. And who knows how excluded she felt? Who could ever know how Lisbeth felt? But we were doing the best we could. It was just never good enough, that was all. It was never adequate to the need.

Part of it was, she didn't have anything to do. She ate and slept and went to the bathroom and sat. And listened to the TV. She always wanted the TV on, and I didn't know anything to do but turn it on, but sometimes I doubted she was really listening. It was just racket, background noise for her sitting. Or when Mitchy was teaching she stood by the door. That was the big break in her routine! We tried to think of things for her to do, of course. At the Home, I thought, they must have kept her occupied with something. Here there was nothing. She was bound to be bored. No wonder she was getting worse.

Even Patti tried. It wasn't her responsibility, but she tried. She checked out educational toys from the Psychology Department at the university and brought them over for us to try. For the most part, though, Lisbeth couldn't get the point, or her hands didn't work right. Designed for five-year-olds, they were too hard for her. Or she wasn't interested.

Something useful, I thought. She's an adult; naturally she doesn't want toys, she wants real work. I tried bread-making, figuring she could knead the dough—she pulled back at the first touch. I tried knitting. For hours and hours I sat, straining, putting her hands through every motion, every stitch, while she got more and more fretful and the kids got into a dog mess in the back yard and used it for war paint. I did teach her to fold socks. That was our one success. But you can't take up a whole day with sock-folding.

"You've got to find something," Mitchy would say. "A day camp, something."

"Oh, yes, *I've* got to, *I'd* better do that."

He got the point, and apologized. We didn't either of us have any ideas.

So everything was already going downhill. And then there was the party.

After the divorce became final, I wanted to give a party to celebrate. Not exactly to celebrate the end of my marriage. I was sorry about it—relieved and resentful, but sorry too. I felt sad that it hadn't worked out. What I really felt like celebrating was the end of the process itself, all that prolonged nastiness. That, and being free now to get on with it—whatever "it" turned out to be.

So I gave a party. Several of Rob's and Patti's friends from school came, people I had done typing for. And some neighbors. Some of them brought bottles of wine and offered their congratulations, so I felt like the real star of the occasion in the old beaded sweater and long skirt that I had dug out to wear. Beep came by herself, late, and some of Mitchy's musician friends. All in all, it was a good, lively, varied group. I had been worried about the refreshments, because naturally I couldn't afford to spend much, but with what people brought we had plenty—dips and cheeses and crackers, and lots of wine and beer. A couple of people asked for Perrier, and I was embarrassed not to have thought to get any—that was a new social wrinkle, as far as I was concerned—but otherwise it seemed like a great success, as far as food and drink.

In other respects, though, it was pretty much a disaster. Lisbeth was determined to plant herself squarely in the middle of things and latch on to everyone who came along, whether they wanted to be latched on to or not. Most did not. Her face was startling enough. It sounds cruel to say, but it's true. When this grossly malformed-looking person came up and grabbed them, they didn't know how to react. And when I tried to get her to leave people alone, to talk to them if she wanted to but not grab them, she gave one of her usual performances, stamping her foot and gritting her teeth in fine style. Rob, bless him, was able to smooth things over, but the damage was done, people were uncomfortable, and I saw my party going down the drain.

It was a complicated evening. Rob was standing back, trying, I could tell, not to act proprietary, but helping me with Lisbeth made that a tricky balancing act. Beep turned on the charm and made such a play for Rob you'd have thought she had no idea we had anything going. My own sister! It was so obvious that I heard a couple of people making jokes about it. I was really steamed. And in the living room Mitchy was having a busman's holiday playing bar-style piano—which is great for a party, of course, but I found it unsettling to see him sharing the bench with a fellow, the two of them brushing against each other and giggling like a couple of flirts. He was drinking a lot too, getting quietly, or actually not too quietly, drunk.

About twelve o'clock, when most people had already left and things were winding down, when I had come out of my shoes, when Lisbeth was finally asleep in my room, everything very mellow, Mitchy took offense at someone's setting a glass on his piano and came roaring up, calling him names, staggering around. It was an ugly scene. He was ready to fight. Rob had to get between them, not because the other guy wanted to fight too—he was as amazed as everyone else—but purely because of the way Mitchy was going at him. Naturally that did it. Everyone left, and the party wound up seeming like a bad idea.

After that, everything seemed like a bad idea. Nothing was working. The grand experiment of having Mitchy move in with us hadn't fixed things up after all. His own disorder, which I had thought to straighten out by bringing him in to help out with mine, was instead getting worse. Our money situation was getting worse. Lisbeth was getting worse. Dr. Krawitz had been trying out first one and then another medication to control her behavior. And sometimes, for a week or two, she would really seem better. But then some little something would happen, she would knock over the salt shaker or step on Gail's foot, and off she would go into screaming fits that might last two hours—two hours of screaming and stamping her foot and hitting herself. Was it any wonder that the kids were getting big-eyed and quiet? Or that Davey was regressing in his toilet training? I knew how they felt. I could remember feeling the same way myself. Only it must have been worse for them, because she was grown now, big. Looming over them, she must have seemed like a monster.

So I was worried about her effect on them, but also, besides that worry, my own tolerance of her was simply wearing out. Mitchy's willingness to spell me with her had ended pretty quickly, and Rob was working so hard on his thesis, trying to finish up, that for him to give up an afternoon was a real act of heroism. He still did it once in a while, and once in a while Patti took her—I was their social experiment, in a way—but they couldn't do it often, and I couldn't expect them to. So all in all that meant I had very little relief from her, very little breathing space. I felt cornered, trapped—more utterly trapped even than I had felt with Stan.

18

c✄c✄c✄

AND THEN, Davey's tonsils became inflamed.

Partly, of course, Davey's ear problems and throat problems were also a money problem. Try as I did to get by without running the kids to the doctor every other day, as Stan had always said I did, I couldn't just ignore it when he was running a fever and whimpering. And so, of course, Dr. Krawitz's bill went up faster than I could pay it. We hadn't allowed enough for doctor bills when setting child support. Once Mama and Daddy sent a check, and with that I almost got caught up at the doctor's office. But mostly I had to let it go. I got used to looking the receptionist in the eye and saying I would send a check next week.

Dr. Krawitz must have known it, but he never pressed me to pay. Half the time he didn't mark down the full charge for our visits on the form he gave me to leave at the desk on my way out. He would enter the office visit but not the shot he had given or the lab work he had ordered, things like that. And he would always check on Lisbeth while we were there without charging extra. He seemed really interested in helping her, really hopeful that he could wave a chemical magic wand and set her straight—as straight as it was possible for Lisbeth to be. Once, when she was having an especially bad couple of days, he even came by the house to check on her. I don't know what I would have done without Dr. Krawitz during that time.

About a week after my party, Davey got sick again and Dr. Krawitz said this was it, we had to get his tonsils out.

It's funny, in a way—the day he told me, he finally made that pass I'd had fantasies about for so long, and when he did I didn't even recognize it. After checking Davey's throat, he asked the nurse to stay in the examining room with the kids for a minute so he could explain what was involved and set things up. We went down the hall to his office, and as he closed the door behind me, his hand dropped and sort of slid down my rear, but like an accident. I didn't think anything about it. He went over and started fumbling through some kind of reference book he had pulled off the shelf. Of course, I thought he wanted to show me something about tonsils. I walked up behind him to look, and when I did he turned, with one arm sort of held out—starting to explain something, I thought—but instead we wound up more or less in a clench. Only I still didn't get it. I was still thinking he wanted to explain tonsillectomies. So I jumped back and started apologizing for having crowded him like that, so clumsy, I was so sorry, etc. He colored and said, "Don't think of it."

It was only later that I realized what had been happening. So that was why he had come by the house to check on Lisbeth that time! But at this point it didn't really matter. I had other things to think about.

Fortunately, the kids were still carried on Stan's hospitalization. That had been part of our settlement. But there was a deductible to pay, and as things stood I didn't know how I was going to pay it, or even half of it—assuming I could get Stan to go halves. I tried talking to Mitchy about it, but those days it was hard to catch him sober enough to make sense. I couldn't face asking Rob. Even if I could have, he was a student, he didn't have that kind of money.

So I had no choice but to try Stan. After all, it was his child, and you don't plan on things like tonsillectomies when you make a support agreement. Surprisingly enough, he didn't yell and rant about it. I almost wished he had. Instead, he went into this long rigmarole: So I had finally decided I needed old Stan, had I? When things got tough, I knew where to turn, did I? If I was wanting to talk about making up, he guessed he was willing to listen.

All I wanted to talk about, I told him, was Davey's tonsils. Nothing else.

In the end, he paid, but I would almost rather he hadn't.

Davey went into the hospital one morning and stayed overnight till about noon the next day. Of course I had to stay with him. So I don't know what I would have done without Rob. He took off work to stay with Gail and Lisbeth, and when we came home he took Davey's prescriptions to the drugstore and got them filled. But I don't know, there was a kind of finality to it. As soon as he had us settled in again, he left to get on with his own things.

When I took Davey to be checked the third day after surgery, I hit another low. He refused to walk; I had to carry him. Gail felt neglected, I guess, and kept clinging to my leg. And Lisbeth was having a distinctly bad day. She kept grinding her teeth and wavering her eyes, a tantrum looking for an excuse to happen. I was all strung out, my hair was dirty and straggling down, and I didn't have so much as a dollar in my purse.

Davey was fine. But Dr. Krawitz took one look at me and called me down to his office again. I really should consider placing Lisbeth, he said. I could not go on like this.

"Fine," I said, barked really. "Do you have any particular place in mind? Or maybe a couple, so I can choose?" I should have remembered how much money I owed him and tried to be more civil. After all, he was thinking about my welfare. But I was getting tired of good advice with nothing to go on.

When I got home, Patti was there and I told her what he had said.

"He's right, of course," she pointed out.

So what else was new? It was still impossible. "What I really need," I said, "is a job. But that's impossible too."

"Why?"

"Come on, Patti. What am I going to do with the kids? What am I going to do with Lisbeth? But then how are we going to get by otherwise? You see?"

She nodded and left. Later in the afternoon, though,

she phoned back with an idea. "Mitchy's there in the morning anyway, right? I know that doesn't help with the kids, of course, because he's sleeping and they have to have somebody watching them. But Lisbeth doesn't have to be watched every minute, does she? I mean, if someone's there in case of a problem. Wouldn't she make enough noise to wake him up if something was wrong? Once she's had breakfast and gotten dressed, isn't she just going to listen to the TV anyway? So why couldn't you settle her on the sofa and take the kids to a nursery, and Mitchy would be there just in case?"

It sounded pretty good to me. I told her I'd think it over.

So that's how Davey's tonsils precipitated another change. They pushed me back to the desperation point, which was where I had to be to make a decision. That, and the absoluteness with which Dr. Krawitz said I couldn't go on the way I was. I was always inclined to believe Dr. Krawitz.

About a week after Davey had his tonsils out, I decided it was time to try Patti's idea, so I went out and got a job. It wasn't much, just checking and stocking at Walgreen's three days a week, eight to two, but I figured I'd better start small and see how it went.

I didn't tell Mitchy until after I had it all lined up, day care and all. When I did, he was not exactly enthusiastic. Since when did I assume he felt like taking care of *her?* Besides, when did I expect him to sleep? After all, he did need to sleep some time.

Well, nobody had asked me if I felt like taking care of

her either. And if he didn't want me to work, I said, he could start paying what he had agreed to when he moved in.

I shouldn't have said it that way, as if he had just decided on his own to move in on me. That wasn't true. But I was feeling cornered, and somebody who feels cornered is going to lash out once in a while. So I lashed out, and he flung himself out of his chair and went off down the hall. Then in a minute he was back, and we had a real fight, the first real fight we'd had since he'd been there.

I hated it. I had never been any good at fighting— maybe if I had been I could have fought with Stan and we would have been better off. Now here I was having to fight with Mitchy.

We threw accusations at each other and mostly missed but hit often enough, and when we did it hurt. My "poor Meg" routine that got him into this; his boozing; my putting out for Our Favorite Intellectual, who was nothing but a freeloader; his putting out for every limp wrist who came along, or did he have to pay them? Oh, it got ugly.

We yelled ourselves red in the face, with the kids looking from one to the other, until I noticed Lisbeth, rocking violently back and forth with her hands over her ears. That stopped me. I said, "Good Christ, Mitchy, what are we doing?" He dropped onto the sofa and put his head in his hands and it was over.

But I couldn't let that part about Rob go by un-challenged. It seemed so unfair, after he had been so nice. So I had to add, but quietly, "Anyway, Rob's not a free-loader. He gave me money for Davey's prescriptions just last week. Which was more than you did."

"More than the Honor Graduate did, either," he pointed out (not entirely accurately). "Or had you forgotten about him?"

So there was still a little lightning playing around the horizon, but the real storm was over. In a minute he got up and went off to his room. Later on, before he went to work, he was back at me, but from a different angle, an angle I hadn't expected. I didn't really take money from Rob, did I? It was bad enough, right there in the same house, but if he thought I took money from him. . . His hands actually shook, he was that worked up over it.

I saw then what he was getting at. And that was when I honestly began to worry about Mitchy. If he could think something as crazy as that—!

Rob came over that night, for the first time in about a week. He saw right off that I was upset and wanted to know what was wrong. I couldn't tell him, of course. I told him I was worried about Mitchy's drinking—and that was true enough. Thin, red eyed, shakes in the morning. Twenty-five years old and a drinking problem, and what could I do for him? Nothing.

We sat at the kitchen table and drank coffee, the way we had so many times, and about midnight we went to bed. And it was still good, it was OK. But it was more like we were keeping up the forms of something: The forms were good forms, but the substance was missing. After a while he said he guessed he'd better go on back to his place. He had to be up early, to get some work done on that last chapter.

Rob was always so nice about things.

So I started my job. And it worked out pretty well, for a

while. The children clung to me and cried the first couple of times I left them at the day-care center, but I had expected that. I knew they would get over it, and they did. Getting ready in the morning was probably the hardest part. I had to rush around like mad getting everybody breakfasted and dressed and getting Lisbeth squared away in front of the TV, so I could leave the house at 7:30.

A couple of times when Rob was there he took over part of the routine so I could sit over my coffee and get my eyes open, and once he even dropped the kids off for me on his way to the campus. That was great—the send-off at the door, the good-bye kiss, all that. But then it was almost as if he realized this was going to start me thinking along lines that might be dangerous. I could practically see him realizing it. And after that he was never around on a work morning again.

In fact, he wasn't around much at all. There wasn't a drastic change, anything I could put my finger on, just a dwindling away. But I was too taken up with other things, with Lisbeth and the kids and with money, to take very much notice of what was going on, or wasn't, anyway. Sometimes I think if I had gotten to know Rob at another time, when there wasn't so much else going on, who knows? He was so sweet, such a sweet guy. But I was so bound up with thinking all the time what am I going to do, what am I going to do, trying to figure it out, trying to manage everything and juggle everything, and then trying to sound cheery and nice to Lisbeth even when I didn't feel cheery and nice, because she noticed tone of voice and would get upset if I didn't, that there simply wasn't any of me left for Rob. Or for

Mitchy. Or for myself, for that matter. But especially not for Rob.

Twice in my first couple of weeks on the job I was late to work because of Lisbeth. Once she got upset because her shoelace broke, and screamed and threw things for ten minutes and took all her clothes off, so I had to persuade her to get dressed again. The other time she had a sudden attack of diarrhea just as I was walking out the door. I had to peel her jeans off her and hose them off in the backyard, jeans and underpants both, yelling at the dog the whole time to keep away, and then put her through two bath waters and get her dressed again and scrub the slick, stinking bathtub. So I was late. And the assistant manager, of course, saw fit to remind me that I was on probation for the first three months and one thing they would be watching for was reliability.

Still, I kept telling myself it was going to be all right, we were going to make it. I was only clearing $35 a week after I paid the day-care center, but it was better than nothing. It was enough to pay the utilities, even in July, with the air conditioner going night and day. And with Mitchy still not holding up his end, that was a big help. Probably I would have felt like we were doing pretty well, if everything else had been going OK.

But it wasn't. Lisbeth seemed to get worse and worse, more difficult, more unreasonable. Nothing pleased her, everything set her off. And the worse she got, the crabbier I got and the harder it was to keep from snapping at her. And if I did, if she detected even the least edge in my voice, she got all upset. It was a losing situation. Not all the medications Dr. Krawitz could prescribe, not whole cocktails of tranquilizers, could turn it around.

I began to understand why Mama had had such tension lines around her mouth. Not that I hadn't understood before, in a way, but now I understood more clearly.

That was one thing. Add to that the fact that Mitchy was flaking out more and more. He complained that he wasn't getting enough sleep, that the TV kept him awake in the mornings, no matter how low I turned it. He complained that things came up that he needed to go out to do before I got home, and he couldn't do them because of having to take care of Lisbeth. He complained it was "just so damn depressing" being with her. "You can't look at that face day in day out and try to deal with everything that goes with it and not get depressed."

"You're telling me that?"

"All right," he admitted, "you oughta know. But you're better at holding up to things than I am."

From the doorway, Lisbeth put in, "Holding up to what?" We had thought she was busy eating her lunch. It was impossible to have a conversation.

I made lame excuses, but she knew, she had to know.

I had been worried about Mitchy's drinking ever since he moved in with us. For some weeks now I had thought it was getting worse. A couple of times I had thought I heard people bring him in after work, and on the mornings after those times I couldn't seem to rouse him to say I was leaving for work. I liked to do that, to make sure he knew I was going and he was on duty. Once he was still asleep when I came in, at two-thirty. Lisbeth hadn't had any lunch, and the lamp on my bedside table was knocked over. I could only guess that she had lost her bearings, maybe after going to the bathroom, and wandered around the house for a while before finding her way back to the family room. I knew how upsetting that would have been for her.

Then one afternoon, when I pulled into the driveway, I saw her standing in the back yard beside the fence. It must have been 105, one of those late-summer scorchers, and there she stood with the sun beating down on her, red in the face and burning up. The back door was locked. She had actually been locked out.

Inside, the house smelled of pot, and I could hear giggling from Mitchy's bedroom.

I knew right then that that was it, I couldn't leave her with Mitchy that way anymore. My second big experiment had failed.

19

THE FIRST thing I did was call Walgreen's and tell them there was a serious illness in the family and I wouldn't be in for a few days. The second was tell Mitchy to get out. After I got Sister something to drink and then some lunch, I went back and amended that to: "Find a place to move and get out."

Later, considerably later, after he apologized, I said OK, he could stay, but no pot in the house and no drinking in the daytime and he'd have to start paying his share.

And I think he meant to live up to that. But of course I knew he never would.

I spent the next week trying to think what to do. Mostly I sat at the kitchen table and drank tea. The kids didn't know what to think. They would get up in the morning, eat dry cereal with their fingers, and go play tents with their bed sheets. Once, Gail inquired, "School?" Looking at bills and writing lists of options, I shook my head. "Not today," I told her. "Let's stay home today."

At least that was one thing working at Walgreen's had gotten me: a supply of yellow pads to make my lists on. That and a little cushion of money in the bank—not enough to pay the rent, due in ten days, plus the bills I had counted up, some $210. But my child-support check was due before the rent, and with that I could cover them.

A couple of little typing jobs came in during that week, but I was so distracted I made mistakes all the time and thought I would never get them done. When someone called with an eighty-page thesis, which I should have greeted with rejoicing, I said I couldn't do it.

Rob was there at the time, I remember. He couldn't believe it. Hadn't I just been saying I needed money? "I hope you won't turn mine down," he said. "You know, it won't be long now." He looked at me sharply. "You do know that, don't you? That I'm nearly through?"

I put my pen down and looked at him, really looked at him, for the first time in weeks, I guess. It struck me how young he looked, like a sandy-haired kid almost—leaner, tireder, but with just that clean-cut, open look of expectancy. It reminded me of Davey's look when he wanted me to admire some picture he'd colored at the nursery and I was too tired, too taken up with everything else. He must have been telling me all this time that he was nearly through, and I hadn't been listening.

"My God, Rob," I said. "When you say it won't be long, how long do you mean?"

Maybe a month, he said, two at the most.

I asked him what he was going to do then.

He shrugged. "Pursue truth, I guess. Stand on the street corner with a sign—Philosopher."

"What about your doctorate?"

He looked away. "Who knows?" With a quick look at his watch, he said he'd better be going. Could I make him a sandwich to eat on his break? And maybe put in a banana to go with it? I fixed it for him while he went to the bathroom and washed up. When he came back through he had his billfold out.

"Here," he said, "for some of what I've been eating off of you." It was a twenty and a ten, folded together. I took them without argument. "Oh, and I won't be back after I get off," he added.

"OK," I said. "See you tomorrow." I was already back into my planning sheets before he started his car.

Patti came over later to report in. She had been coming over practically every day since I gave up on my job, to help me plan my future. Not that she had any ideas either, but she seemed to think if we kept at it we'd sooner or later strike a spark. She was determined I had to get out from under Lisbeth. That's how she put it—out from under her. And it was accurate enough. More and more I felt like some great weight had settled over me and I was struggling along under it. Every day we sat and discussed my options, or actually my lack of them, in low voices, not wanting Lisbeth to know we were trying to find someplace to put her, to send her away. We would look up and there she would be, listening, and we wouldn't know how much she had heard.

Patti had taken it on, like a cause. She kept phoning

around to state agencies, mostly in Austin, tracing down one lead after another, trying to find a place for her. She even found an agency for agencies, a kind of watchdog office for helping people get what they were entitled to from the other agencies. I think she called that one about every day, trying to push them to turn something up besides the places we already knew about, that had already turned out to be dead ends. Fortunately, they had an 800 number.

I appreciated her efforts. She had about the most energetic idea of friendship I had ever seen. She was like Rob that way. If they saw something that needed to be done, they did it. They both seemed to have this confidence that things could be fixed, that all problems had solutions. I didn't. So all her telephoning and investigating was like something going on out on the periphery. In the center, surrounded by more immediate questions, I was just hoping to deal with things as they were. Things like making a living: I had to get a job, and a full-time job, no more of this eighteen hours a week. That meant I needed someone to watch Lisbeth. I couldn't count on Mitchy, that was for sure. I couldn't count on anyone.

My first idea was to find an older woman to come in and stay with all three of them. I spent half a day phoning baby-sitter agencies, then churches in poorer parts of town, which might have members needing a small income. And I got a few leads, all right. But they all expected me to drive across town to pick them up and take them home, and they all backed off when they heard about Lisbeth.

Next I tried Stan. I figured, given that he cared about the kids' welfare, he would naturally want to help me help them. Of course, what I was leaving out was a lot of complications, plus he didn't at all want to help me help Lisbeth. But I ignored that and phoned him up. My idea was, if he could switch to the early shift at work, I might get some kind of hospital job on a three to eleven shift. I could drop the kids at his place and pick them up on my way home. Or he could let them sleep over and drop them off on his way to work the next morning. He wouldn't have to give them breakfast or anything, just wake them up, get them out to the car, and drop them off. And for that I would knock $75 a month off his child support.

At first, before he realized I meant Lisbeth too, he seemed inclined to think about it. Or at least he seemed to want to talk about it, or to talk, period. He gave me a long spiel about how much he missed us and how lonely he was and how he knew I wouldn't have done what I did if I had known I was ruining his life. I could have felt very sorry for him if I had let myself. But I was learning better; I was toughening up.

"How about it?" I said. "I need to get a job, I can't wait around with four mouths to feed."

Of course, that did it. He picked up on the "four mouths" right away. What did I think this was, anyway? Why should he knock himself out trying to deal with that mental defective? No one had ever known what to do with her, so why should he? And whose fault was it I had four mouths to feed anyway? Hadn't he told me to get rid of her?

He hung up on me, then called back in ten minutes to say he was coming over, maybe we could work something out. I told him no way, any talking we had to do could be done on the phone. I still remembered the last time he had come over. He kept begging—please, please, he needed me, he needed the children, he missed us so much; if I'd just get Lisbeth out of there he'd come back to me in a minute, in spite of it all. He kept going on like that till I just hung up. Then he came over anyway, barged right in, and when he saw Rob standing by the sink with a peach in his hand he called me names—bitch, whore, about what you'd expect—and stormed back out. I was just relieved he hadn't done any worse.

So much for that idea.

I guess what I kept hoping was that Rob would surprise me and move in with us. Funny, I never even thought of wanting him to marry me. It never even occurred to me. He was younger, he was different—even without Patti's efforts to warn me to put the brakes on, I knew he wasn't marriage-able. By then I had found out too that he was seeing Beep once in a while. That was Beep for you. But he was sweet, and I would have enjoyed having him around on a regular basis, at least for a while. Also, as it turned out, he was my last resort.

A few days after Stan's blowup, the child support was due. The day came and went—no check, and then a couple more days—no check. It didn't even occur to me that he might be getting back at me by not paying. Stan wasn't like that. But when it still didn't come, I finally decided to call him. His phone had been disconnected. I felt a chill; what was I going to do? Call the garage, of course; I could find him that way. They said he had quit.

It's funny how things come together. I was sitting there

with the phone in my hand, trying to let it sink in that Stan had really completely run out on me, when it rang and there was Rob telling me he was going away. He'd had a fellowship offer to start on his Ph.D. Not the greatest, but not the worst either—L.S.U. He had just that minute opened the letter, he said, and he couldn't wait to tell me in person, he had to call right away.

"Rob, that's great," I said. "That's really wonderful." And it was, I meant it. It was exactly what he had wanted. And how often do people get exactly what they want? I was just sorry I had too much on my mind to give it the reception it deserved.

The funny thing was, I didn't feel a bit sorry that he wasn't asking me to go along. That wasn't even part of it. I didn't think of that till later, that it hadn't even been part of it. I had my own problems, and I was too busy groping around for a way out of them to waste time being sorry for something that wasn't in the cards.

He was so excited. He said he was going to make some more calls and fill out his acceptance form, and I said great, I was so happy for him. I hoped he didn't notice that my heart wasn't really in it.

After that I just sat and tried to think what to do. That meant trying to ignore the backdrop of Lisbeth's TV game show and the kids' carrying on in their room, where they were supposed to be taking a nap. Think—I had to think. What to do now?

Gail and Davey stole out from their room in their underwear, staying close together, expecting to be sent back. I ignored them.

Lisbeth came to tell me about the Meow Mix commercial. "Cats ask for by name! Oh, gosh!" That commercial bowled her over every time. Yes, yes, Lisbeth, that's really funny. Finish the show and I'll make you and the kids some Kool-Aid in a minute. Or some chocolate milk, if we have any milk.

Family. What would we do without family? I had too much of it, in a way, but for dealing with problems, not enough. Like right now, for this. It ought to be family trying to deal with this, not just me.

What could I do but make one last try with Mama and Daddy? Or no, not with them this time but with her, just her. He was the one who couldn't take it. He left first. She hung in there for a few more years, until she got us up to survival age. She ought to understand something about reliability.

Reliability: a concept Daddy never got hold of. He was the sweeter of the two, the one I loved. And oh, how I had wished for good reason to go on loving him!

I remember sitting on his lap behind the steering wheel, as round as my arms would reach, peering through the middle space and turning in intent jerks. He knew not to let me see his one finger backing me up. Or standing on the kitchen chair and punching the keys of his accordion, or the chord buttons, while he worked the bellows. He laughed and laughed. When we woke up the baby, he didn't even care. We were having too much fun to stop laughing so soon. But there were more of the other times. Daddy holding Beep on his lap and reading, reading while Mama got dinner, or rolling Mitchy on the grass with the football somewhere in between. I was out of it. Or even worse, shoving us all away to retreat behind his cigarette and newspaper. I guess that's where I learned to hate newspapers; I'm still a poor newspaper reader, a skimmer and a forgetter. I remember his bending over Mama where she sat hemming something, and his hand sliding down over her breast, and the frown he got for it. I remember his being gone so much, and then gone for good.

Stan was a lot like him, actually—changeable, unreliable.

I never loved Mama that way. But she was the one I needed now. She was the only one I had any hope in.

It was nearly three-thirty. I would wait till five, when the rates went down, and then start calling and keep calling till I got someone. Person-to-person, to her, not him. That was the only way.

I started to call Patti and see what she thought of the idea. I knew she had been saying all along it was their responsibility more than mine—which didn't do a lot of good—and society's responsibility most of all, which so far hadn't done any good at all. But I decided against it. Patti was a great help; anyway, she kept on trying to be. Rob, on the other hand, had been a great help, but now seemed to have gotten tired of it. Yes: I had to face that. Anybody wears out, no matter how nice they are. But this was for me to decide on, and to do. It wasn't for either one of them. I was on my own.

I sat right there and watched the clock. For nearly two hours that was all I did except to put out sandwiches and carrot sticks for the kids' supper. The three kids, that is. I didn't feel like cooking or like anything else. They dragged toys out all over, banged on Mitchy's piano, cut up the Sears catalog. I left them alone and watched the clock. Five came, and I waited a half hour more, for no reason. Then I started calling.

Person-to-person was the way to do it, all right. And I got her on the third try. At first the man at the office said she wasn't there. But he must have decided it had to be important for me to keep on trying and to pay for person-to-person at that. Either that or she really had been out when he said she was. Anyway, on the third try he said, "Just a minute" and brought her to the phone.

When she answered, in that hard, careful voice I knew so well, I wanted to cry and cry. It all came over me at once, all of it together: Beep's wildness and her good looks, which I didn't know how to handle; Mitchy's drinking, which I didn't know what to do about; his screwing around with other guys as aimless as himself, which I was trying to accept but hadn't managed to yet; my failing with Stan—yes, failing, I might as well admit that's what it was; Rob; Sister. Everything about Sister—the absolute nothing she had to look forward to and my failure to make anything better for her, besides the problem she was for me. It all gathered in my throat and behind my nose, and I could have hung on to the receiver and cried for hours. But it wouldn't do. I couldn't let all that out; she would be utterly overwhelmed, there would be no way she could even begin to respond.

So I held on and said, "Mama, this is it. I'm asking you one more time, isn't there something you can do? Stan hasn't sent the child support this month and his phone's disconnected and I don't know what to do. I can't go on without some real help."

"Isn't Mitchy . . ."

"Mitchy's falling apart himself, Mama. He can't help. It's too complicated to go into now. What I'm telling you is, I've got to get a job, but I can't get anyone to take care of Lisbeth, and—"

"Your father told you, we can't do a whole lot."

"I know, Mama, but—"

"We'll send something next month if we can."

"Mama, I'm telling you, this is it. I'm going to have to do something right away. Tomorrow. I can't keep her, Mama. Are you hearing me? *I cannot keep Lisbeth.* I've done all I can do, Mama. I can't help it. Can't you take her? Because if you can't take her, I'm going to have to . . ." I hadn't known until that minute what I was going to have to do. Then suddenly, right in a flash, I did know. But I couldn't say it.

"I'm telling you, Mama, I can't keep her here anymore. Now can you do it or not?"

There was a silence and then a sound of crying, and I knew we were at the same place, facing the same impossibility. There wasn't any use going on.

"I'm sorry, Mama," I said. "I'm sorry I called you like this. I'll write. I'm going now, Mama." I waited a minute in case she wanted to say anything else and then hung up.

And there stood Lisbeth in the door; of course she would be there, rolling her eyes up.

"What do you mean, can't keep me?"

20

I WENT out the next morning and found us a place to move.

I had gone through the classifieds with a red marker the night before till midnight. Then I lay down on the sofa instead of going to bed, so I would be sure to wake up when Mitchy came in. I didn't wake up after all, but luckily he roused me to find out what I was doing there.

When I could clear my head, I asked him whether he wanted to go on living with the kids and me. He seemed to think that was a pretty big question for 3:00 A.M., but after a minute he said yes, he did. So I told him fine, that was what I needed to know, because I was going to find us a cheaper place, and I had to know whether to look for two bedrooms or three.

He didn't ask a thing, just nodded, and we both went to bed.

The next morning I left the kids at the day-care center

and Lisbeth with Mitchy so I could move fast. It only took me a couple of hours. The third place I looked at was an old frame house needing paint, in an area overlooked by two elevated freeways—one of those neighborhoods where streets merge into tire-packed yards through melancholy strips of gravel and Quarter Pounder boxes. It was pretty close to where Mitchy had lived before. But the house was nicer inside than the one he had lived in, and the freeways were far enough away that noise didn't seem to be a problem. I decided at once to take it.

The owner was a scrawny little man of seventy or so who looked like a sharp dealer. I had an idea he wouldn't be very tolerant of people who got behind on their rent. But he seemed to take a liking to me. After we talked a while he agreed to come down on the rent, which was already pretty reasonable, in exchange for scraping and painting the house. I pretended to think it over.

"You buy the paint, right?"

He tried to look indignant, but underneath he was laughing. "You drive a hard bargain, girl, you know that? Yes, I'll buy the paint. That way I'll know what I'm getting. You better do a good job, you hear?"

I paid him the first month on the spot, with the money for the rent that was overdue at the other place. I didn't feel good about it; I had never walked out on a bill before. But life brings you to do things you never expected to, sometimes. My plan was to move out quickly and quietly, without giving notice and without leaving any forwarding address. That was the main thing—no forwarding address. So people would have trouble finding us.

On the way home I stopped at two grocery stores and filled up the car with boxes, and as soon as I could give the kids their lunch I went into action, chucking things in any old way. Mitchy took a couple of cartons back to his room and packed what he couldn't cram into his dresser drawers. When he came back for another one to start on bathroom towels, I told him never mind boxes, just spread out a sheet, pile them on, and tie it up. This was going to be a fast move.

We spurred each other on: the faster one worked, the faster the other did. By four we had maybe not most, but anyway a lot of it ready to go.

Mitchy hadn't asked where, how much, or anything except whether it had air-conditioning.

"Sorry, no air-conditioning," I said. "Summer's nearly over. We can stand it."

I knew I ought to tell him about the painting deal, but I figured he might as well keep on with what he was doing and not worry about it. He was going to have to quit soon enough anyway, to shower and go to work. I needed every minute's work I could get out of him.

When Rob stopped by on his way to the drugstore, he could hardly believe it. In the first place, Mitchy's car was still sitting in front—and I'd told him I was throwing Mitchy out. Then he came in and found the whole place dismantled, without a word of warning.

I didn't have time for long explanations.

"We're moving," I said. "I'll explain later. No, don't kiss me, I'm too sweaty. But listen, I need you to do something." I went on working while I talked. He just stood there; I don't think it had sunk in yet. "Phone around and find us a truck to rent. You can pick it up on your way to work, if you will, and then bring it when you get off. Can you do that? We're loading tonight, while it's dark. I hope you'll help." I more than hoped. I had counted on him.

"Hey, wait, hold on, I think I've missed something." He laughed and caught me for a kiss on my way by, sweaty or not. "When did you decide to move?"

"Last night. Now go on, we don't have much time. Oh, and if you know a couple of guys who might help us, I can pay them twenty apiece, if you can line them up."

He wouldn't give up, though. Was I going to tell him what this was all about? He wasn't doing one thing till I did. Where was I going, anyway?

"Just a cheaper place," I said. Which was the truth, but not the whole truth. I hesitated. "Come on, Rob. You don't want to know any more."

I think he guessed it then. He had been looking so high, about the fellowship, of course—which I hadn't even thought to mention. But now his grin dropped away, and he gave a long sigh and said under his breath, "Oh, boy." Just that, not another word. And he went off to phone truck-rental places.

After he got that taken care of, he said he'd better be going, but he'd call from work to try to line up some help. "But listen," he said, "did you think about the piano?"

The piano! I had thought of everything else, but not that. "Damn!" I exclaimed. "Do you think we could do it ourselves?" We looked at each other. He was waiting for me to say it. "No," I conceded, "you're right. We couldn't. What time is it now?"

It was five.

"Let me get started calling. I've got to get somebody here first thing in the morning."

I had visions of our landlord chaining the piano to the toilet, or something, till we paid him what we owed. Which we couldn't do, since I had used the money to rent the other place, so that was that. Besides, I didn't want to leave any leads. I didn't want him to have any information to give out, if somebody asked him.

Lisbeth came to the door and listened while I tried to line up a piano mover. That was another one of those little things she did that got under my skin, always listening in while I talked on the phone. Not that it mattered so much. Ninety percent of the time I didn't have anything to talk about anyway. It just got me, that's all. And then I felt guilty because it did. One more thing to feel guilty about.

All afternoon she had sat on the sofa listening to the commotion going on around her without asking a thing about it. And we hadn't told her anything either. Not a thing. I didn't know if she was wondering about it or not. I hoped not.

Now, though, she listened to every word I said, her eyes rolling intently. I looked at her and knew she understood what I was saying. But I had to get this lined up; I didn't have any choice. Anyway, she had to find out some time, so it might as well be sooner as later.

When I had finally found someone who could come at seven-thirty the next morning to move the piano, and I'd arranged all the details and hung up, she asked me just one question: "Will they move that door too?" That door: the folding door that shut her out from Mitchy's lessons.

I told her no, we'd have to leave the door here.

She said, "Oh," and went away, but came back after a minute to add, "It's a good door."

That was all. She never asked another question. Maybe she couldn't think of any.

The kids thought it was a great game, of course. All afternoon they hid behind boxes and sat on the bundles of linens and poked through the cans and spice jars from the kitchen cabinets as if they had never seen groceries before. About five-thirty I told them we'd better take a rest.

I had already planned what to do about their night's sleep while we loaded. I would take the beds apart after supper and put their mattresses on the floor. They could go to sleep on them there. If I got everything else out of their room, or everything I could, we wouldn't be having to go in there a lot and wake them up. Even so, there was no way they were going to get a regular night's sleep, I knew that. And I wasn't going to get any at all. So I figured we could all use a little nap before supper.

Naps together were always taken on my bed, lying crossways. I don't know why, that was just the way we did it. The bed seemed to feel extra comfortable that way, for naps. So I kicked off my shoes and made sure Davey didn't need to go potty, and we lay down, Gail next to the pillows, her favorite place, me next, and Davey toward the foot.

I hadn't thought to say anything to Lisbeth. She never wanted to take a nap anyway. But she came on her own and lay down with us, wedging herself in between Davey and me and holding both our hands.

That was when I came the closest to crying, but I wouldn't do it. I couldn't. If I once let that get started, there wouldn't be any stopping it. It was so bad. It was the worst thing I'd ever had to do. But no use crying about it now.

I remembered then something I hadn't thought of in years that must have seemed to Mama like the worst thing she had ever had to do.

When Lisbeth was just a little thing, six or seven, I guess, she had been taken away to the state school for the blind. I had no awareness of what went into the decision to send her there. I was a year younger, of course, and so, mercifully, shielded from it in unawareness. It must have been terrible, coming to the conclusion that there was no way but that. I'm sure there were no local schools for her, and something had to be done, so there was no choice.

There must have been lists of things to bring and instructions for labeling every sock. I'm sure there were, judging by later years when I was more aware of what went on, every year, for the beginning of school. They must have worked on it for weeks, buying, labeling, checking and rechecking, packing. And then, all together, we took her up there and left her. A child of six, blind and confused—we just took her there and left her.

I can still remember the scene in that dormitory. Young as I was, it stayed with me. The children were sorted out by age, of course. We were in the place for the youngest ones. All these little blind kids being brought to this strange place, away from home for the first time probably, and being told good-bye and then left there, terrified and holding on to each other and crying as hard and as loud as they could cry. And Mama trying to unpack Lisbeth's things in the middle of that uproar and count out socks, underpants, pajamas, while the housemother checked them off on a list. I remember how her hands shook, while she counted them out. When we left, Lisbeth tried to hold on to Daddy, then to me and to Mama. They had to pull her away, crying, her distorted face distorted all the more.

"Don't worry," the woman said, "she'll get over it."

And now I was about to do the same thing. Or worse, in a way. But what else could I do? I had thought and thought, and I couldn't see any way to go on.

The three of them dropped off to sleep right away, and I was just starting to feel drowsy myself when I heard the back door slam and Patti's voice calling through the house, "Me-eg, Me-eg." Rob must have called her when he got to work. I slipped away from the bed and met her in the hall, holding my finger up for quiet, and we went back to the kitchen to talk.

She was pretty clear on what I was doing, even without my telling her. Had I thought about this? she asked. Was I sure I could live with it? "This isn't like you," she said. "You usually think things over more. You usually ask the rest of us what we think."

The rest of us—so we were a family now! She was right, of course; usually I did. But this was something I had to do myself.

"Look," I pointed out. "You've been telling me I couldn't go on this way."

"Yes, but I didn't think . . ."

"Well, you were right. I couldn't."

She nodded slowly, uncomfortably, wanting to say more and not knowing how much to say. Oh, I knew what she was thinking. Finally she came out with it: "But we were looking for a good place for her. We were going to get her well taken care of."

I went to the sink and looked out. Mutt was mulling over an old stick. What a mess that dog could make of a yard! Yes, we were going to take care of her. We were going to do a lot of things. But we might as well face it: We couldn't.

I would have to take Mutt with us, of course. You can't just abandon a dog. Not a dog, anyway.

"That woman in Austin," she went on. "She was going to look into it and call me back. She was going to see—"

I waved her off. "Patti, there isn't a good place. There just isn't. It doesn't exist. You've been great, you've tried to help, you've gone to a lot of trouble. But it's no use."

"There has to be a place."

"There isn't. Places for the blind don't want her because she's retarded. Places for the retarded don't want her because she's blind. Not to mention disturbed. She throws things at people. Like rocking chairs." She looked up. "Yes, rocking chairs. One time I saw her pick up a wooden rocker and throw it at Mama. How are you going to live with that?"

Lisbeth's voice broke in, "What do you mean, don't want me?"

We looked at each other. Think fast now, think fast.

"Don't want you to get too tired," I said. "They want me to make sure you get enough rest. That's why we had a nap."

She turned away.

The subject was closed. Not resolved, just closed. There was nothing more to be said.

Patti picked up her keys and billfold. "Can I bring over some supper in a little while?" she offered. "Just something simple?"

I said thanks, that'd be great. And if she'd bring paper plates I could go ahead and pack the rest of the dishes. That would be a big help.

I let the kids sleep for another half hour while I got Lisbeth's things together. Everything she owned went into one big suitcase. I left out an outfit for tomorrow and started one last load of wash, so I could get all her underwear and things in. There would be time after dinner to put them through the dryer. Then I woke up the kids and started taking beds apart.

As soon as Rob got back, about ten, we started loading. He had backed the truck up the driveway so we could load through the back door and hope not to be noticed from the street.

There was something about doing all that in the dark, with flashlights inside the truck picking out spots of scuffed wall, that heightened the sense of urgency. We rushed back and forth, loading things any old way, just to get them in. Even if we had had time to do the job right, we couldn't have seen to.

When Mitchy came in, a little earlier than usual, we

had the first load nearly done. He changed and took out some boxes and two kitchen chairs, and that was it.

I noticed Rob's friend starting to load boxes from the garage onto his pickup and told him just to leave them. Most of that stuff was Stan's anyway. Why should I go on carting it around? If there was anything of mine in those boxes, I could get along without it.

We did get the lawnmower into the pickup, though, and the red wagon and the two garbage cans. And Mutt's doghouse. Then they left to take that load, and I stayed behind with the kids. I filled up the car trunk and half the back seat with little things and clothes and then wandered around looking for something else I could throw into boxes. We still had three or four empties. I found some toys, my makeup, several pairs of shoes. After a while, when I couldn't figure out what else to do and they still weren't back, I lay down on the edge of Sister's roll-away bed. She seemed to be sleeping pretty well, thank God. That had made everything easier.

I seemed to have just dropped off, but it might have been five minutes or thirty, when they were back, voices all around me, something heavy going out. I jumped up, trying to clear my head. Then they were back in, standing around, hands on hips, breathing in gulps and wiping brows on shirtsleeves with little quick shoulder motions, seeing what was left, what to get next. I poured little paper cups of milk for them, all that was left in the refrigerator. What we'd do for breakfast I didn't know. Worry about that then.

When they finally got away with the second load, it was about four-thirty. We had thought we would finish sooner, but we kept looking around and seeing something else to carry out. The kids' mattresses went on at the very back by the door, so they could be first off.

At the last minute I had carried first Gail and then Davey out to Mitchy's car, sound asleep, and laid them on the back seat. We figured even if they woke up, they'd go back to sleep when he carried them in at the other end. But it looked like they'd sleep right through it. They didn't even stir.

After they all left again, I lay down once more in my clothes, this time on the floor next to Lisbeth's bed. She had roused several times during that last couple of hours, but had gone right back to sleep, and she seemed to be still resting pretty well. One hand was dangling over the side, and I held it. That was a mistake. It always made me feel like crying to touch her hands, they were so thin and undeveloped and helpless; but especially now. But I held it anyway.

And then in no time the doorbell was ringing and I saw that it was seven-thirty and realized it must be the piano movers. Lisbeth was already sitting up, bleary-eyed and confused. I told her I'd be right back, and went to let them in.

This was it.

By the time they had the piano loaded, Lisbeth was dressed and her teeth brushed and her toothbrush, toothpaste, and pajamas packed into the suitcase. Right on top, before I closed the lid, I put a short letter I had written to the people at the Home.

After I gave the movers the address of the new place and told them there would be someone there to meet them and pay the bill, I took one more look around the house. A square of soft, matted dust marked where the refrigerator had been, and two more like it marked the washer and dryer. In every room, in corners, along baseboards, lay the evidence of how poor a housekeeper I had been. I would have liked to have left the place cleaner. But then, I would have liked to have done a lot of things better. Nothing about this was the way I wished it had been.

With careful good cheer, I said to Lisbeth, "Guess what? We're having breakfast at McDonald's today! How about that?"

"McDonald's?" She sounded doubtful. "We don't usually." She thought about it a minute, then stood up with a jerk, and a pleased look spread over her face. "Oh yeah," she said. "Egg McMuffin."

"You don't listen to TV for nothing, do you, girl?"

She liked that. "Don't listen for nothing! Oh, gah!"

I first folded up the roll-away bed, then got Sister out to the car and told her I had to go back for something. We had figured I could get the bed into the trunk, but I had trouble. I had to open it again there in the driveway, take out the mattress, and load frame and mattress separately, nervous as a cat the whole time for fear the landlord was going to drive up and ruin everything. Another minute and I would have left it there.

By the time I got both pieces loaded, it was nearly nine-thirty and hot as blazes. I ran back in for the suitcase and my purse and left the keys to the house on the kitchen counter where they could be found easily. We had just a little over an hour. Her bus was at ten-forty.

With the roll-away bed in the trunk, I had to put the suitcase in the back seat. When I did, Lisbeth reached back and felt what it was. I guess that was the first time she realized she was going away. She scowled and said we didn't have to take her suitcase to McDonald's.

I had known this moment was coming, of course. There had to be a time when she caught on, and even if she hadn't I would have had to tell her. But I still cheated.

"This is the day you're going back to the Home, remember?" I tried to sound as if we had planned this and talked about it and she had just forgotten. I don't know if she believed me or not, but she didn't argue. She did keep the traces of a frown, as she turned it over and over in her mind. I talked on about this and that, trying to distract her, so maybe when her mind came back to it she would accept it and think, oh yes, we really had talked about that and she knew she was going back, she had just forgotten. If that's how she thought about things. That's what I was hoping.

All through breakfast she was very quiet, dawdling with her food. I didn't dare tell her to hurry, for fear I'd get her upset and have trouble getting her onto the bus. But I was worrying about the time. As soon as she took her last bite and her last drink of juice, I had her wipe her hands, got her out to the car, and drove as fast as I could to the station.

Then, after all, we were early. There was no line at the ticket counter at all.

I bought a one-way ticket to Austin, checked her bag, and pinned to the front of her dress an abbreviated version of the letter I had put inside her suitcase. It said,

Dear Superintendent Smit:
I know you said I should make alternate plans, but I
couldn't. You will have to keep her or find a place.

On the envelope I had written her name and the address and phone number of the Home, so someone at the bus station in Austin could get her where she was going. But not my address or phone number—not mine. That was the whole idea. They wouldn't be able to find me again, ever, to tell me I had to take her. They would have to find a place for her themselves.

We had about a fifteen-minute wait. I didn't know what to talk about. After a few minutes I asked her if she wanted a can of Coke in case she got thirsty on the bus. She liked that idea, of course, so we found a machine and got one. It wasn't as cold as it should have been, but I figured she wouldn't wait long enough for it to get really hot, so it wouldn't be too bad.

When they called her bus and we stood up to go, I still didn't know what to say. But she seemed to have something in mind to say to me. I asked her what it was. She stopped and, putting her face up close to mine, confided, "Mama didn't want me either. She didn't say it, like you did, but she didn't want me. You didn't, any of you."

She merely stated it as a fact, not bitterly, just telling me that home truth. I wondered if she wanted to relieve me of the responsibility of having let her down, by letting me know she had never had any illusions on that score anyway. Or was that too much, from Lisbeth?

There was nothing I could say, nothing at all. Why

should I lie now and try to claim that of course we had wanted her, we had always wanted her? She knew! All those years she had known and had kept that knowledge to herself, protecting us from it, helping us keep up the pretense that she was wanted. And I didn't know why she had told me now, unless it was to let me off that hook. I also didn't know whether I felt better about it now or worse. With some things, you can't tell.

I couldn't kiss her good-bye or even say good-bye, I was so afraid I would break down.

So I just made sure she knew where her claim check was and said, "See you."

"See you," she said back, and the driver helped her on.

I had meant to leave then, before the bus pulled out, but I couldn't make myself go.

It was so hard; it was the hardest thing I had ever done. Much harder than the break with Stan. Why did she have to have so little? She had nothing. I could see, like a picture right there before me or like a real object, the thing itself, the nothing she had or would ever have, how much she needed and how little there was to fill that need. And now here I was making that little even less. Dumping her.

Oh, I saw it all very clearly. But what I couldn't see was any way out of it. There was just nothing I could do for her. Her need was too great. I didn't know where to start. I had the kids to take care of and I had myself and, in a way, I had Mitchy. So that was all I could do.

But I did stay there in the bay of the bus station and wait until they pulled out. I could do that much, anyway, for whatever it was worth. Not much. When they did start up and the bus turned into the street, I saw her in the window. She was drinking her Coke and looking like she felt OK.

So then I got in the car and went on. I had kids to feed and a household to put in order and, in a couple of days, a job to find. It dawned on me that maybe I could get Mitchy to look for a job too. He was a trained auto mechanic. Maybe he would be better off if he worked in a garage during the day and just played piano jobs once in a while, instead of every night. Maybe he could pull himself together.

I didn't know. We'd see. First I had to get back and see how things were going. I decided to stop at a phone booth on the way and get our phone disconnected. That way, when they called from the Home later on, they would get the message.

There were just some things I couldn't do anything about. And those I could, no one was going to do for me. So I might as well get started.

would get the